Ext

3 9077 03319 4393

W9-BZP-454

ERD   Erdrich, Louise.

The bingo palace.

$25.95   EXT 4393

DATE			

Extension Department
Rochester Public Library
115 South Avenue
Rochester NY 14604-1896

NOV 1 0 1994   BAKER & TAYLOR

THE BINGO PALACE

THE
BINGO
PALACE

Louise Erdrich

WHEELER
PUBLISHING, INC.

★ AN AMERICAN COMPANY ★

EXT 4393

Copyright © 1994 by Louise Erdrich.

All rights reserved.

Published in Large Print by arrangement with
HarperCollins Publishers, Inc. in the United States and
Canada.

All the characters in this book are products of the
author's imagination. Any resemblance they bear to
persons living or dead is pure coincidence.

Parts of this book have been published in the following:
Chapter Seven as "The Bingo Van" in *The New Yorker*,
Chapter Twelve as "Fleur's Luck" in the *Georgia Review*,
Chapter Twenty-four as "I'm a Mad Dog Biting Myself
for Sympathy" in *Granta*.

Wheeler Large Print Book Series.

Set in 16 pt. Plantin.

Library of Congress Cataloging-in-Publication Data

Erdrich, Louise.
    The bingo palace / Louise Erdrich.
        p.   cm.—(Wheeler large print book series)
    ISBN 1-56895-073-X (cloth) : $25.95
    1. Indians of North America—North Dakota—Fiction.   2. Man-
woman relationships—North Dakota—Fiction.   3. Bingo—North
Dakota—Fiction.   4. Large type books.   I. Title.   II. Series.
    [PS3555.R42B5   1994b]
    813'.54—dc20   94-8054

To Michael,
U R lucky 4 me

ACKNOWLEDGMENTS

Megwitch, Merci, B-4 and after 4 bingo guidance, Susan Moldow, Lise, Angela and Heid Ellen Erdrich, Delia Bebonang, Thelma Stiffarm and Duane Bird Bear family, Pat Steun, Peter Brandvold, Alan Quint, Gail Hand, Pauline Russette, Laurie SunChild, Marlin Gourneau, Chris Gourneau, Bob and Peggy Treuer and family, Two Martin, Trent Duffy, Tom MacDonald, Michael Dorris, as ever, for his generous devotion to this book. Thanks go to my father, Ralph Erdrich, for keeping track of bingo life, and again, my grandfather, Pat Gourneau, who played so many cards at once.

CONTENTS

Chapter One
  The Message   1

Chapter Two
  Lipsha Morrissey   12

Chapter Three
  Solitary   26

Chapter Four
  Lipsha's Luck   29

Chapter Five
  Transportation   40

Chapter Six
  June's Luck   64

Chapter Seven
  The Bingo Van   68

Chapter Eight
  Lyman's Luck   97

Chapter Nine
  Insulation   108

Chapter Ten
  Shawnee's Luck   131

Chapter Eleven
  Mindemoya   139

Chapter Twelve
  Fleur's Luck   157

Chapter Thirteen
Lyman's Dream   164

Chapter Fourteen
Religious Wars   168

Chapter Fifteen
Redford's Luck   192

Chapter Sixteen
Shawnee Dancing   203

Chapter Seventeen
Getting Nowhere Fast   207

Chapter Eighteen
Lyman Dancing   229

Chapter Nineteen
Albertine's Luck   232

Chapter Twenty
A Little Vision   240

Chapter Twenty-one
Gerry's Luck   248

Chapter Twenty-two
Escape   254

Chapter Twenty-three
Zelda's Luck   268

Chapter Twenty-four
I'm a Mad Dog Biting Myself for
Sympathy   276

Chapter Twenty-five
Lulu's Capture   290

Chapter Twenty-six
Shawnee's Morning   296

Chapter Twenty-seven
Pillager Bones   299

CHAPTER ONE

THE MESSAGE

On most winter days, Lulu Lamartine did not stir until the sun cast a patch of warmth for her to bask in and purr. She then rose, brewed fresh coffee, heated a pan of cream, and drank the mix from a china cup at her apartment table. Sipping, brooding, she entered the snowy world. A pale sweet roll, a doughnut gem, occasionally a bowl of cereal, followed that coffee, then more coffee, and on and on, until finally Lulu pronounced herself awake and took on the day's business of running the tribe. We know her routine—many of us even shared it—so when she was sighted before her normal get-up time approaching her car door in the unsheltered cold of the parking lot, we called on others to look. Sure enough, she was dressed for action. She got into her brown Citation wearing hosiery, spike-heeled boots, and, beneath her puffy purple winter coat, a flowered dress cut evening low. She adjusted her rearview mirror, settled her eyeglasses on her nose. She started the engine, pulled away onto the downslope winding road. From the hill, we saw her pass into the heart of the reservation.

She rolled along in quiet purpose, stopping at the signs, even yielding, traveling toward one of two places open at that early hour. The gas pumps—she could be starting out on a longer

1

trip—or the post office. These were the two choices that we figured out among ourselves. When she passed the first, we knew it must be the second, and from there, we relied on Day Twin Horse to tell us how Lulu entered the post office beneath the flags of the United States, the Great Seal of North Dakota, and the emblem of our Chippewa Nation, and then lingered, looking all around, warming herself like a cat at the heat register and tapping at her lips with a painted fingernail.

Day Twin Horse watched her, that is, until she turned, saw him looking, and set confusion into motion. First she glared a witch gaze that caused him to tape a finger to the postal scale. The tape seemed to have a surprising life all of its own so that, as he leaned over, extracting the finger, balling up the tape, Day Twin Horse became more and more agitated. For while he struggled with the sticky underside, Mrs. Josette Bizhieu entered, impatient as always, carrying three packages. Tending to her needs, Postmaster Twin Horse was unable to keep an eye on Lulu as she wandered, flicking at the dials of the tiny boxes that held other people's bills. He did not see her pause to read the directions on the Xerox machine, or lean over the glass display case showing pen sets, stamp mugs, albums that could be purchased by collectors. He did not see her stop before the wanted posters, flick through quickly, silently, riffling the heavy roll until she came to the picture of her son.

It was Josette herself, sharp and wary as her namesake bobcat, who tipped her chin down, turned her face just a fraction to watch Lulu

Lamartine as she reached into the fall of criminals and with one quick tug, evenly, as if she were removing a paper towel from a toothed dispenser, tear away government property. Holding the paper, Lulu walked over to the copier. She carefully slid the picture onto the machine's face, inserted two coins into the coin box. Satisfaction lit her face as the machine's drum flashed and whirred. She removed the original, then the copy of the picture as it emerged. She folded it into an envelope and carried it quickly to the Out of Town slot, where Josette now held her packages as if deciding which to mail first. Seeing the drop of Josette's gaze, Lulu quickly posted the letter, but not before Josette caught the city part of the address, already written onto the outside of the stamped envelope.

Fargo, North Dakota. There it was—the well-known whereabouts of that stray grandson whom Lulu Lamartine and Marie Kashpaw shared uneasily between themselves. So Lulu Lamartine was sending the picture of the father to the son. Perhaps it was a summons home. A warning. Surely, it meant something. There was always a reason behind the things Lulu did, although it took a while to find them, to work her ciphers out for meaning. Now Lulu walked directly through the glass front doors, leaving Josette and Day Twin Horse in the post office.

The two gazed after her, frowning and pensive. Around them, suddenly, they felt the drift of chance and possibility, for the post office is a place of near misses, lit by numbers. Their gazes fixed upon the metal postal box doors—so strictly aligned and easily mistaken for one another. And then the racks constructed for the necessary array of identical-looking rubber stamps that nevertheless could send a letter halfway around the world. Of course, there were the stamps themselves, either booklets or sheets sold in waxed cellophane envelopes. Eagles. Flowers. Hot air balloons. Love dogs. Wild Bill Hickok. The ordinary world suddenly seemed tenuous, odd. Josette reared back in suspicion, narrowing her clever eyes. Day Twin Horse regarded his olive-colored tape. The roll again was docile and orderly in his hands. He ran his fingernail across the surface searching for the ridge to pull, the cut, but the plastic was seamless, frustrating, perfect, like the small incident with Lulu. He couldn't find where to pull and yet he knew that in her small act there was complicated motive and a larger story.

As it turned out, however, there was not much more to know about the things Lulu did on that particular day. It was later on that we should have worried about, the long-term consequences. All the same, we tried to keep a close eye upon her doings, so we know that soon after she left the post office Lulu Lamartine purchased, from the fanciest gift shop in Hoopdance, a brass and crystal picture frame. She brought it back to her apartment, laid it down upon her kitchen table. Josette, who sat right there with a glass of water, winding down from all her errands, told how Lulu used her nail file to press aside the tiny clamps that held in the backing. She removed the fuzz-coated cardboard, then the inner corrugated square, and lastly, the flimsy reproduction of a

4

happy wedding couple. She tossed the sentimental photograph aside, positioned the wanted poster against the glass. She smoothed down the cheap paper, replaced the backing, then turned the portrait around front to gaze upon the latest picture of her famous criminal boy.

Even in the mug-shot photographer's flash, the Nanapush eyes showed, Pillager bones, the gleam of one earring at his cheek. Gerry Nanapush had a shy rage, serious wonder, a lot of hair. She looked for traces of herself—the nose surely—and of his father—the grin, the smile held in and hidden, wolf-white, gleaming. Looking down the length of her rounded arms, her face was thoughtful, Josette said, too shrewd, bent on calculation. In fact, we never thought Lulu Lamartine wore the proper expression anyway—that of a mother resigned. Her undevout eyes were always dangerously bright, her grin was always trying to get loose and work a spell. Her face was supple, her arms strong, and even touched with arthritis, she had the hands of a safecracker. Still, we thought the business would end with the picture sitting on the shelf. After all, he was recently caught and locked up again for good. We never thought she'd go so far as she finally managed. We believed Lulu Lamartine would content herself with changing the picture's resting spot, carrying it back and forth until she finally centered it upon her knickknack shelf, a place where you couldn't help noticing it upon first entering her apartment.

Lulu's totaling glance followed Josette that day, not the picture's rigid stare, but the two pairs of

5

eyes were so alike that it always took a decision of avoidance to enter the place. Some of us tried to resist, yet were pulled in just the same. We were curious to know more, even though we'd never grasp the whole of it. The story comes around, pushing at our brains, and soon we are trying to ravel back to the beginning, trying to put families into order and make sense of things. But we start with one person, and soon another and another follows, and still another, until we are lost in the connections.

We could pull any string from Lulu, anyway, it wouldn't matter, it would all come out the same degree of tangle. Start with her wanted-poster boy, Gerry Nanapush, for example. Go down the line of her sons, the brothers and half brothers, until you get to the youngest, Lyman Lamartine. Here was a man everybody knew and yet did not know, a dark-minded schemer, a bitter and yet shaman-pleasant entrepreneur who skipped money from behind the ears of Uncle Sam, who joked to pull the wool down, who carved up this reservation the way his blood father Nector Kashpaw did, who had his own interest so mingled with his people's that he couldn't tell his personal ambition from the pride of the Kashpaws. Lyman went so far as to court a much younger woman. He loved and failed, but that has never kept down Kashpaws, or a Lamartine either, for very long.

Keep a hand on the frail rope. There's a storm coming up, a blizzard. June Morrissey still walks through that sudden Easter snow. She was a beautiful woman, much loved and very troubled. She left her son to die and left his father to the mercy

6

of another woman and left her suitcase packed in her room to which the doorknob was missing. Her memory never was recovered except within the thoughts of her niece, Albertine—a Kashpaw, a Johnson, a little of everything, but free of nothing.

We see Albertine dancing at the powwow, long braid down her back and shawl a blue swirl. We see her hunched over the medical library books resisting a cigarette ever since anatomy class. We see her doing what the *zhaginash* call *her level best*, which is going at it, going at it until she thinks her head will fall off into her hands. It seems her task to rise and sink, to rush at things fast and from all directions like the wind, to bowl down every adversary with her drama. We see her hurt when the strong rush fails. We see her spring back, collecting power.

We shake our heads, try to go at it one way, then another. The red rope between the mother and her baby is the hope of our nation. It pulls, it sings, it snags, it feeds and holds. How it holds. The shock of throwing yourself to the end of that rope has brought many a wild young woman up short, slammed her down, left her dusting herself off, outraged and tender. Shawnee Ray, Shawnee Ray Toose and her little boy, for instance. The old men shut their eyes and try not to look directly at this young woman's beauty because a hot flame still leaps to life, focused and blue, and what can they do about it? Better to let the tongue clack. We've heard Shawnee Ray talks to spirits in the sweat lodge in such a sweet way, in such an old-time way, respectful, that they can't help but answer. We don't know how she's going to get

7

by that boss *ikwe* Zelda Kashpaw, who put up a stockade around her own heart since the days when she herself was a girl. We don't know how it will work out, come to pass, which is why we watch so hard, all of us alike, one arguing voice.

We do know that no one gets wise enough to really understand the heart of another, though it is the task of our life to try. We chew the tough skins, we wonder. We think about the Pillager woman, Fleur, who was always half spirit anyway. A foot on the death road, a quick shuffle backwards, her dance wearies us. Yet some of us wish she'd come out of the woods. We don't fear her anymore—like death, she is an old friend who has been waiting quietly, a patient companion. We know she's dawdling, hanging back as long as she can, waiting for another to take her place, but in a different way from when she put her death song into other people's mouths. This time she's waiting for a young one, a successor, someone to carry on her knowledge, and since we know who that person must be, our knowledge makes us pity her. We think she's wrong. We think Fleur Pillager should settle her bones in the sun with us and take a rest, instead of wasting her last words on that medicine boy.

Lipsha Morrissey.

We're all disgusted with the son of that wanted poster. We give up on that Morrissey boy Marie Kashpaw rescued from the slough. Spirits pulled his fingers when he was a baby, yet he doesn't appreciate his powers. His touch was strong, but he shorted it out. Going back and forth to the city weakened and confused him and now he flails in

8

a circle with his own tail in his teeth. He shoots across the road like a coyote, dodging between the wheels, and then you see him on the playground, swinging in a swing, and again he has made himself stupid with his dope pipe. He tires us. We try to stand by him, to bring him back, give him advice. We tell him that he should ground himself, sit on the earth and bury his hands in the dirt and beg the Manitous. We have done so much for him and even so, the truth is, he has done nothing yet of wide importance.

We wish that we could report back different since he last told his story, but here's the fact: that boy crossed the line back to the reservation, proud in his mother's blue Firebird car, and then he let his chances slip. For a while it looked like he'd amount to something. He stuck with high school, scored high in the state of North Dakota in the college tests. He gave us all a shock, for we thought he was just a waste, a load, one of those sad reservation statistics. Offers came into his Grandma Marie's mailbox—everything from diesel mechanics to piloting aircraft. But then he proved us right. For nothing captured his interest. Nothing held him. Nothing sparked.

He got onto a crew that was turning an old abandoned railroad depot into a first-class restaurant, which was the fad in renovation. It came out picture-perfect, except that when the trains came through plates fell, glasses shook, and water spilled. Next, he worked in a factory that made tomahawks. He helped to bring that enterprise down around his own ears, and didn't stay to clean up the mess, either, but skipped off down to

Fargo. There, he found work in a sugar beet plant, shoveling sugar. He shoveled mountains of it, all day, moving it from here to there. He called back on the party line, always collect, to his Grandma Marie, and always he was complaining.

Well, we could imagine. What kind of job was that anyway, for a Chippewa? We weren't very pleased with the picture. When he got back to his room, he held a dustpan underneath his shoes and socks and emptied the sugar in a little pile. He shook his pants in the bathtub and brushed his hair and washed the sugar down the drain. Still, the grains crackled underfoot and the carpet thickened. The shag strands stuck together, the sweetness drew roaches and silverfish, which he sprayed dead. Nothing was ever clean, he told Marie, us listening. The sugar settled into syrup and the spray acted like a seal, so that layers of sticky glaze collected and hardened.

Just like him. He was building up a seal of corrosion, hardening himself, packing himself under. We heard from sources we don't like to talk about that he was seen down in the bars, the tougher spots, the dealer hangouts and areas beneath the bridges where so much beyond the law gets passed hand to mouth. Like father, we thought, only moving our eyes to say it, like father, there he goes. And then one day Lulu's mailed picture of Gerry Nanapush arrived in Fargo, a wanted-poster message regarding his father that evidently made the boy stop and look around himself. This was his life—a fact we could have told him from the first phone call. There he was, sitting at the fake wood-grain table, listening to cars go by in the street below. He was covered with a sugary chip-proof mist of chemicals, preserved, suspended, trapped like a bug in a plastic weight. He was caught in a foreign skin, drowned in drugs and sugar and money, baked hard in a concrete pie.

We didn't know him, we didn't want to, and to tell the truth we didn't care. *Who he is is just the habit of who he always was*, we warned Marie. *If he's not careful, who he'll be is the result.*

Perhaps a drumming teased in the bones of his fingers, or maybe his whole face smarted as if he'd slapped himself out of a long daze. Anyway, he stood up and found himself out the door taking what he could carry—jackets, money, boom box, clothes, books, and tapes. He walked down the hall and stairs, out into the street. He stuffed his car full and then, once he got behind the wheel, all that mattered was the drive.

We saw him immediately as he entered the gym during the winter powwow. He slid through the crowd during the middle of an Intertribal song. We saw him edge against the wall to watch the whirling bright dancers, and immediately we had to notice that there was no place the boy could fit. He was not a tribal council honcho, not a powwow organizer, not a medic in the cop's car in the parking lot, no one we would trust with our life. He was not a member of a drum group, not a singer, not a candy-bar seller. Not a little old Cree lady with a scarf tied under her chin, a thin pocket-book in her lap, and a wax cup of Coke, not one of us. He was not a fancy dancer with a mirror on his head and bobbing porcupine-hair roach, not a

11

traditional, not a shawl girl whose parents beaded her from head to foot. He was not our grandfather, either, with the face like clean old-time chewed leather, who prayed over the microphone, head bowed. He was not even one of those gathered at the soda machines outside the doors, the ones who wouldn't go into the warm and grassy air because of being drunk or too much in love or just bashful. He was not the Chippewa with rings pierced in her nose or the old aunt with water dripping through her fingers or the announcer with a ragged face and a drift of plumes on his indoor hat.

He was none of these, only Lipsha, come home.

CHAPTER TWO

LIPSHA

LIPSHA MORRISSEY

Walking into the lights of the high school gym that evening, I stop as if to ask directions to a place I've always known. The drums pound, lighting my blood. My heart jumps. I am all at once confused and shy-faced and back where I belong without a place to fit, a person to turn to, a friend to greet. Of course, it doesn't take long before I glimpse satin, the trademark of my cousin Albertine Johnson. Her patience with that slippery fabric is well known, and sure enough, as if I'd even imagined the sky blue color, the darker shadows she would pick, my eyes latch right onto her the first time she circles past and catches me with the corner of her gaze.

I watch her. A dusky blue eagle spreads its beaded wings across her back, and she carries a blue shawl with all shades from navy to turquoise fringe swinging from the borders. Her leggings are beaded blue and her moccasins are that same color. She's put her red-brown hair in one simple braid right down her back, a tapering rope held on each side with a matching rosette and a white plume that lifts softly with each of her steps. Right about here, I ordinarily would begin to tell you all about Albertine: how she went away to school, how her life got so complicated and advanced. However, because she's dancing along with a friend, my story doesn't turn out to be a record of Albertine at all. She comes later. No, the hero of my tale, the mad light, the hope, is the second woman I see dancing at the winter powwow.

Our own Miss Little Shell.

I follow the soft light of Albertine's expression to where it catches the harder radiance of Shawnee Ray Toose, who takes that glow of my cousin's and somehow beams it at me, in a complex ricochet that leaves me, as they sway by, with the dazzling impression of lights glinting off Shawnee's teeth. I step forward, to catch a better glimpse of them both, but my eyes somehow stay hooked to Shawnee Ray. The back view of her jingle dress, which is made of something snaky and gleaming dark red, grabs me hard and won't let go. The material fits so close, and her belt, labeled Miss Little Shell in blazing beads, so tight around her waist.

13

I blink and shake my head. My eyes want to see more, more, closer, but my hands save me, as I fold my arms and press myself back into the crowd. Still, every time those two women sweep by me I am fixed. I can't ignore the display of Shawnee Ray's sewn-in breasts, carried in a circle, around and around, like prizes in a basket, and those jingles sewn all over her in Vs, so that each wet-looking red curve goes by ringing with her body music. I catch her profile, tough and bold. Her hair is twisted into some kind of braid that looks stitched onto her head, and a crown is pinned there, made of winking stones. Once, when I look too long at her, I think she feels the touch of my attention, because all of a sudden she tips onto her toes, high, higher. She rises into the popcorn air, and she begins to step free and unearthly as a spirit panther, so weightless that I think of clouds, of sun, of air above the snow light.

Then she lands, bounds lower, and puts a hand to her hip. She raises her other arm, proud, and poises her fan high.

Shawnee carries the entire wing and shoulder of a big mother eagle. I picture her lifting off, snagging that bird midflight, and then neatly lopping it in half. You can see Shawnee Ray deep in the past, running down a buffalo on a little paint warhorse, or maybe on her own limber legs. You can see her felling the animal with one punch to the brain. Or standing bent-elbowed with a lance. You can see her throwing that spear without hesitation right through a cavalry man or a mastodon. Shawnee Ray, she is the best of our past, our present, our hope of a future.

14

There are her parents, I see now. Elward Strong Ribs, second husband to big Irene Toose. They are back to the reservation for a visit. Shawnee's real dad died a while ago in a bad accident, and after Irene married again the new couple went to work in Minot. Shawnee Ray was left here on the reservation to finish high school and, oh yes, to have her baby, which everyone now takes for granted.

Tonight, Elward and Irene are sitting as far apart as they can place themselves on side-by-side folding chairs, trying not to look at their girl too often, or to seem too pleased with her or not pleased enough with one another. They try not to notice that Irene's other daughters, the Toose girls, are not in the gym but most likely out in the parking lot or farther off, drinking in the dark hills beyond. They try not to notice their own position, the best one, right in front but not too near the Rising Wind drum, and try not to talk too long to any one person or show their favor although they nod in agreement with the medium-stout woman in the heavy black-velvet beaded dress who stands next to them with a child in her arms.

Zelda Kashpaw.

When women age into their power, no wind can upset them, no hand turn aside their knowledge; no fact can deflect their point of view. It is like that with the woman I was raised to think of as a sister and call aunt in respect, the velvet beaded lady holding Shawnee Ray's little boy. Upon seeing Zelda Kashpaw, I remember to dread her goodness. I remember to fear her pity, her helping

15

ways. She is, in fact the main reason coming home is never simple: with Zelda, I am always in for something I cannot see but that is already built, in its final stages, erected all around. It is invisible, a house of pulled strings, a net of unforced will, a perfect cat's cradle that will spring to life as soon as Zelda is aware of me. I step back. Her head whips around. What am I thinking? My aunt knows all there is to know. She has a deep instinct for running things. She should have more children or at least a small nation to control. Instead, forced narrow, her talents run to getting people to do things they don't want to do for other people they don't like. Zelda is the author of grit-jawed charity on the reservation, the instigator of good works that always get chalked up to her credit.

Zelda stands firm, a woman to whom much is obliged. She moves within an aura of repayment schedules, and, as always, it is clear I owe her big even though I don't yet know what for. This happens in many different and mysterious ways. How amazed I am so often in my life to find myself acting, as I believe, from true and deep motivations, only to discover later that Zelda has planned what I am doing.

For instance, she knows all about my return. My summons by Grandma Lulu. No words needed. Zelda has now left the Strong Ribs and Toose family and moved over next to me. She carries Shawnee Ray's little boy, Redford, carefully in her arms, but he is only bait for calculations. I know that much by this time. It is no matter that I have driven the back roads. No matter that I haven't talked to or in any way

16

informed my aunt of my traveling decisions. It turns out that all along, without knowing it, I am just following her mental directions.

"I told them you'd make it," she says, putting down the boy, who runs directly into the circle and manages somehow to evade the trampling moccasins of the big-bellied war dancers who lurch past, too proud and heavy with bone plate and paint to lift their knees. Redford zips straight to his mother's side and she scoops him immediately close. His roundcheeked face sweetens, his eyes go big and tender, light with dark fascination. Nobody talks too much about Redford's father, for it often seems that his presence is everywhere—he has a foot through every basket, a nose for scams and schemes. If I say it out, it is only to introduce what is known and whispered. The boy is the son of my half uncle and former boss, Lyman Lamartine.

I often brag on Lyman, for even though I think of him as a big, bland Velveeta, I am proud I am related to this reservation's biggest cheese. The fact is, a tribal go-getter has to pasteurize himself. He has to please every tribal faction. He has to be slick, offend nobody, keep his opinions hid. By way of doing this, Lyman has run so many businesses that nobody can keep track—cafés, gas pumps, a factory that made tomahawks, a flower shop, an Indian Taco concession, a bar which he has added to and parlayed from a penny-card bingo hall and kitchen-table blackjack parlor into something bigger, something we don't know the name of yet, something with dollar signs that crowd the meaning from our brain. My uncle took

17

an interest in me after my A.C.T. scores turned out so high, though I don't think he ever personally liked me. It is well known that he and Shawnee Ray are long-term engaged, that dates for a wedding keep getting set, wrangled over, broken. What isn't clear to anyone is just who does the breaking or the setting, whose feet are hot, whose cold.

"Redford's big," I remark to Zelda. She is fanning herself with a paper plate she has stored in her beaded bag, and waits for me to say more. Zelda was once called raven-haired and never forgot, so on special occasions her hair, which truly is an amazing natural feature, still sweeps its fierce wing down the middle of her back. She wears her grandmother Rushes Bear's skinning knife at her strong hip, and she touches the beaded sheath now, as if to invoke her ancestor.

My aunt recently launched herself into the local public eye when Shawnee let it be known she would keep her baby. With her parents moving off, and her sisters' drinking habits a bad legend, Shawnee needed a place to stay. Zelda took her in for the price of free-rein interference. She stepped to the front and erected a structure for the whole situation. She swept, tidied, and maneuvered an explanation and a future that would fit expectations and satisfy all hearts.

Through furious gossip, Zelda has got Shawnee and her man semi-engaged, and is doing her best to make arrangements for them both to marry. A pang shoots through me, now, when I think of marriage between Shawnee Ray and Lyman. I am

18

surprised to find that I experience the disappointment of a hope I never knew I harbored.

Most people are jealous of Lyman, and maybe I am no better. He is an island of *have* in a sea of *have-nots*. And even more than that, he's always been a little special, picked out. Though short, he is a guy with naturally football-padded shoulders, a dentist grin, a shrewd and power-cleaned presence in a room. Lyman owns a beautiful Italian-cut three-piece suit. His shirts are sparkling white, his collars ringless, his bolo-tie stones not glass but semiprecious rocks. Some think that he is following in the footsteps of his old man, Nector Kashpaw, and will eventually go off to Washington to rise into the Indian stratosphere. Some green envy talk has him quitting the local bingo, running for an elected office, making politician's hay. As if business and popularity are athletic events, he keeps himself in tip-top shape, especially for a guy his age. His vested middle is made for a woman to throw herself at, clawing the buttons, which are sewn on double-tight. A girl could do an entire load of laundry on his washboard stomach. I know, because I've seen him bench press, that his biceps are smooth, rounded, and hard as the stones in lakes.

I could go on and on about Lyman. The truth is, our relationship is complicated by some factors over which we have no control. His real father was my stepfather. His mother is my grandmother. His half brother is my father. I have an instant crush upon his girl.

Reading is my number-one hobby, and I have browsed a few of the plays of the old-time Greeks.

19

If you read about a thing like Lyman and me happening in those days, one or both of us would surely have to die. But us Indians, we're so used to inner plot twists that we just laugh. We're born heavier, but scales don't weigh us. From day one, we're loaded down. History, personal politics, tangled bloodlines. We're too preoccupied with setting things right around us to get rich.

Except for Lyman, who does a whole lot of both.

As an under-the-table half sister, Zelda Kashpaw is in his corner, and she tries to help him out in the community. She blesses his and Redford's future in a hundred conversations via phone and tribal mall, asks positive input from the priests, from her friends the Sisters. She leads novenas for unwed mothers. She helps Shawnee in every way—would have had the baby for her if she could, and nursed it too, with the rich, self-satisfying milk of her own famous kindness. It's gotten so, by this time, no one can mention the current situation of Redford and Shawnee Ray without acknowledging Zelda's goodness in the same breath.

"Isn't that a fine thing Zelda's doing?" people repeat to each other. "Shawnee Ray is lucky to have her take such an interest."

Yes, Zelda racks points up sky high with her tireless energy. She fixes it for Redford to get a naming ceremony and she arranges files and blood quantums in the tribal office where she works, so that he is enrolled as a full-blood. She gathers WIC food to feed him, and is always at the Sisters' door when they open it to sell or give away donated clothing. People let her snatch what she wants, knowing it is for the child, who is always, at every moment, dressed like an ad in a magazine. Even if Shawnee Ray sews his outfit, as she has the one he wears right now—old-time leggings, a ribbon shirt of dotted calico—the word soon leaks that Zelda bought the "special" fabric.

Just to check, I point at Redford.

"Nice fabric," I observe.

Zelda draws herself up with a penetrating air.

"*You* might think so," she answers. "But it was not what I wanted. They never have exactly what you're looking for! I had to go to three shops, then finally I gave up and drove all the way to Hoopdance." She frowns, shakes her head remembering the gasoline expended and the many unworthy bolts that passed between her critical thumb and first finger.

"And Shawnee Ray, she looks like she's doing pretty good." I am casual, unable to help myself from mentioning her name.

"Pretty good." Zelda's hand goes into that beaded bag. She draws out a foil-wrapped brick and presses it toward me. The thing is heavy as a doorstop. I don't need to ask—it is Zelda's old-time holiday fruitcake, made with traditional hand-gathered ingredients, chokecherries pounded with the pits still in them, dried buffalo meat, molasses, raisins, prunes, and anything else that carries weight. Winter traction, I think as I heft it. I thank her, and then, when that is not enough, thank her again for saving it for me through the new year and its aftermath.

Accepting my gratitude, Zelda turns her atten-

21

tion full onto me. I can feel her scan my brain with the sudden zero-gaze of medical machines. A map of my feelings springs up in blue light, a map that Zelda focuses to read.

Miss Little Shell.

Suddenly I am watching so hard for the flash and wave of red that I miss Zelda's reaction, which is too bad, because if I could only have seen what she was rerouting and recasting to fit her intentions and visions, I could perhaps have headed off all that came to pass. But too late. I have this impression that my regard of Shawnee Ray, my watching of her, is natural. So I stand there and continue looking, as in me there begins to form some vague swell of feeling. I believe at the time it is fate at work, but of course, it turns out to be Zelda.

You may undergo your own incarceration. You may witness your demise piece by piece. You may be one kind of fool who never gets enough or another who gets too much. Lipsha, I tell myself, you didn't have to come back. You got your father's poster in the mail, courtesy of Grandma Lulu. Staring at this haunted face, you had the impulse to change your life. But to put that moment into operation is more complicated than you thought. You are looking for a quick solution, as usual, but once you get into Zelda's range that won't matter. Something else is at work. I have to ask myself if there is more—am I drawn back specifically to watch the circle where that pretty Toose now appears? And Shawnee Ray herself, our hope of a future, is she aware, too, and has

22

she rolled me into each one of her snuff-can-top jingles? Sewed me into her dress with a fine needle? In/out. In/out. Lipsha Morrissey. My man. Can it be possible?

Once I allow myself to consider anything, it is almost sure those thoughts don't quit, so I sink down holding Zelda's gift. I find myself in a bland steel chair and I wait, watching the floor, dazzled with new prospects. I am out of shape for being told what to do by everything around me. I've been out in a world where nobody cares to manipulate me, and maybe I take this unseen plotting as a sign of concern, even comfort, and fall back under its spell. That might be it, because even when another part of the design comes clear, soon after, I don't register its meaning.

Lyman Lamartine attacks the polished wood floor with his pounding feet. He whips by me and I hardly glance up except to register that he is now good at yet another thing. Lyman has inherited, and wears now, the outfit of his champion grass-dancing brother Henry. It is old-timey looking compared to the other yarn-draped and ribboned ones, but there is something classical about it, too. His antique roach has white fluffies bobbing on the wrapped springs of two car chokes, long silky fringes from an upholstery outlet, a beautifully beaded necktie and a pointed collar, matching armbands, and over his forehead, shading his shifty eyes, a heart-shaped mirror.

Lyman gets bigger when people stare at him, his chest goes out, his nostrils flare. He grows visibly as he swings into motion. Which is maybe

23

why he is so good at dancing. The more people who watch him the faster and huger he spins, as if he feeds off their stares. He takes the title of his dance literally and plays out a drama in his head. He believes in himself like nobody else. Now I watch close, closer, and get lost in things I see: a guy on the lookout, quick footed, nervous, sneaking up on someone unsuspecting. Crouching. Snaking down in long grass. The grass, it closes over him. You only see its movement as he creeps along, as he knits himself into the scene. Wind riffles through, bending, charming the stems and stalks and plumes. The sneaking what . . . warrior? No, *lover*, pokes his head up. Puts it down. Now he's getting close. More grass blows, waves. His victim sleeps on. Suddenly Lyman springs. Four times, right on the drumbeat, he jumps in a circle, his feet landing in a powerful stance, his heart mirror shining like a headlight, glancing sharp, piercing, pointing, straight into the deep brown eyes of Shawnee Ray, who winces, blinks, then opens her eyes wide and skeptical to take in his crazed and sudden dancing.

Aunt Zelda, of course, stands right next to Shawnee, focusing that love light to a narrow laser. She leans over, accomplishing through small remarks great articles of destiny. As she talks, she jiggles Redford, whose dark brown hair and beaming eyes are fixed upon his father. Shawnee Ray turns away from Lyman. Zelda pops a piece of candy into Redford's mouth so as not to distract the two. Shameless, playing on resistless baby greed, Zelda keeps the boy occupied and totally set

24

on the hand that contains the rest of the packaged sweets.

Hold on now, the tangle, the plot, the music of homecoming thickens. Lyman has one great advantage. Zelda shoots her webs right at him from a distance, and he allows them to stick. They are in on this together, although he doesn't know it yet. Sensing that invisible-string guide ropes have been erected to assist his approach, Lyman simply walks over, smiling at his own son. He is friendly, unconcerned over looks and whispers. He says hello to Shawnee Ray, reaches into Zelda's embrace and takes Redford, who strains toward him with thrilled arms and an open face. Zelda's lips press together, sealed on her own directions like an envelope. Having insisted everything should be up front and normal, these are the fruits, her reward.

I have to admire Lyman right then, for he clearly has kept a firm connection with his little boy. Perhaps I should take lessons from him, but I don't. I don't have the broad vision, or I am otherwise unprepared. Maybe the net that whirls clean around him falls by accident, with firm links, over me. I hardly know what happens next, although I hear it coming, the sounds of her approach. Then those steak-rare, ringing hips are suddenly before me, eye level, and I look up, over what the basket carries, into Shawnee's downcast and commanding eyes.

"You're back," she states. "For good?"

"For bad," I joke.

She doesn't laugh.

I glance away from her, anywhere but at her,

25

and try to compose myself. I have the sense of weight descending, and then of some powerful movement from below. I have this sudden knowledge that no matter what I do with my life, no matter how far away I go, or change, or grow and gain, I will never get away from here. I will always be the subject of a plan greater than myself, an order that works mechanically, so that no matter what I do it will come down to this. Me and Shawnee Ray, impossible, unlikely. I don't know if I give in then, or if I respond to the sight of her slender, silver-ringed, strong, and pointed fingers resting for a moment on my own bare hands. I only know that I close my ears to the drum music, my heart to the blowing wind, and stare at the random swirls of plastic within plastic, the stained linoleum on the gym floor that spreads so calm and thick beneath my feet, and changes each time I blink my eyes so that a leaping bull becomes a howitzer and then an apple tree tipped with small candles, or a hill into which a pleasant little door opens, into more doors than I can count, darker ones that lead farther back, intricately, toward spaces I have never seen and no place I can name.

CHAPTER THREE

SOLITARY

Even in direct and skilled competition with death itself, Albertine did not escape the iron shadow of her mother's repressed history. Her name was the feminine of the middle name of her mother's first

26

boyfriend, Xavier Albert Toose. When, as a little girl, she had complained about it to her mother, Zelda had looked sternly at her and asked if she would rather have been named after Swede, her father, morose and handsome in a fading photograph.

Recently, in a ceremony that Xavier Toose himself had run, and in the presence of Fleur Pillager, she had received a traditional name, one belonging originally to a woman she had heard of spoken in her grandmother's low voice as a healer. Since then, whenever she had a moment, Albertine worked her way through notebooks and trapper's diaries and fitful church records to try to find some reference to Four Soul.

She'd sunk deep in the scattered records of the Pillagers, into the slim and strange substance of the times and names. The words soaked into her, the names almost hurt with the intimations of unknown personality. Ogimaakwe, Boss Woman; Chokecherry Girl; Bineshii, Small Bird, also known as Josette. There was Unknown Cloud. Red Cradle. Comes from Above. Strikes the Water.

And there was Four Soul, only a scratch on the record of Chippewa taken down by Father Damien in that first decade when people, squeezed westward, starving, came to the reservation to receive rations and then allotted land.

Everywhere she looked, once she got up from the desk, reminders of her mother's notorious benefactions—books, hair clips, many sets of earrings, food by the item and box, lacy note cards, pictures. Her suitcase for home was always halfway packed, her heart dutifully filling, a holy-water font for guilt. Albertine was one of those who took on too much in order to remain perpetually dissatisfied with herself. It worked—a plume of spent fuel trailed her days, headlong in concentration, and her nights were black. Exhaustion was her pleasure, usually, but tonight she was too keyed up to settle into sleep and she switched on the television.

A vibrant, low-pitched, and authoritative male voice described a microwaved meal. Albertine dropped her head back, sank into the knitted pillow on her couch, wrapped one of Zelda's patchworked afghans around herself, and tucked it under her chin. Next the voice described the careful recording of all personal and phone conversation and showed a long and shining corridor of white paint, linoleum tile, blue and brown lines. An hour of gym a day, metal rings. SORT team. A description of headgear, helmets, pads. Albertine leaned forward, turned up the volume, stared intently into the screen. A different voice began to speak on the subject of penitentiary life.

I spend my time dwelling on revenge and try to deal with the monsters crawling out of the ashes.

And still another voice.

Chained and spread-eagled in the isolation four days.

And then his face, impossibly smiling, but different, a soft wilderness, a temple of unconfused purpose, much different from the man she had known, in person. That Gerry Nanapush had absorbed and cushioned insults with a lopsided jolt of humor. He had been a man whose eyes

28

lighted, who shed sparks, who had once leaped out a hospital window and popped a wheelie at the hospital entrance to mark his daughter's birth. Gerry's look now was so hungry and his gaze so razor desperate that there seemed no depth or end to the moment that the two confronted one another across blank space.

At his trial, as the verdict was handed over, when the voice dropped the words into the paneled courtroom the spectators in the back of the room had risen, startled from the benches to their feet shouting *no* at once, in one thrilled and throttled voice, breaking it across the air. *No. No.*

Albertine said it out loud now, again, at the sight of Gerry. *No.* But he was frozen air now, caught in the shadows of the beamed videotape just as he was in the Xeroxed posters and Insty-Printed newsletters and movies and stories of appeal. The television image dissolved, but as if the ink blackened and spread, her mind continued to leak apprehension until the air dimmed, until the constant and underlying level of fatigue hooked her under.

CHAPTER FOUR

LIPSHA'S LUCK

Marie Kashpaw sat at the round wooden table in her Senior Citizens apartment, touching her wracked hands together lightly. Through sheer nylon drapes, the winter sun cast a buttery light on the table, warming her knobbed fingers. She

29

knew that her youngest would come by to visit soon, and she was gathering peace. She prayed to no saints, but she believed in steadiness and luck. This one worried her. He was different from the others, wilder, anxious. She had taken him in as abandoned, but he had felt like her own from the beginning. Though he was grown, she still babied him, kept his school pictures taped to her refrigerator, still bought his clothes on sale, still saved money for him in a jar.

Maybe she had put her fierceness into guarding children for so long that she didn't know how to quit. Maybe she petted him too much, gave in too easy, spoiled him with her mercy. Lulu Lamartine said so, but Marie did not agree. Long ago, she had decided to grant Lipsha extra. Because of the way he was found in the slough, half drowned, he needed more than other children. She had tried to mother his mother, June, but it had been too late to really save her. June had worn out the world with her hurt, headlong chase. June was damaged goods, found once freezing in an outhouse, in a ditch, on the steps of the Sisters, and at last starving in the woods. Some children, you could not repair.

As a baby, Lipsha knew how to make his hands into burrs that would not unstick from Marie's clothing. He gripped her so strongly that he left small marks on her skin. And even older, he hugged her, desperate, when the others weren't looking. Sometimes she caught him holding to his face a piece of soft leather that she had given him as a doll. She had caught him weeping for no

30

reason. She had caught him playing dead in a pile of leaves and dirt.

Now Marie heard his footsteps in the hall, his knock on the door, and she stroked the doeskin bag that held Nector's pipe. The quilled parcel was laid out before her, carefully, on a crocheted place mat.

Peendigaen.

Lipsha came in looking ragged, his hair a chopped off mass that touched his shoulders, his mustache thin hairs curving down beside his lips. His skin was clear and mild, a pale brown like his mother's, and his eyes were hers too, beautiful and slightly upturned at the corners. He gave her a serene and foolishly sweet look, shrugged, sat down at the table.

"What's this?"

"Nector's pipe."

He was wearing a black baseball jacket, black jeans, a white shirt full of slogans. She said nothing more and he swallowed his carelessness into a quiet and attentive frown. For a few moments, they listened to snow drip from the eaves over the window, and gathered in the brilliance of sun, strained through the net of curtains. The pipe in its bag rested between them and their thoughts were small fractions, shards of sight. Lipsha remembered and saw the calm way that Nector's supple hands tamped down kinnikinnick in the bowl. Marie heard his voice speaking the old language in chunky phrases, his prayers that went on too long and always included everyone. Nector's eyes had always slightly crossed into the

31

distance, his arms made a light swaying motion with the pipe as he asked for favors.

"You know how to use it," Marie said. "He taught you."

Lipsha raised his face to hers and let the warmth of her intentions fill him until a shy smile rippled nervously over his features and he blinked, looked down at the bag, and made his face serious again. He still seemed unbelieving when she put the pipe into his hands. As he held it in his open palms he seemed about to speak. Once or twice he cleared his throat, shook his head, but he didn't find words.

An hour or two of asking around for jobs made Lipsha restless, and he decided to take a break and play a few video games at the newly built tribal mall, a complex erected to keep cash revenues in local hands. His initials soon lighted the bottoms of two screens, his scores were highest. When he got bored he wandered out of the dim hole-in-the-wall and sat on a scarred wooden bench bolted to the floor. One wish led to another and he soon persuaded himself that it wouldn't hurt to call up Shawnee Ray, just to talk. He walked to the pay phone, hopeful, and took it as a sign when it was not taped up and broken, but in working order. He knew the number because he was raised at the old Kashpaw place where Shawnee now lived with Zelda. He dialed and forgot to breathe. He didn't expect her to say anything important right off, but she answered his sudden offhand question whether she wanted to go out with him the way she danced, put her foot right down on the beat.

32

"Sure."

A raw hot space bloomed in Lipsha's chest.

"Hey. Are you there?"

Shawnee sounded worried, and the small note of concern in her voice charmed and exalted Lipsha. He stammered and an eager grin formed on his face. Ideas galloped at him right and left and he couldn't stop them, tame them. He tried to make small talk for a few more minutes, set a time to pick up Shawnee, said good-bye, and then stood in the entryway of the mall building with the phone clutched in his fingers. He looked down at the tiny black holes of the mouthpiece and it suddenly occurred to him that it had been brushed by many, many lips, maybe even Shawnee's. Tenderly, he placed the receiver on its cradle. With his sleeve, he smoothed the shining chrome rectangle beside it. Passing public phones, he usually slipped his hand into the dark apertures of their coin boxes in the hope of a stray quarter. A wholly different impulse gripped him now. He took an extra coin from his pocket and fed it into the slot in the machine's forehead. He pushed his arms into the air, pulled them down tight, in fear and pleasure, whispered, "Yes!"

That night, he drove to Zelda's and waited outside the front door of the little house. Although the night was cold, Shawnee Ray was sitting on the steps and now she rose, walked quickly to Lipsha's car, hands shoved in her jacket pockets. The door opened and Zelda posed in the kitchen light, waving slowly, once, twice, solemn but with an unreadable expression of satisfaction on her face. Lipsha put down his car window, waved back, and Zelda disappeared. Shawnee slid into the front bucket seat and latched herself securely.

"Is this a date?" Shawnee's voice was worried.

There was a long still space in which the car bounced slowly over the winding access road.

"I always hated dates, where you plan out fun." Lipsha talked quickly, nervous. "It always seems like no matter what you do you're not having enough of it, or having it only for the other person's benefit, or not having the kind of fun you are supposed to be having. It seems like your fun is suspect, or that your fun is really no fun, you know?"

"Because I'd rather this wasn't a date," continued Shawnee Ray.

"How about we go to Canada?" Lipsha suggested. "Ho Wun's."

"Why not?"

Lipsha could almost feel Shawnee's smile open in the dark. The nearest Chinese restaurant was located in a tiny town across the border and it was a romantic place, the walls covered in red paper patterned with flocked lanterns, signs for happiness, benevolence, and luck. Black bean sauce shrimp. Dumplings. Flower petal soup. All of these were on the menu. Rich foods, exotically chopped vegetables that they could exclaim over. They headed into the black north along a new stretch of highway.

"So, how's Lyman?" asked Lipsha, then bit his lip, surprised he'd spoken Lyman's name right out like that. He didn't know why he'd said it so abruptly, it was just that he wondered so hard about Shawnee and Lyman, whether or how they were involved, and his tongue had slipped.

"He's okay, I guess." Shawnee Ray's tone was careful, stiff.

"How's your uncle Xavier?"

"Okay."

"How's your mom?"

"Fine."

"How's Zelda?"

"Good."

"How, how, how," said Lipsha. "I feel like a Hollywood Sioux."

Shawnee laughed once, abruptly, and then immediately the atmosphere inside the car thickened and grew rubbery. Everything Lipsha said from then on bounced back at him unchanged, so he turned on the radio and twisted the dial to find something besides the Christian preaching that jammed the airwaves. *Sometimes His ego raps to me*, a male voice said. Quickly he switched the station and the miles zoomed by until they reached the lighted building next to the highway, the checkpoint people from the reservation always breezed through when they went up to Canada.

Lipsha rolled down his window to answer the usual questions, but here's where it started, that little wrinkle in destiny which he somehow came to believe that Zelda might have arranged. The incident grew out of nothing more than a border guard's dark mood, or maybe an unfilled quota, or just a fit of thoroughness. The guard, an elderly clean-cut type with a deep crisp voice, asked Lipsha to step out of the car. Lipsha turned off the ignition and did so. The officer reached to the

35

dashboard and gently removed the ashtray and brought it beneath the floodlit awning to examine. Lipsha got back into the driver's seat, tried to smile confidently at Shawnee, but she wasn't looking at him. The guard took a long time poking through the ashes with a ballpoint pen before he came up with something. He walked back, leaned down to the car window.

"I have bad news," he said, holding between his thumb and forefinger what looked like a tiny seed. His voice was formal and neutral. "I am compelled to search this vehicle."

Carefully, hands folded before them, heads bowed, Lipsha and Shawnee stepped out of the car, into the linoleum-floored and fluorescent-lighted room, and sat down across from one another on hard benches.

Shawnee Ray was wearing a big fluffy parka that made her shoulders huge. She tapered like a bodybuilder to her hips. Her hair had been sprayed-curled and it punched out all over her head, as if frozen stiff in fear or rage. Her eyes were irritated, not at all afraid. Lipsha sat down next to her, breathed her sharp perfume in deep breaths, narrowed his eyes against the harsh overhead glare. Shawnee Ray stared at her hands, calm in her lap. She found the patterned stitching on the back of her green knit gloves of exquisite interest and seemed so fascinated that Lipsha didn't dare drag her away from her involvement. Meanwhile, in the parking lot outside, he could hear the cheerful sound of boxes and bags thumping the asphalt.

36

"Sorry. I almost feel like this trouble's my fault."

"It is your fault," said Shawnee. "Where'd that seed come from?"

"I don't know."

"And another thing. Zelda told me you'd call, right after the powwow. How'd she know?"

"I guess she saw me looking at you."

Shawnee glanced up and then froze, caught in the lock of Lipsha's stare, so direct he scared himself at first, until he found he was looking hopefully and peacefully into Shawnee's eyes as into a beautiful and complicated new computer game whose pleasures and secrets he could not yet and might never measure. Shawnee's face transformed as she returned his frank stare, her outer features melting with her inner warmth. If the electricity went off, Lipsha felt sure, thinking of this moment later, she would have glowed with her own blossoming light. Her hair softened into a cloud, ready to be touched by welcome hands.

Lipsha's heart pumped hard, thinking for itself. He could hear things put back into his car now—from outside there was the sound of jamming, squeezing, slamming. What did he care? It was time to change this false configuration. The *not yet* of his potential life was the perfect match for Shawnee's *I am*, her *is*, he reasoned, while Lyman's *always was* fit precisely with the *no doubt* of some other unnamed and successful woman. The structure of this date had been strictly arranged, he now understood. Zelda was behind it, as with everything in which she had an interest. Lyman was along, too—not in the backseat, but certainly stuck between them in spirit. In the all-revealing light and silence of that waiting room, Lipsha believed he saw that whatever love there was between Shawnee and Lyman was canned love, love they ate from Zelda's shelf, love they couldn't even admit to not having because of the *should be* of the whole situation. That is, Lyman should be in love with Shawnee because he had fathered her child, and Shawnee should welcome him back into her arms for the same reason.

As for Lipsha, he remembered Zelda's mysterious parting look, and a word from his high school chemistry class sprang into his head. She intended him to be that third element introduced so that two neutral substances would strongly react. He was a drop of jealousy—strong, clear, and bitter: a catalyst. He pondered this with all of his powers, but the understanding that he almost reached flew from his hands and was of no consequence anyway, for just as he was about to try to rearrange Zelda's plans by driving all other men but himself from Shawnee's mind—he was concentrating all these thoughts into what he hoped would be a shattering kiss—it was as if Zelda knew. It was as if she sensed this danger and with swift magic counteracted Lipsha from a distance.

The guard stepped back into the door with the small, foil-wrapped brick of Zelda's old-time pemmican fruitcake resting in the open palm of one hand. In the other, he carried the elaborate bag that contained the sacred pipe that had once belonged to Nector Kashpaw.

"You'll be staying here until I can get you picked up," the guard said, jingling Lipsha's car keys. "You're in federal protective custody until I can get a lab analysis on this."

"But," Lipsha began, "that's—"

"Don't bother," said the guard, not unkind. He almost smiled, grim with satisfaction. "I've heard it all and I've seen it all. But this is a pipe and I know hash."

And then, staring calmly at the two, the guard put down the fruit bread, opened the quilled bag, and took out the bowl of the pipe and the long, carved stem. He held out his hands and there, as they watched, under the strong lights, he looked from one piece to the other and decided to connect the pipe as one. So many things would happen in the next months, soon after, that Lipsha wouldn't have time to take in or understand. But always, he would think back to that action, which seemed to happen slowly and to last for timeless moments. It seemed, on thinking back, that there, in the little border station, in the hands of the first non-Indian who ever attached that pipe together, sky would crash to earth.

"Please, don't," Lipsha whispered.

But the frowning man carefully and methodically pressed the carved stem to the bowl and began to turn it and jam it until the two sections locked into place. The eagle feather hung down, the old trade beads clicked against each other three times. Then there was silence, except for the buzzing lights. The guard turned to make his phone call, walked counterclockwise, around the room and desk. The pipe hung from his hand, backwards, casual as a bat. The eagle feather

39

dragged lower, lower, until it finally touched the floor.

CHAPTER FIVE

LIPSHA

TRANSPORTATION

When I think of all of the uncertainties to follow, the collisions with truth and disaster, I want to dive, to touch and lift that broad feather. I want to go back in time and spin the Firebird around, screeching with a movie flourish, to zoom back into the story, separate the pipe, swallow that one lone seed. And yet, as there is no retreating from the moment, the only art left to me is understanding how I can accept the consequence. For the backwardness, the wrongness, the brush of heaven to the ground in dust, is a part of our human nature. Especially mine, it appears.

As I sit with Shawnee Ray in that blinding room, waiting for the police to drive up wailing their sirens, I talk fast. I am trying to edge out the one idea I do not want Shawnee Ray to pursue.

"Just picture the lab analysis when it comes back," I try to joke. "Raisins, dried buffalo meat, *pukkons*, suet, prunes, tire rubber . . ."

She doesn't answer. Her head stays bowed.

"You're thinking," I venture.

She just sighs, gets up, and walks over to the phone.

40

It only takes Lyman Lamartine a half hour to respond to the call that ricochets from Shawnee to Zelda and probably on all through the tribal party-line wire. He drives into the border station yard with a powerful crackle of his studded snow tires. I can't help but hope he might slide through to Canada, but Lyman never slips off course. Each tiny silver nail bites ice. Standing at the window, both Shawnee Ray and I watch as he confers with the guard, using soothing hand gestures, shaking his head, smiling briefly, and then examining with zealous eyes the pipe offered to him, holding forth then, explaining tradition with a simple courtesy I wish that I could imitate. He wears a tie and silver-bowed eyeglasses. His hair is long, but cut in a careful shag that brushes the collar of his overcoat. After a while, the conversation seems to take on a friendlier overtone, for the guard nods his head once, and then straightens with an air of discovery.

"Zelda must have called him," says Shawnee Ray. Her face, in its frame of harsh feathers, is flushed and anxious. I am going to ask her just how I should conduct myself in this unusual situation, what to say, whether she can give me any clues, when Lyman and the guard come inside.

Shawnee doesn't turn to greet Lyman, her stare just widens as she continues to gaze out the window, seemingly struck by the view of parking lot asphalt and dark-night snowy earth. I am at such a loss that I act completely normal, and walk over to Lyman to talk to him, far enough away so she will not hear our conversation. There aren't

41

enough words on the reservation for our line of kin anymore. It's less confusing to decide on one thing to call them and leave out the tangles.

"Hello, my uncle," I say, once the guard has busied himself with a phone call and paperwork. "It's decent of you to show up and get this straightened out, so I just want to say thanks, and to assure you that Shawnee Ray had nothing to do with the mess."

"I never dreamed she did."

"And, see, you were right."

Lyman still holds the pipe carefully in his two hands. Weighing it, he slowly disconnects the bowl and stem. I reach to take them, but he keeps turning the pieces around and around in his hands as though they were magnetized. The stem is long as my arm, double barreled, one of a kind. It is quilled the old way, and the bowl is carved by some expert long forgot, the red stone traded from South Dakota.

"I'll give you three hundred," he says.

I don't register his meaning at first. I stand still, waiting for him to finish his inspection. Passed to Nector from his old man, Resounding Sky, that pipe is that very same one smoked when the treaty was drawn with the U.S. government. So there are some who say that it was badly used and has to be reblessed, and it is, I don't argue, a pipe that capped off the making of a big fat mistake. This is the same pipe refused by Pillagers who would not give away our land, the same one that solemnized the naming ceremony of a visiting United States president's wife, but it is also the pipe that started the ten-summer sundance. It is a kind of

42

public relations pipe, yet with historical weight. Personal too. This pipe is my inheritance from Nector. I feel his love dishonored by the rude treatment it received from the guard, on my account. Standing there regarding it, guilty, I wait for the sky to drop. I wait for the earth to split, for something to go terribly wrong, but the only thing that happens is I take a job.

"I suppose," says Lyman, putting the pipe reluctantly back into my hands, "you don't have a place to keep this museum piece."

"I'm kind of between places," I acknowledge. "I had the pipe stowed in a little suitcase in my car trunk."

Lyman drops his chin low and looks up at me from under his brows.

"You working?"

"I'm between jobs, too."

"Maybe," says Lyman, his teeth showing a little, "you could work for me again. Close by. Where I could keep an eye on you."

Neither of us glances at Shawnee Ray, but we both automatically lower our voices.

"Could be," I put the pipe in its bag, tuck it back into my jacket, against my heart, "I'll take you up on that. Stay close. Where I can keep an eye on you, too."

So that's how I am hired to rise early and clean out the bingo hall. Once in a while, I substitute bartend too. My place of employment is an all-purpose warehouse containing an area for gambling that Lyman hopes to enlarge, a bingo floor that converts to a dance area, and a bar, and

43

there are even a few older makes of video games blinking dimly against one wall. At five each morning I roll from bed in a room behind the bar, fill a bucket with hot water, add a splash of pink soap, wring out my mop, and set to work. After I swab the linoleum, I sling my rag across the seats and counters. I wash down the walls where people stagger, reach their hands out to break their fall, hands they've used to fix cars, calm horses, tie steel in the new interstate highway, hands that have slipped low with the oil of popcorn. Hands that are blood-related to my own hands, knuckle and bone.

It is my duty to retrieve what people drop when their nerves go numb in the lounge. Every morning, I pick up all that has fallen from their pockets, wedged beneath the plastic seats of booths. All the evidence of the night before comes to me, and as I accumulate what was lost, I feel lighter, as if the keys and the pens and the pennies and the dimes have no gravity, as if they drop off a weightless planet. As I clean, I see and hear all of the dramas replayed. Scenes resurrect from their own peaceful wreckage and surround me with the echoes of crashing noise.

In those still blue hours, the drunks and the nuns who pray for them are the only other people with their eyes open. I sometimes imagine those Sisters up the hill with clouds floating above their brains. Pure white clouds full of milk. As their lips move, the clouds pass over us, raining drops of mercy on the undeserving and the good.

Wisps of vapor, on the other hand, pour from the ears of my brothers and sisters in the deeps of

44

their binges and write, in vague ballooned letters over their heads at this hour, *Where the fuck can I get the next one?*

The answer: *Here. Just hang tough till seven.*

From outside, my place of work is a factorylike Quonset hut—aqua and black—one big half-cylinder of false hope that sits off the highway between here and Hoopdance. By day, the place looks shabby and raw—a rutted dirt parking lot bounds the rippled tin walls. Bare and glittering with broken glass, the wide expanse is pocked by deep holes. The Pabst sign hangs crooked and the flat wooden door sags as if it was shoved shut in too many faces, against hard fists. But you can't see dents in the walls or rips or litter once darkness falls. Then, because the palace is decked with bands of Christmas tree lights and traveling neon disks that wink and flicker, it comes at you across the flat dim land like a Disney setup, like a circus show, a spaceship, a constellation that's collapsed.

Inside it's always sour twilight. The atmosphere is dense and low, as if a storm is on the wind. You don't walk through the door, it's more like you're swallowed, like God's servant who the fish gulped down. Steel ribs arch overhead and the floor is damp. I can't get it dry even with a fan. The booths are covered in a thick plastic torn and carved in old patterns, glued back together in raised scars where I've fixed them with Vinyl-repair. But nobody notices how it looks after nine o'clock.

On one side, the bar is fixed so all the bottles are backed by mirrors and the bartender can see

45

the customers even when his hands are busy with the pumps. The popcorn machine is at the end of the counter, and it's the best lighted spot in the house. The bulbs in the hood flood golden radiance down on four or five barstools where women gravitate. They know how the light makes their eyes soft and dark, how the salt and butter clings to them, gets into their clothes, and mixes with sweat, cologne, and Salem smoke to produce a smell that is almost a substance, a kind of magic food that leaves a man emptier and hungrier after one whiff.

The bingo palace drives itself through wet nights according to these hungers. Except for the bright glow of the glass case of yellow popcorn, and the stage, bathed in purple, the great low room is a murk that hazes over and warms. Lovers in the booths or the unmatched dinette sets wrap their arms and legs together and send charged looks through rings of smoke. Smoke hangs low like a heavy cloud, collects at one level, shifts and bobs above the heads of the players and dancers. Smoke deepens, poised calm as a lake, over the tables.

People come and go underneath the cloud. Some to the bar, some to the bingo. There are the road workers, in construction, slab muscled and riding temporary money, new pickups with expensive options and airbrushed curlicues on the doors. Local businessmen with French names and Cree blood, guys with green eyes and black hair, talk in the quieter corners, making deals with flat hand gestures. Farmers visit—a Scandinavian family group or two—always quiet and half asleep and worked raw. When the men take off their Grain Belt or John Deere hats, the upper halves of their pale foreheads float and bob in the dark as they nod and talk.

Indian men, old ones with slicked-back gray hair, black-framed Indian Health Service glasses, and spotless white shirts of western cut and pearl snaps, sit straight up at the tables. Although they speak in low, soft voices, you can hear everything they say through the din. Within their company, there's sometimes a woman in a flowered pantsuit, hair swept into a bead rosette. She sips her beer, nods, adds a word at the right moment, and through the force of her quiet, runs the entire show.

Near the radiant circle at the popcorn machine, against the Lally poles, around the back entrance, lounge the younger Indian guys. Without seeming to notice the eyes that turn on them, or don't— and I know because I'm usually attempting to be one of them—these guys strut like prairie grouse. Some wear straw Stetsons with side or front medallions of pheasant feathers, and some wear mesh CAT hats, black and gold, with beaded brims. A few have long ponytails that flood to their waist, or thick loose hair they toss back over their shoulders. Some leave on their dark glasses, even inside. Some wear rude-colored western shirts, or fancy ones with roses and briars and embroideries of rising suns. Heavy-metal leather, surfer shirts, glow-in-the-dark rings around a few necks. Anything to make a girl look. There are tall men already with hard, belligerent paunches and slender boys with mysterious, clear faces and

47

sly ways with their hands. But all of us, every one, wear boots and jeans within which our hips move, proud, with lazy joy, smooth as if oiled with warm crankcase or the same butter that the women at the bar lick off their fingers and smear on the men's hands when they dance—or go elsewhere. For the large unlit parking lot behind the palace is full of empty-looking cars that shudder, rock on their springs, or moan and sigh as the night wears on.

Now, you say, what about that truth and disaster I mentioned? It starts here at the bingo palace, with one of those ladies I just told you about who runs things by sitting quiet in the middle of the room. Aunt Zelda, of course.

Every time Aunt Zelda got annoyed with life in general she came to sit in Lyman's bar—not to drink, but to disapprove of her surroundings. On the night I get my luck fixed, I feel my aunt's presence the moment she steps through the doors. Her eyes flick and probe the dark booths as she sails forward, and her mouth twitches in righteous shock. I don't even have to turn around or look in the mirror to know it is her. She clicks across the floor loud as a calculator, then scrubs the end stool clean with a hankie fished from her sleeve.

"A tonic water, please," she requests in a controlled voice. I reach over and splash the stuff into a glass with ice. Then I squeeze a rag carefully to wipe the counter, and I set her glass on a little white square napkin from a special pile, unsoiled by liquor slogans or printed bathroom jokes. Cautiously, I put forth the question. "Lime?" She gives a short nod, a little yank of her cuffs. Her shoulders shrug slightly down. I spear not one, but two lime chunks on a little plastic sword and dunk them into her glass.

Only then does she take possession of her stool.

"On the house." I wave away the open metal jaws of her tiny purse. She snaps it shut, thanks me, cranks up her posture one more notch.

"You give this place just what it needs," I tell her, "an air of class."

When she doesn't respond, I repeat the compliment again, with more conviction, and she smiles, curving the corners of the pointed lips she has carefully painted upon her mouth.

"Salute," she toasts with light sophistication. Her sip prints the glass with her sharp lip-print, blurring her determined mouth further yet.

It will take glass after glass of formal prepared tonic waters very gradually laced with gin to bring the human shape back to her face. My motive is good—to make Shawnee Ray's life a little easier, for once the slight amounts of alcohol start having their effect, Zelda's basic niceness is free to shine forth. Right and left, she always forgives the multitude. Her smile relaxes—gleaming, melted pearls. From her corner she sheds a more benign opinion like a balm. No matter how bad things get, on those nights when Zelda stays long enough, there is eventually the flooding appeasement of her smile. It is like having a household saint.

But you have to light a candle, make a sacrifice. Zelda is aware that her chemistry experiment has had unexpected results—here I am mixing drinks for my boss, the intended husband of the girl she fostered, while that girl herself, Shawnee Ray, is not out with Lyman Lamartine but at

49

home intensively mothering her little boy. Zelda shouldn't play so hard and loose with the unexpected, that is my opinion. People's hearts are constructed of unknowable elements and even now, I feel sure, there is some unexplainable interest in me on the part of Shawnee Ray. I have to admit that our first date wasn't much. Still, she has consented to talk to me on the phone once or twice since that night.

I don't push my luck, but just go along for a while tending to my job, allowing the others to run interference with Zelda. As usual, she has a lot of people to maneuver, and so she hasn't had the time to concentrate full force on me. I am satisfied, want to stay that way. I like my aunt, even though I find it difficult to keep from getting run over by her unseen intentions.

Eighteen-wheeler trucks. Semis, fully loaded, with a belly dump. You never know what is coming at you when Zelda takes the road. Maybe it is the wariness, maybe I just want to head her off. Maybe I am stepping out in front of her with a red flag, or maybe I forget to put on my orange Day-Glo vest. Whatever happens, the fact is I get careless with Zelda's drinks. The trade is slow. I suppose I am tired and forget to measure. I add just that little bit too much to Zelda's tonics that sends her barreling at me full throttle. Too bad I am standing on the center line.

Starting out, she explains to me how my great grandmother, that dangerous Fleur Pillager, tried to kill herself by loading her pockets with stones and marching into Matchimanito Lake. Only, here's what stones she picked: the very ones that rested by her bedside, the very ones that she had always talked to. The perfect ones. The round ones. They knew her and so they helped her. They wouldn't let her sink. Spirit stones, they floated her up.

Aunt Zelda next confides to me the identity of her first boyfriend, the only man she ever loved. That is Shawnee Ray's uncle, Xavier Toose. Zelda says right out, strangely, that he lost his fingers for touching her. Then she falls silent, stares long at the mirror behind me, just moving her lips. I try to change the subject of her brooding thoughts by asking her how Redford is doing, but as though I have prodded a tape back into the reel she begins to speak again of Xavier, well-known traditional singer whom I last saw at the powwow, hand cupped at his ear like an animal paw. As he drummed, his voice shivered all the high notes with the Rising Wind singers.

Again she stops. "So, do you want me to tell it?" she asks.

"Tell what?"

"Do you want me to tell you this here story?"

I want to say no, to gently tap the faucet of her words shut, but her eyes are too brilliant, her need too harsh.

"It's what you might call," she says, her face both dreamy and sharp of sight, "a tale of burning love."

It's a concept with which I'm very recently familiar, so I lean closer, and I open my ears.

"Xavier Toose was the lookingest man around here, and a smart one too, but he wasn't the man

51

I was saving myself to marry. That special man had to be white, so he would take me away from the reservation to the Cities, where I'd planned my life all out from catalogs and magazines. I resisted Xavier Toose, and yet my heart annoyed me when he sat down in our kitchen. Beating so loud, beating out the rabbit dance, beating hard enough to choke my throat, my heart pounded when I watched him stretch his slim legs from the wooden chair. He knew that when he spoke, my ears caught the lower registers, the love line underscoring all he said, the real and hidden meanings.

"There were other things. I lighted candles to the saints to stop my thoughts, but they did no good. I dreamed of him every single night. I think he knew it. I think he doctored my tea. Yet, he was wrong for me, didn't fit into my futures, where I saw myself holding a pan over a little white stove. In those wish dreams, I was dressed in pink, dressed in pale blue. I was someone with an upstairs to her downstairs, a two-story woman.

"Not Xavier. He was a man who would live in an old-time cabin. He was heading for a life of happy-time powwowing, if he didn't get caught up in drink. Oh yes, those days he drank some. I saw him doing the circuits, singing and drumming. He would hold down a low-pay job to support the bigger task it was to be an Indian. Now he's a ceremony man, Xavier, religious and quiet, but then he had a little of the devil in him.

"Time went on, and I refused him once a season. Spring. Summer. Fall. Then came winter. The question would be asked for the last time. The fourth time, in the old ways, you accept or

52

refuse forever. So it seemed like we were down to a pitched battle. He visited every night and people assumed I'd said yes. But I hadn't said that word to Xavier because he hadn't asked outright although he kept looking at me, staring at me, with patient determination.

"Then came Saint Lucy's, the longest night of the year. He came over to our house and as the light ran soft and dusky he whispered, smiled, flashed the new ring on the tip of his finger. Unwilling, I followed him out to the barn, placing no in my mouth like a pebble to throw. Once inside, we stood by the dark stalls and he showed me the golden French band he'd bought with haying money.

" 'Want it?' he asked.

"I couldn't find the courage to talk so I shook my head *no*.

" 'Sure?'

"My heart was giving out on me, going fast. My face curved to meet his. Staring into his eyes, my gaze lost focus.

" 'Go away,' I said.

" 'I'm not going to leave tonight until you tell me the truth. You love me but you want a white man, I know the way you are. You wouldn't be happy, though. You need a guy like me.'

"Xavier had stashed a bottle of whiskey in the manger, underneath some hay, and now he brought it out, offered me a drink. I took a sip and the burn almost choked me, I took another and my head cleared.

" 'I won't leave. I'll sit outside your window

lighting matches all night.' He laughed. 'I'll get drunk on your doorstep. Say yes!'

"I turned away from him and slammed back into the house, mad, yet my heart was dancing to return to the stalls, the warmth of his hands, already seamed with so much work. But I was strong, this just goes to show you. I did not go back. From the wide bed I shared with my little sisters, I pulled a blanket around my shoulders and I watched. After the lights were out I saw his matches, one after the other, flare in the windless night. One small light, then another. I dozed off and still saw those small flickers in the depth of blue, against the blue snow.

"The next morning, my brothers brought him in. They found Xavier hunched and frozen, still sitting in a curl of drifted snow. One hand was on his heart, they said, the other clutched the bottle. It was the hand on his heart that froze, though, and from that hand he lost his fingers."

Zelda stops, drinks long, and then looks me steady in the eye to see how I react.

"Go home now, Auntie, please go home," I beg.

But she will not, in fact, she's just getting started, one story hinging into the next. She tells me how my grandma Lulu found a dead man in the woods, and how she herself stood by to watch her own father burning down the Lamartine's house. She tells me that is why she's glad that she refused Xavier Toose. "Love wrecks things, love is a burning letter in the sky, a nuisance," she growls. She says things that she should keep to

54

herself, keep quiet about, never speak. She goes and tells me why I owe her everything.

"You're sweet," Zelda sways forward, her hair semifrowzled.

"I got it from the time I worked the sugar beet plant," I explain.

"You got it from yourself." Her black eyes wander. "Not from your mother."

"My mother?"

I can't help it, my ears flare for more. So I ball up my rag, lean on the counter, and ask the thing I shouldn't ask.

"What about her?"

And then Zelda tells me the raw specifics of how my mother left me with Grandma. She tells me facts that make me miserable. She does the worst thing of all: she tells me the truth.

"I don't know how she could have done it." Zelda shakes her head, her mouth rolled tight.

"What?"

"I hate to talk about it in front of you." She hedges to draw out the intensity. "But then, you already heard about the gunnysack."

My aunt is enjoying herself. She pretends not to, but actually loves giving out the facts and the painful details. I could stop her, but the mention of my mother makes me helpless. No matter what June Morrissey has done to me, no matter that she's gone, I still love her so. I can't hear enough, or so I believe.

"That gunnysack was a joke." I speak confident. "Grandma kidded me once that my real mom was about to throw me in the slough. But no mother—"

Zelda interrupts me, nods agreement. "No mother, she was sure no true mother. June Morrissey, Kashpaw, whatever she was, she threw you in."

"*N'missae*," I say now, real slow, calling her my oldest sister. "You had a little extra to drink tonight. I spiked your tonic. Don't get mad at me. It's on the house."

But she is shaking her head at my version of the subject that has risen in her memory.

"She chucked you," Aunt Zelda continues. "I should know. It was me who dragged you out."

"You never said that before." I check the gin bottle. I cannot tell exactly how much I've poured.

"I was always a watcher, the one who saw. I was sitting on the back steps when I looked down the hill. There was June, slinging a little bundle into the slough."

"That's gin talking," I say. I tell her right out like that, and even throw down my rag on the counter. But I cannot turn away or stop listening as she continues in a voice that grows more hoarse, fascinated and too believable.

"I'll never forget that moment, Lipsha. Cloudy summer's day. I was all sly and I waited until June left. Then I went to see for myself what she had tossed into the water." Zelda stops here, bites her lower lip, and twists the glass in her hands. "I don't know how long I waited. If I'd known it was you, I would have ran down right away."

"Wasn't me." I make my voice firm, loud. "Wasn't Lipsha. No mother . . ."

56

No use. Zelda hardly notices me. She's talking about the moment she lived through at the edge of that pothole of water brown as coffee and sprouting cattails and lilies and harboring at its edges ducks and mudhens and flashy mallards.

"I waded in." Her voice grows strong, definite and sure. "I went in mud up to my knees and then into water over my head, so I had to swim around and try to remember where June had aimed the gunnysack. I started diving and must have made three, four tries before I touched the bag's edge. It took me two more dives to haul it up because"—now Zelda pauses for emphasis, glaring through me like I'm not there—"June had added *rocks*. I lugged that heavy sack to dry land, pulled it out. Then I packed it with the rocks banging, through the woods and into the field." Zelda bites her straw as she remembers me once more. "I would have opened it as soon as I got it out, Lipsha, if I'd known it was you."

I am getting this feeling now, this sick wrench that comes upon a person when they don't want to witness what is happening right in front of them.

"It wasn't me!" My voice is loud and one or two bleary loungers look over, curious. My mind is buzzing. My arms are weakening, deadening with the feeling that they want something big to hold on to, a tree, a rooted sapling, a hunkered crowd of earth, another person. But Zelda isn't someone to tolerate surprises. I can't grab her, and anyway she is the source of my confusion, so I stand my ground, even though I feel a tremble starting down low in my feet. I don't move as her voice continues.

57

"I opened that sack once I was out of the woods. I cried when I saw it was a baby! When you saw me you blinked your eyes wide and then you smiled. You were in that sack for twenty minutes, though, maybe half an hour."

"I was not."

"Maybe longer." She takes no argument. "Something else has always bothered me though." She scratches at the counter with a swizzle. "Lipsha, you were in that slough a long time."

"No, I wasn't."

She stops completely and stares at me, and then she whispers.

"So why weren't you drowned?"

And because I am mad at her for making up that stupid fucking story and all, I stare right back.

"Watch out," I snap my eyes at her. *"You'll take my place!"*

I hiss these words into Zelda's face, using the same dangerous threat that my great grandmother, Fleur Pillager, is supposed to have said to her long-ago rescuer, who died soon and took her place on death's road. I employ the family warning, and Zelda does draw back. A tiny light of fear strikes itself in and out of her eyes as quick as a motel match. But she isn't one to accept into herself a curse. She is too strong a boss woman, and veers off my Pillager words with a quick sign of the cross.

I would like to do the same with hers, but odd thing is, I can't. I tell myself that in her cups she became inventive, that she embroidered my case history in her memory, beadworked it with a colorful stitch. She's wrong, I keep promising myself. Wrong as wrong.

Wrong, I repeat, turning in that night. *Wrong*, I keep insisting in my mind as I turn out the lights. *Wrong, wrong, wrong*, I fall into my dreams. I tell myself that Zelda scared the story up, she made it happen. She never found me in a gunnysack. I remind myself that I believe what Grandma Kashpaw told me—that I was given to her in a sad but understandable way by a mother who was beautiful but too wild to have raised a boy on her own. I had come to terms with that story, forgave how June was so far out on the edge of life that she couldn't properly care for me.

I want to keep that firm ground, that knowledge, but my dreams are frightening water.

That night, deeper places draw me down. I sink into black softness, my heart beating fast, straining in the trap of my chest. I wake with a thump, as though I've hit the bottom of my waterbed. I jump onto the floor and pull on my jeans, switch on the lights, decide to make a round, a kind of house check, and maybe, although I rarely do indulge, drink down a free drink.

I walk quietly into the shadowy echoes of emptiness. I pass the bar, then steer around to the other side. I am just in the process of selecting a bottle, when I look into the mirror.

And see June.

Her face is a paler blur than the dark, her eyes are lake quartz, and she gazes with sad assurance at me out of the empty silence. She wears a pink top that glows faintly, as does the Bailey's Irish

59

Cream filling her small glass. Her hair is black, sweeps down along her chin in two smooth feathers. There is no age to her—ancient, brand-new, slim as a girl. Take your pick. She is anyone, everyone. She is my mother.

She looks the way she did when I was little, those times I glimpsed her walking back from her trips to town. She looks the way she should have if she stayed and kept the good ways and became old and graceful. She watches me across the long, low room. There is no smoke to part, to make way for her gaze. There is no noise to hear over. I can't claim that she is obscured. I can't claim her voice is covered.

June carefully opens her purse and taps out a cigarette. Darkness moves in front of her and by the time I turn around and shuffle to the other side of the room, her chair is empty. She has moved. My hair freezes on my neck to see her on the other side of the bar. I get a prickle down my back and I go fainting and weak all over. Stumbling, I almost turn tail.

"You have to face her," I tell myself, trying to calm my heart. "She's visiting for a reason."

In places, the concrete base of the bar has humped beneath the flooring and buckled. On cold nights, from my little den, I hear it shift. I catch that low sound now, a thump and crack. Then there is a still moment when nothing moves. Outside, there is no wind, not a faraway motor. No voice raised. No sound in the open fields. No dog barks, nothing.

Suddenly the furnace breathes out and

60

complains. Ice tumbles in the freezer slot of the refrigerator.

I shake.

Now I always told myself before that there was a good side to ghosts. My reasoning goes along on the base of the following uncertainties: Beyond this world, is there another? Dimensions, how many? Which afterlife? Whose God will I face if there is one, whose court? A ghost could answer the basic question, at least, as to whether there is anything besides the world I know, the things I touch. If I see a ghost, possibilities will open. I have told myself all this, and yet, finally in the presence of one, I shake.

I keep telling myself that my mother means me no harm and besides, it can't have been easy for her to appear. She has surely walked through fire, crossed water, passed through the great homely divide of fenced pasture and fields scoured flat by the snow. She has walked the three-day road back, the road of the dead. She has put herself out royally to get here, is what I'm saying. I tell myself I should at least have the guts to find out why.

I take a deep breath and enter the vast, still plain of the bingo palace. I flick on the lights, but they are low-watt anyway, so dim they hardly make a difference. Each step I take, I stop and listen for the echo, the trail. Each time I stop, I hear the silence, loud as a rush of heat. My heart pushes the blood to my head in pulses that glow behind my eyelids, and my fingers burn at the tips as if they were dipped in ice. I reach the stool, the one where I've seen her sitting, and then I touch

61

it with my palm and it seems to me the back is warm.

"Where's my car?" she asks right beside me, then, as if we are continuing a conversation in time. "I came back because I was just wondering where you put it. Where the hell is my car?"

"It's outside," I answer, but my voice sounds like I'm talking from a hollow well.

"What did you do with it?" Her tone is pointed. "Crack it up?"

"No."

"Well, what?"

"It's kind of stalled," I tell her.

" 'Kind of'? What do you mean 'kind of'?"

"All it needs is a little jump-start."

"I'll give you jump-start. Shit!"

She throws herself down at a table, angry, and nods at the chair. I am now in a weakened state, my legs wobble, soft rags. If I'd known that accepting the blue Firebird paid for with the insurance money from her death would piss her off this bad—even from beyond the grave—well, forget it. Even after what Zelda said, I guess I still imagined my mother as gentle toward me, hopefully guilt-struck, but either that was wishful thinking or she is in a mood that night. Her voice is hard and she has no time for small talk. I figure that there is maybe some trouble, something disagreeable going on wherever she has come from, a situation from which she needs relief, or at least transportation.

After sitting there and stewing in our own silence for what seems a long time to me, I get the nerve to speak.

"June . . . Mom," I gently begin, surprised to hear how the last word sounds in my voice, "what do you want from me?"

Lukewarm puffs of smoke quiver in the air between us, and she frowns.

"I'm in a rush. I gotta go, but listen here. Do you play bingo?"

"I never did yet," I inform her. "Well, hardly ever."

"Now you do."

She dangles the lighted cigarette from her lips and again opens her purse, searches with both hands, carefully draws out a flimsy booklet, and pushes it across the table between us. I see that the papers are bingo tickets, marked with little squares containing letters and numbers. I begin to flip through the book politely, the way you look at photos of someone's vacation to Sturgis, wondering what her intention could be, but there is nothing in the tickets that looks out of the ordinary. When I lift my head to thank her, no one is there. She has evaporated into the spent daze of smoke that wreathes her chair.

I run outside, coatless in the freezing black air, and I call my mother's name but there is no answer. Above me, in the heaven where she came from, cold stars ring down and stabs of ancient light glitter, delicate and lonely. Grand forms twist out of unearthly dust. As I watch, then, sure enough, one star breaks from its rank and plunges.

It is happening. I know it. My luck is finally shifting. I go back inside and crawl into my sleeping bag bed, and eventually I begin to lose the sense of fear and of excitement, to float down

63

through the connections. I wake slightly, once, imagining that from beyond the thickly insulated walls of the bar, I hear the muffled rev of an engine. I worry vaguely about my car, but sleep is a deep wave's trough. I turn over, roll down the watery slope.

CHAPTER SIX

JUNE'S LUCK

At first it was just that June's mother went clumsy, knocking the tin cups from their nails, the bucket hollow against the stove. In the middle of the night, she sang an old round-dance song and laughter screamed out from her place behind the curtain. Dawn came and June rose by herself, found a little cold bannock in the unfired oven. She scraped ashes off and put it into her mouth, chewed the sweet, burnt crumbles. June left for the school bus but then, halfway down the path, a cloud spun into her face. She ran back, touched her sleeping mother on the cheek, jumped away, and was gone once she stirred.

Lucille Lazarre was thin through the hips and arms, but her stomach was thick and solid as a tree trunk. She looked huge standing at the door when June came home from the Sisters' school. June had made good marks that day and had won a scapular of bronze felt. Her older brother, Geezhig, who had stayed in town the night before, elbowed roughly past his mother but Lucille grabbed him and hugged him against her. He

64

looked down at his feet and held his neck stiff while she rubbed at his hair with her warm palms. She didn't stop, kept rubbing harder.

"Let me go."

She pushed him away, turned to June. Her eyes were red around the edges, burning, her lips were dry and purple. Her long hair fell almost to her waist. When, on good days, she sat in a chair making baskets and let June braid and brush, June imagined that she wore her mother's hair, that she sat inside its safe tent.

June reached out now, tried to catch a strand, a mistake she realized even before her mother's hand slapped. Still, it happened so quickly that June did not react at first. She squinted across the sting of the blow at Lucille's blouse, at the blue patterns of teapots, turned upside down. Lucille's tan skirt was long and stained as though she had been standing near fire and the smoke had drifted up her body. Now, because of the slap, the clothing seemed covered with a strange glaze, a shining, beaded substance that winked fiercely. June rubbed her eyes, turned away, then ran outside, pushing off the sand of her mother's voice. For the next few hours she sat high in her tree.

When June went into the house again, her mother's face looked chalked in, coated with white dust. She was sitting on the chair, alone and still. There was no bottle in her hand, none to see anywhere, and June crept past her to the corner of heaped blankets where she slept with Geezhig. It was soon completely dark, and she rolled against

Geezhig's bony back, slept until he tapped on her face, lightly, calling her awake.

"Run off in the bush," he said. "Go on, little sister."

Lucille's boyfriend was there, a man named Leonard whom they both made fun of for his big red lips. His body was a powerful lump, short and thick, and he thrust out his head before him as he moved, like a wedge. He wore his hair short, bristling, so they called him porcupine. His nose was darker than the rest of his face, but he didn't smell sour like a porcupine, he smelled wonderful. He wore some kind of *zhaginash* juice that sweetened him for Lucille.

The air around June's face seemed cold. She sank lower, under the scratchy old army blankets, where her body had hollowed a nest. Usually, her mother had to hit Geezhig anyway, and got to her only when she wasn't so angry, when her arm had gone slack and lazy. June curled up and shut away Geezhig's voice. It was too cold outside to sleep covered over with leaves. She stayed. The voices boomed around her with great and muffled drumming sounds and filled her body with a loose warmth. In sleep, she didn't have to hear them, and so she relaxed into their cries and curled against a wall of noise.

Light blared. June's head, thick, rang. Then she flew and hit. Sprawled flat, she gagged for breath. Her chest was pressed flat as pages. She saw the center of a yellow wheel, churning, throwing off sparks that filled big sails.

Across golden water, her mother screamed. *"Where is he?"* June's air bubbled in and out and fear shot her toward the doorway. She nearly slipped by, twisting like a cat, but Leonard's hands were loaded springs and he caught her and scuffled her down. June's mother cuffed her once, not too hard. But then, different than ever before, she kneeled with her knees pinching in June's waist and with a string of cotton clothesline fastened complicated tangles around her arms and tied her daughter to the leg of the cast-iron stove.

"No more running away!"

Lucille's breath rushed in and out, ragged, sick. She got the bottle and went off, tilting it over her with every other step. June twisted against the knots, tried to scramble or bite herself free, but the ropes were put on every which way and tightened the harder she fought. Leonard's feet clumped down once, but he never came near. Then she heard him walk over to the lean-to door, near where her mother kept her bed, and although the floor was rough dirt, the dust choking, cold, she went dreamy. Finally, sleep sifted into her brain.

She felt his hand across her mouth, big and heavy with tough pads. She smelled the sweetness, spice, the incense of his perfumes and under it the sour yeast and heavy flowers of his armpits. He touched her, his hands like hot bells. He took off her ropes but kept her bound up with his fingers. They were steel clamps. They found her, found her, until she galloped against him. No matter where she went, his tongue came down. Then the wheel sang again, flew off its spokes and banged into a brilliant wall. There was a way a man could get into her body and she never knew. Pain rang

67

everywhere. June tried to climb out of it, but his chin held her shoulder. She tried to roll from underneath, but he was on every side. Skeins of sparks buzzed down, covered her eyes and face. Then she was so small she was just a burning dot, a flung star moving, speeding through the blackness, the air, faster and faster and with no letup until she finally escaped into a part of her mind, where she made one promise before she went out.

Nobody ever hold me again.

Chapter Seven

LIPSHA

THE BINGO VAN

When I walk into bingo that night in late winter I am a player like any regular person, drenched in casual wishes, in hopes. Upon first entering, I look for any friends I might have from the past or the present, or any relations, and right off, I see Grandma Lulu. She has five tickets spread in front of her. Her neighbors each have only one. When the numbers roll, she picks up a bingo dauber in each hand. It is the Early Birds' game, one-hundred-dollar prize, and nobody has got too wound up yet or serious.

"Lipsha, go get me a Coke," commands Lulu when someone else bingos. "Yourself too."

I hit the concession, snag our soft drinks and come back, set them down, pull up to the table,

68

and lay out my ticket. Like I say, my grand-mother, she plays five, which is how you get the big money. In the long run, much more than even, she is one of those rare Chippewas who actually profit by bingo. But then again, these days it is her preferred way of gambling. No pull-tabs. No blackjack. No slot machines for her. She never goes into the back room, never drinks. She banks all of her cash. I think I can learn from Lulu Lamartine, so I watch her close.

Concentration. Before the numbers even start, she sits down in her lucky place, a chair that nobody else dares take, fourth row and fourth to the right by the eastern wall. She composes her face to calm, snaps her purse shut. She shakes her daubers upside down so that the foam-rubber tips are thoroughly inked. She looks at the time on her watch. The Coke, she takes a drink of that, but no more than a sip. She is a narrow-eyed woman with a round jaw, curled hair. Her eyeglasses, blue plastic, hang from her neck by two chains. She raises the ovals to her eyes as the caller takes the stand. She holds her daubers poised while he plucks the ball from the chute. He reads it out. B-7. Then she is absorbed, scanning, dabbing, into the game. She doesn't mutter. She has no lucky piece to touch in front of her. And afterward, even if she loses a blackout by one square she never sighs or complains.

All business, that's Lulu. And all business pays.

I believe I could be all business too, like her, if not for the van that sits behind the curtain. I don't know it right away, but that is the prize that will change the order of my life. Because of the van,

69

I'll have to get stupid first, then wise. I'll have to keep floundering, trying to catch my bearings in the world. It all sits ahead of me, spread out in the sun like a naming giveaway. More than anything, I want to be the man who can impress Shawnee Ray.

"Lipsha Morrissey, you got to go for a vocation," says Grandma Lulu, during break.

"Maybe I'll win at bingo," I say to her, in hope.

Her smile is still and curved as a cat's, her cheeks round and soft, her fingernails perfect claws of blazing tropic pink.

"Win at bingo," she repeats my words thoughtfully. "Everybody wins once. It's the next time and the next time you got to worry about."

But she doesn't know that I am playing bingo on the advice of a ghost, and I haven't mentioned my position as night watchman at the bar. I suppose I want her to think of me as more successful than I really am, so I keep my mouth shut although, after all, I shouldn't be so shy. The job earns me a place to sleep, twenty dollars per week, and as much beef jerky, beer nuts, and spicy sausage sticks as I can eat.

I am now composed of these three false substances. No food in a bar has a shelf life of less than forty months. If you are what you eat, I will live forever, I decide.

And then they pull aside the curtain, and I forget my prediction. I see that I wouldn't want to live as long as I have coming, unless I own *the van*. It has every option you can believe—blue plush on the steering wheel, diamond side windows, and complete carpeting interior. The seats are easy chairs, with little built-in head-phones, and it is wired all through the walls. You can walk up close during intermission and touch the sides. The paint is cream, except for the design picked out in blue, which is a Sioux Drum border. In the back there is a small refrigerator and a padded platform for sleeping. It is a starter home, a portable den with front-wheel drive, a place where I can shack with Shawnee Ray and her little boy, if she will consent. If she won't live there, though, at least she will be impressed.

Now, I know that what I feel is a symptom of the national decline. You'll scoff at me, scorn me, say what right does that waste Lipsha Morrissey, who makes his living guarding beer, have to comment outside of his own tribal boundary? But I am able to investigate the larger picture, thanks to my mother's directions and thanks to Lulu, from whom I soon learn to be one-minded in my pursuit of a material object.

After that first sighting, I go play the bingo whenever I can get off from bar duty or cleanup. Lyman never stops me, for I think it seems economical for his workers to return their profits to the palace by spending off-hours at the long tables or drinking beers. Every bit of time that I spend listening for bingo numbers, I grow more certain I am close. There is only one game per night at which the van is offered, a blackout game, in which you have to fill every slot. The more cards you buy, the more your chance increases. I try to play five numbers like Grandma Lulu, but they cost five bucks each.

To get my van, I have to shake hands with greed.

I get unprincipled. As I might have already said, my one talent in this life is a healing power I get passed down through the Pillager branch of my background. It's in my hands. I snap my fingers together so hard they almost spark. Then I blank out my mind, and I put on the touch. I have a reputation up to now for curing sore joints and veins. I can relieve ailments caused in an old person by one half century of grinding stoopover work. I have a power in myself that flows out, resistless. I have a richness in my dreams and waking thoughts. But I do not realize I will have to give up my healing source once I start charging for my service.

You know how it is about charging. People suddenly think you are worth something. Used to be, I'd go anyplace I was called, take any price offered or take nothing. Once I let it go around that I expect a twenty for my basic work, however, the phone at the bar rings off the hook.

"Where's that medicine boy?" they want to know. "Where's Lipsha?"

I take their money. And it's not like beneath the pressure of a twenty I don't try, for I do try even harder than before. I skip my palms together, snap my fingers, position them where the touch inhabiting them should flow. But when it comes to blanking out my mind, I consistently fail. For each time, in the center of the cloud that comes down into my brain, in perfect focus, the van is now parked.

72

One afternoon, Grandma Lulu leaves word that I should come over to her apartment to work on a patient, and though she doesn't name money, I know from her voice it is an important customer. Maybe he's her latest boyfriend. For sure, he has a job or some SSI. So I go over there. Entering her place, as usual, I exchange salutes with my own father from his picture on her shelf of little china mementos.

"I'd like you to meet Russell Kashpaw," Grandma says, and with that, I shake the hand of our state's most decorated war hero, who is recovering from multiple strokes and antique shrapnel wounds. Russell sits in a wheelchair. His job, at which he does the most business after the bars close, is tattooing people with pictures of roses, skulls, Harleys, and kung fu dragons. He lives down a curved road, off in the bush, and you can see his work displayed on almost any night.

Russell looks like a statue, not the type you see in history books, I don't mean those, but the kind you see for sale as you drive along the highway. He is a native Paul Bunyan, carved with a chain saw. He is rough-looking, finished in big strokes. I shake Russell Kashpaw's hand, hoping to feel some pulse surge, some information. I shake it longer, waiting for electrical input, but there is nothing.

"Sometimes there's a lot of static in these old war wounds," I say out loud. "Where do you feel the knot?"

In a low and commanding voice, heavy on the details, he begins to describe his aches, his pains,

73

his spasms, his creaks and cricks. My two grandmas and their neighbor, that gossiper Mrs. Josette Bizhieu, are in the room with me. The three of them nod and tut at every one of Russell Kashpaw's symptoms and in glowing words assure him that he's come to the right place for a cure. So I rub my hands together hard and fast, inspired, then I press my burning palms to the sides of his shoulders, for it is the back of his neck and spine that are giving him the worst aggravations today. But though I knead him like I see Grandma making her buns and rolls, and though I heat my hands up again like a lightning strike, and though I twist my fingers into wire pretzels, I cannot set the touch upon him proper.

He was so shot up there's metal in him, shorting out my energy. He is so full of scars and holes and I can't smooth him straight. I don't give up, though. I try and I try until I even seem to hurt him worse, gripping desperate, with all my might.

"Holy buckets," he yells.

"Damn, Mr. Kashpaw. I'm sorry!"

I'm all balled up like some kind of tangled yarn of impulse. I'm a mess of conflicting feedback, a miserable lump of burnt string. And worst of all, the eyes of my Grandmas are on me with increasing letdown and disappointment, as I fail, and fail my patient once again. Russell pays me but he isn't happy, and neither am I, for I know, as soon as right now, the talk will gather and flash from lip to lip starting at the Senior Citizens and fanning through the houses, down the roads. My touch has deserted me. My hands are shocked out, useless. I am again no more than the simple nothing that I always was before.

I suppose after that I begin to place my desperations in the bingo. I long for the van like I've started to wish for Shawnee. And then, there comes an incident that sets me back in my quest.

Instead of going for the van with everything, saving up to buy as many cards as I can play when they get to the special game, I go short-term for variety with U-Pick-em cards, the kind where you have to choose the numbers for yourself.

First off, I write down my shoe and pants size. So much for me. I take my birth date and a double of it after that. Still no go. I write down the numbers of my Grandma's address and her anniversary dates. Nothing. Then I realize if my U-Pick-em is going to win, it will be more like revealed, rather than a forced kind of thing. So I shut my eyes right there in the middle of the long bingo table and I let my mind white out, fizzing like the screen of a television, until something forms. The van, as always. But on its tail this time a license plate is officially fixed and bolted. I use that number, write it down in the boxes.

And then I bingo.

I get two hundred dollars from that imaginary license. It is in my pocket when I leave that night. The next morning, I have fifty cents. But it's not like you think it is with Shawnee Ray, and I'll explain that. She doesn't want something from me, she never cares if I have money and never asks for it. Her idea is to go into business. To pay

75

for college, she wants to sell her original clothing designs, of which she has six books.

I have gotten to know Shawnee a little better with each phone call, but the time has come that I can't think up another excuse to dial her number. She is so decided in her future that she intimidates me—it is her A+ attitude, her gallons of talents and hobbies. Though I want to ask her out again, the embarrassing memory of our first date keeps intruding on my mind. Finally I tell myself, "Lipsha, you're a nice-looking guy. You're a winner. You know the washer's always broken at Zelda's house. Pretend to run into Shawnee at the laundry."

So I scout the place for days until she finally shows, then I go right up to her at the Coin-Op and I make a face of surprise, which against my better judgment gets taken over by immediate joy. Just seeing her makes my head spin and my hands clench my chest. For the hundredth time, I apologize for how I've gotten her in trouble. Then I say, "Care to dance?" which is a joke. There isn't anyplace to dance at a laundromat. Yet, I can tell she likes me at least as much as the week before. We eat a sandwich and a cookie from the machine and then while her clean clothing dries Shawnee says she wants to take a drive, so we tag along with some others in the back of their car. They go straight south, toward Hoopdance, where action is taking place.

"Shawnee Ray," I whisper as we drive along, "I can't stop thinking of you."

"Lipsha." She smiles. "I can't stop thinking of you too."

I don't say anything about Lyman Lamartine and neither does she, but I have this sudden sense of him right then as perched behind us in the back window, head bobbing side to side like a toy car dog. Even so, Shawnee Ray and I move close together on the car seat. My hand is on my knee, and I think of a couple different ways I could gesture, casually pretend to let it fall on hers, how maybe if I talk fast she won't notice, in the heat of the moment, her hand in mine, us holding hands, our lips drawn to one another. But then I decide to give it all up, to boldly take courage, to cradle her hand as at the same time I look into her eyes. I do this. In the front, the others talk between themselves. We just sit there. Her mouth turns raw and hot underneath the weight of my eyes and I bend forward. She leans backward. "You want to kiss me?" she asks. But I answer, not planning how the words will come out, "Not here. Our first kiss has to be a magic moment only we can share."

Her eyes flare softer than I'd ever imagined, then widen like a deer's, and her big smile blooms. Her skin is dark, her long hair a burnt brown-black color. She wears no jewelry, no rings, that night, just the clothing she has sewed from her own designs—a suit jacket and a pair of pants the tan of eggshells, with symbols picked out in blue thread on the borders, the cuffs, and the hem. I take her in, admiring, for some time on that drive before I realize that the reason Shawnee Ray's cute outfit nags me so is on account of she is dressed up to match my bingo van. I can hardly tell her this surprising coincidence, but it does convince me that the time is perfect, the time is right.

They let us off at a certain place and we get out, hardly breaking our gaze from each other. You want to know what this place is. I'll tell you. Okay. So it is a motel, a long low double row of rooms painted white on the outside with brown wooden doors. There is a beautiful sign set up featuring a lake with some fish jumping out of it. We stand beside the painted water.

"I haven't done this since Redford," she says in a nervous voice. "I have to call Zelda and tell her I'll be late."

There is a phone outside the office, inside a plastic shell. She walks over there. I know without even listening that when Shawnee Ray asks whether it is okay with Zelda to stay out later than usual no names will be mentioned but Lyman's will probably be implied.

"He's sleeping," she says when she returns.

I go into the office, stand before the metal counter. There is a number floating in my mind.

"Is room twenty-two available?" I ask for no reason.

I suppose, looking at me, I look too much like an Indian. The owner, a big woman in a shiny black blouse, notices that. You get so you see it cross their face the way wind blows a disturbance on water. There is a period of contemplation, a struggle in this woman's thinking. Behind her the television whispers. Her mouth opens but I take the words from it.

"This here is Andrew Jackson," I say, offering the bill. "Known for booting our southern relatives onto the trail of tears. And to keep him company, we got two Mr. Hamiltons."

The woman turns shrewd, and takes the bills.

"No parties." She holds out a key attached to a square of orange plastic.

"Just sex." I cannot help but reassure her. But that is talk, big talk from a person with hardly any experience and nothing that resembles a birth control device. I am not one of those so-called studs who can't open up their wallets without dropping out a foil-wrapped square. No, Lipsha Morrissey is deep at heart a romantic, a wild-minded kind of guy, I tell myself, a fool with no letup. I go out to Shawnee Ray, and take her hand in mine. I am shaking inside but my voice is steady and my hands are cool.

"Let's go in." I show the key. "Let's not think about tomorrow."

"That's how I got Redford," says Shawnee Ray. So we stand there.

"I'll go in," she says at last. "Down two blocks, there's an all-night gas station. They sell 'em."

Okay. Life in this day and age might be less romantic in some ways. It seems so in the hard twenty-four-hour light, trying to choose what I needed from the rack by the counter. It is quite a display, there are dazzling choices—textures, shapes, even colors. I notice I am being watched, and I suddenly grab what is near my hand, two boxes, economy size.

"Heavy date?" my watcher asks.

I suppose the guy on the late shift is bored, can't

resist. His T-shirt says Big Sky Country. He is grinning in an ugly way. So I answer.

"Not really. Fixing up a bunch of my white buddies from Montana. Trying to keep down the sheep population."

His grin stays fixed. Maybe he has heard a lot of jokes about Montana blondes, or maybe he is from somewhere else. I look at the boxes in my hand, put one back.

"Let me help you out," the guy says. "What you need is a bag of these."

He takes down a plastic sack of little oblong party balloons, Day-Glo pinks and oranges and blues.

"Too bright," I say. "My girlfriend's a designer. She hates clashing colors." I am breathing hard suddenly, and so is he. Our eyes meet and take fire.

"What does she design?" he asks. "Bedsheets?"

"What does yours design?" I reply. "Wool sweaters?"

I put money between us. "For your information," I say, "my girlfriend's not only beautiful, but she and I are the same species."

He pauses, asks me which species.

"Take the money," I order him. "Hand over my change and I'll be out of here. Don't make me do something I'd regret."

"I'd be real threatened." The guy turns from me, ringing up my sale. "I'd be shaking, except I know you Indian guys are chickenshit."

As I turn away with my purchase, I hear him mutter something and I stop. I thought I heard it, but I wasn't sure I heard it. Prairie nigger.

80

"What?" I turn. "What'd you say?"

"Nothing."

The guy just looks at me, lifts his shoulders once, and stares me in the eyes. His are light, cold, empty. And mine, as I turn away, mine burn.

I take my package, take my change.

"Baah . . . ," I cry, and beat it out of there.

It's strange how a bashful kind of person like me gets talkative in some of our less pleasant border-town situations. I take a roundabout way back to room twenty-two and tap on the door. There is a little window right beside it. Shawnee Ray pulls the curtains aside, frowns, and lets me in.

"Well," I say in that awkward interval. "Guess we're set."

She takes the bag from my hand and doesn't say a word, just puts it on the little table next to the bed. There are two chairs. Each of us takes one. Then we sit down and turn inward to our own thoughts. The romance isn't in us now for some reason, but there is something invisible that makes me hopeful about the room.

It is a little place just over the reservation line, a modest kind of place, a clean place. You can smell the faint chemical of bug spray the moment you step inside it. You can look at the television hung on the wall, or examine the picture of golden trees and waterfall. You can take a shower for a long time in the cement shower stall, standing on your personal shower mat for safety. There is a little tin desk. You can sit down there and write a letter on a sheet of plain paper. You can read in the Good Book someone has placed in the drawer.

I take it out, New Testament, Psalms, Proverbs. It is a small green book, no bigger than my hand, with a little circle stamped in the corner, a gold ring containing a jug, a flame.

As we sit there in the strumming quiet, I open the book to the last page and read, like I always do, just to see how it ends. I have barely absorbed the last two pages when Shawnee Ray gets curious, touches my hand, asks what I am doing. Her voice is usually bold but at that moment I think of doves on wires. Whatever happens, I think, looking at her, I want to remember. I want a souvenir. I might never be hopeful for the rest of my life the way I am hopeful right now. I suppose it says something about me that the first thing I think of is what I can steal. But there it is, the way I am, always will be, ever was. I think of taking the lampshade, made of reed, pressed and laced tight together. That is possible, but not so romantic. The spread on the double mattress is reddish, a rusty cotton material. Too big, too easy to trace. There is an air conditioner. That might not be noticed until winter finishes. There are ashtrays and matches, a sad, watery mirror, and a couple postcards of the motel itself with its sign of the fish. But what I finally close my hands on, what I put in my pocket, is the little Bible, the bright plastic Gideon's.

"I don't know why we're here," I say at last. "I'm sorry."

Shawnee Ray removes a small brush from her purse.

"Comb my hair?"

I take the brush and sit on the bed just behind

her. I start at the ends, very careful, but there are hardly any tangles to begin with. Her hair is a quiet dark without variation. "Your lamp doesn't go out by night," I whisper, in a dream. She never hears me. My hand follows the brush, smoothing after each stroke, until the fall of her hair is a hypnotizing silk. I lift my hand away from her head and the strands follow, electric to my touch, in soft silk that hangs suspended until I return to the brushing. She never moves, except to switch off the light, and then the television. She sits down again in the total dark and asks me to please keep on and so I do. The air goes thick. Her hair gets lighter, full of blue static, charged so that I am held in place by the attraction. A golden spark jumps on the carpet. Shawnee Ray turns toward me. Her hair floats down around her at that moment like a tent of energy.

Well, the money part is not related to that. I give it all to Shawnee Ray, that's true. Her intention is to buy material and put together the creations that she draws in her notebooks. It is fashion with a Chippewa flair, as she explains it, and sure to win prizes at the state home-ec contest. She promises to pay me interest when she opens her own boutique. It is after the next day, after we have parted, after she has picked up the very-dried-out laundry and after I have checked out the bar I was supposed to night watch, that I go off to the woods to sit and think. Not about the money, which is now Shawnee's and good luck to her, not even about the Bible I have lifted and find myself reading, again, again, whenever I am lonesome. I

83

don't want to think about these things, but about the bigger issue of Shawnee Ray and me.

She is two years younger, yet she has direction while I am aimless, lost in hyperspace, using up my talents which are already fading from my hands. I wonder what our future can hold, even if she breaks it off with Lyman Lamartine. One thing is sure, I'll get fired from my job if Shawnee and I get together. I never knew a man to support his family playing bingo, and ever since the Russell Kashpaw failure the medicine calls for Lipsha are getting fewer by the week, and fewer, as my touch fails to heal people, flees from me, and stays concealed.

I sit on ground where Pillagers once walked. The trees around me are the dense birch and oak of old woods. Matchimanito Lake drifts in, gray waves, white foam in a bobbing lace. Thin gulls line themselves on a sandbar. The sky turns dark. I close my eyes and that is when, into my mind, the little black star shoots. It comes out of the darkness, though it is darkness itself. I see it pass and diminish and remember my mother's visit.

Here's luck. June's moment, a sign to steer me where I go next.

"This is the last night I'm going to try for the van," I tell myself. After my mother's visit, the book of bingo tickets that she gave me disappeared for a while and then, one early morning, cleaning out the bar, I found them stuffed into the seam of a plastic booth. To me, they are full of her magic— ghostly, charged. I never dared use them before. I'll use them now, I decide. This or never is the time. I'll use these last-ditch tickets, and once

84

they're gone I'll make a real decision. I'll quit working for Lyman, go full out for Shawnee Ray, open the Yellow Pages at random and where my finger points, I will take that kind of job.

Of course, I never count on actually winning the van.

I am playing for blackout on the shaded side of those otherworldly tickets. As usual, I sit with Lulu. Her vigilance helps me. She lets me use her extra dauber and she sits and smokes a filter cigarette, observing the quiet frenzy that is taking place around her. Even though that van has sat on the stage five months, even though nobody has yet won it and everyone says it is one of Lyman's scams, when it comes to playing for it most people buy a couple cards. That night, I've just got one, but it is June's.

A girl reads out the numbers from the hopper. Her voice is clear and bright on the microphone. Lulu points out one place I have missed on the winning ticket. Then I have just two squares left to make a bingo and I suddenly sweat, I break into a chill, I go cold and hot at once. After all my pursuit, after all of my plans, I am N-36 and G-52. I narrow myself, shrink into the spaces on the ticket. Each time she reads a number out and it isn't 36 or 52 I sicken, recover, forget to breathe.

I almost faint with every number she reads out before N-36. Then right after that G-52 rolls off her lips.

I scream. I am ashamed to say how loud I yell. That girl comes over, gets Lyman Lamartine from his office in the hallway behind the big room. His

85

face goes raw with irritation when he sees it's me, and then he cross-checks my numbers slow and careful while everyone hushes. He researches the ticket over twice. Then he purses his lips together and wishes he didn't have to say it.

"It's a bingo," he finally tells the crowd.

Noise buzzes to the ceiling, talk of how close some others came, green talk. Every eye is turned and cast on me, which is uncomfortable. I never was the center of looks before, not Lipsha, who everybody takes for granted around here. Not all those looks are for the good either—some are plain envious and ready to believe the first bad thing a sour tongue can pin on me. It makes sense in a way. Of all those who stalked that bingo van over the long months, I am now the only one who has not lost money on the hope.

Okay, so what kind of man does it make Lipsha Morrissey that the keys do not burn his hands one slight degree, and he beats it out that very night, quick as possible, completing only the basic paperwork? I mean to go tell Shawnee Ray, but in my disbelief I just drive around without her, getting used to my new self. In that van, I ride high, and maybe that's the thing. Looking down on others, even if it's only from the seat of a van that a person never really earned, does something to the human mentality. It's hard to say. I change. Just one late evening of riding the reservation roads, passing cars and pickups with a swish of my tires, I start smiling at the homemade hot rods, at the clunkers below, at the old-lady sedans nosing carefully up and down the gravel hills.

86

Once, in the distance, flying through my headlights at a crossroads like a spell, I think I see the blue Firebird, mine formerly and, I presume, now rightfully my mother's. After all, she told me she was coming for it on the night she gave me the bingo tickets. After all, the next morning it was gone. I reported it stolen and I filed a complaint with the tribal police, but that was duty, for the car insurance. I know who has it now. Riding along in my van, I wish her well. I am happy with what I have, alive with satisfaction.

I start saying to myself that I shouldn't visit Shawnee because by then it's late, but I finally do go over to Zelda's anyway. I pull into the driveway with a flourish I cannot help. When the van slips into a pothole, I roar the engine. For a moment, I sit in the dark, letting my headlamps blaze alongside the door until it opens.

The man who glares out at me is Lyman Lamartine.

"Cut the goddamn lights!" he yells. "Redford's sick."

I roll down my window, ask if I can help. I wait in the dark. A dim light switches on behind Lyman and I see some shadows—Zelda, a little form in those pajamas with the feet tacked on, a larger person pacing back and forth. I see Shawnee arguing, then picking up her little boy.

"Come in if you're coming," Lyman calls.

But here's the gist of it. I just say to tell Shawnee hello for me, that I hope Redford is all right, and then I back out of there, down the drive, and leave her to fend for herself. I could have stayed. I could have drawn my touch back from wherever it had

87

left. I could have offered my van to take Redford to the IHS. I could have sat there in silence as a dog guards its mate, its own blood, even though I was jealous. I could have done something other than what I do, which is to hit the road for Hoopdance, looking for a better time.

I cruise until I see where the party house is located that night. I drive the van over the low curb, into the yard, and I park there. I watch until I recognize a couple cars and the outlines of Indians and mixed-bloods, so I know that walking in will not involve me in what the newspapers term an episode. The door is white, stained and raked by a dog, with a tiny fanshaped window. I go through and stand inside. There is movement, a kind of low-key swirl of bright hair and dark hair tossing alongside each other. There are about as many Indians as there aren't. This party is what we call, around here, a hairy buffalo and most people are grouped with paper cups around a big, brown plastic garbage can that serves as the punch bowl for the all-purpose stuff, which is anything that anyone brings, dumped in along with pink Hawaiian Punch. I grew up around a lot of the people, know their nicknames, and I recognize others I don't know so well but am acquainted with by sight. Among those last, there is a young redheaded guy.

It bothers me. I recognize him, but I don't know him. I haven't been to school with him or played against him in any sport. I can't think where I've seen him, until later, when the heat goes up and he takes off his bomber jacket. Then Big Sky Country shows, plain letters on a blue background.

88

I edge around the corner of the room into the hall and stand there to argue with myself. Will he recognize me or am I just another face, a forgotten customer? He probably isn't really from Montana, so he might not have been insulted by our little conversation or even remember it anymore. I reason that he probably picked up the shirt while vacationing. I tell myself that I should calm my nerves, go back into the room, have fun. What keeps me from doing that is the sudden thought of Shawnee, our night together, and what I bought and used.

When I remember, I am lost to the present moment. One part of me catches up with the other.

I have a hard time getting drunk. It's just the way I am. I start thinking and forget to fill the cup, or recall something I have got to do, and end up walking from a party. I have put down a full can of beer before and wandered out to weed my Grandma's rhubarb patch or to work on a cousin's car. But that night, thinking of Lyman's face, I start drinking and keep on going and never remember to quit. I drink so hard because I want to lose my feelings.

I can't stop thinking of you too.

I hear Shawnee Ray's voice say this out loud, just behind me where there is nothing but wall. I push along until I come to a door and then I go through, into a tiny bedroom full of coats, and so far with nobody either making out or unconscious on the floor. I sit on a pile of parkas and jean jackets in this alcove within the rising hum of the party outside. I see a phone and I dial Shawnee Ray's number. Of course, Zelda answers.

"Get off the phone," she says. "We're waiting for the doctor."

"What's wrong with Redford?" I ask. My head is full of ringing coins.

There is a silence, then Shawnee's voice is on the line. "Could you hang up?"

"I'm coming over there," I say.

"No, you're not."

The phone clicks dead. I hold the droning receiver in my hand, and try to refresh my mind. The only thing I see in it clear enough to focus on is the van. I decide this is a sign for me to pile in behind the wheel, drive straight to Zelda's house. So I put my drink on the windowsill, then slip out the door and fall down the steps, only to find them waiting.

I guess he recognized me and I guess he really was from Montana, after all. He has friends, too. They stand around the van and their heads are level with the roof, for they are tall.

"Let's go for a ride," says the T-shirt guy from the all-night gas pump.

He knocks on the window of my van with his knuckles. When I tell him no thanks, he leaps on the hood. He wears black cowboy boots, pointy-toed and walked-down on the heels, and they leave small depressions every time he jumps and lands.

"Thanks anyhow," I repeat. "But the party's not over." I try to get back into the house, but like in a bad dream, the door is stuck or locked. I holler, pound, kick at the very marks that a desperate dog has left, but the music rises and nobody hears. So I end up behind the wheel of the van. They act very gracious. They urge me to drive. They are so polite, I try to tell myself, they aren't all that bad. And sure enough, after we have proceeded along for a while, these Montana guys tell me they have chipped together to buy me a present.

"What is it?" I ask.

"Shut up," says the pump jockey. He is in the front seat next to me, riding shotgun.

"I don't really go for surprises," I say. "What's your name anyhow?"

"Marty."

"I got a cousin named Marty."

"Fuck him."

The guys in the back exchange a grumbling kind of laughter, a knowing set of groans. Marty grins, turns toward me.

"If you really want to know what we're going to give you, I'll tell. It's a map. A map of Montana."

Their laughter turns hyena-crazed and goes on for too long.

"I always liked the state," I allow in a serious voice.

"No shit," says Marty. "Then I hope you like sitting on it." He signals where I should turn and all of a sudden I realize that Russell Kashpaw's place is somewhere ahead. He runs his tattoo den from the basement of his house, keeps his equipment set up and ready for the weekend, and of course, I remember how in his extremity of pain I failed him.

"Whoa." I brake the van. "You can't tattoo a person against his will. It's illegal."

91

"Get your lawyer on it tomorrow." Marty leans in close for me to see his unwinking eyes. I put the van back in gear, but just chug along, desperately, thinking. Russell does a lot of rehabilitation in the old-time sweat lodge, and for income or art has taken up this occupation that he learned overseas and can do sitting down. I don't expect him to have much pity on me, and I graphically imagine needles whirring, dyes, getting stitched and poked, and decide that I'll ask Marty, in a polite kind of way, to beat me up instead. If that fails, I will tell him that there are many states I would not mind so much, like Minnesota with its womanly hourglass for instance, or Rhode Island which is small, or even Hawaii, a soft bunch of circles. I think of Idaho. The panhandle. That has character.

"Are any of you guys from any other state?" I ask, anxious to trade.

"Kansas."

"South Dakota."

It isn't that I really have a thing against those places, understand, it's just that the straight-edged shape is not a Chippewa preference. You look around, and everything you see is round, everything in nature. There are no perfect boundaries, no natural borders except winding rivers. Only human-made things tend toward cubes and squares—the van, for instance. That is an example. Suddenly I realize that I am driving a four-wheeled version of the state of North Dakota.

"Just beat me up, you guys. Let's get this over with."

But they laugh even harder, and then we are at Russell's.

The sign on his basement door reads Come In. I am shoved from behind and strapped together with five pairs of heavy football-toughened hands, so I am the first to see Russell, the first to notice he is not a piece of all the trash and accumulated junk that washes through the concrete-floored cellar, but a person sitting still as any statue, in a corner, on his wheelchair that creaks and sings when he pushes himself toward us with long, powerful old man's arms.

"Please!" I plead with a desperate note in my voice. "I don't want—"

Marty squeezes me around the throat and tousles up my hair.

"Cold feet. Now remember, Mr. Kashpaw, just like we talked about on the phone. Map of Montana. You know where. And put in a lot of detail."

I try to scream.

"Like I was thinking," Marty goes on, "of those maps we did in grade school showing products from each region. Cows' heads, oil wells, missile bases, those little sheaves of wheat and so on. . . ."

Russell Kashpaw looks from Marty to me and back and forth again, skeptical, patient, and then he strokes his rocklike cliff of a chin and considers the situation.

"Tie him up," says Kashpaw at last. His voice is thick, with a military crispness. "Then leave this place."

93

They do. They take my pants and the keys to the van. I hear the engine roar and die away, and I roll side to side in my strict bindings. I feel Russell's hand on my shoulder and suddenly, from out of nowhere, caught in a wrinkle in my brain, words jump like bread into my mouth.

I start babbling. "Please, Russell. I'm here against my will, kidnapped by Montana boys. Take pity!"

"Be still." Russell Kashpaw's voice has changed, now that the others are gone, to a low sound that matches with his appearance and does not seem at all unkind. I fix my pleading gaze upon him. A broke-down God is who he looks like from my worm's-eye view. His eyes are frozen black, his hair crewcut, half dark, half gray, his scarred cheeks shine underneath the blazing tubes of light in the ceiling. You never know where you're going to find your twin in the world, your double. I don't mean in terms of looks, I'm talking about mindset. You never know where you're going to find the same thoughts in another brain, but when it happens you know it right off, just like you were connected by a small electrical wire that suddenly glows red hot and sparks. That's what happens when I stare up at Russell Kashpaw, and he suddenly grins.

He puts a big hand to his jaw.

"I don't have a pattern for Montana," he tells me. He unties my ropes with a few quick jerks, sneering at the clumsiness of the knots. Then he sits back in his chair again, and watches me get my bearings.

"I never wanted anything tattooed on me, Mr.

94

Kashpaw, not that I have anything against a tattoo," I say, so as not to hurt his professional feelings. "It was a kind of revenge plot though."

He sits in silence, a waiting quiet, hands folded and face composed. By now I know I am safe, but I have nowhere to go and so I sit down on a pile of magazines. He asks what revenge, and I tell him the story, the whole thing right from the beginning. I tell him how my mother came to me, and go farther back, past the bingo, from when I entered the winter powwow. I leave out the personal details about Shawnee and me but he gets the picture. I mention all about the van.

"That's an unusual piece of good fortune."

"Have you ever had any? Good fortune?"

"All the time. Those guys paid plenty. Maybe they'll want it back, but then again, why don't you just look sore—you know, kind of rub your ass the next time you see them. Keep them off my back too."

He opens a book on the table, a notebook with plastic pages that clip in and out, and hands it over to me.

"You can pick a design out," he says.

I pretend interest—I don't want to disappoint him—and leaf through the dragons and the hearts, thinking how to refuse. Then suddenly I see the star. It is the same one that scattered my luck in the sky after my mother left me alone that night, it is the sight that came into my head as I sat in the woods. Now here it is. The star falls, shedding rays, reaching for the edge of the page. My luck's uneven, but it's coming back. I have a wild, uncanny hope. I get a thought in my head, clear

95

and vital, that this little star will bring my touch back and convince Shawnee I am serious about her.

"This one. Put it here on my hand."

Russell nods, gives me a rag to bite, and plugs in his needle.

Now my hand won't let me rest. It throbs and aches as if it came alive again after a hard frost. I know I'm going somewhere, taking this hand to Shawnee Ray. Even walking down the road in a pair of big-waisted green pants belonging to Russell Kashpaw, toward the bingo palace, where I keep everything I own in life, I'm going forward. My hand is a ball of pins, but when I look down I see the little star shooting across the sky.

I'm ready for what will come next. That's why I don't fall on the ground and I don't yell when I come across the van parked in a field. At first, I think it is the dream van, the way I always see it in my vision. Then I notice it's the real vehicle. Totaled.

My bingo van is dented on the sides, kicked and scratched, and the insides are scattered. Ripped pieces of carpet, stereo wires, glass, are spread here and there in the new sprouts of wheat. I force open a door that is bent inward. I wedge myself behind the wheel, tipped over at a crazy angle, and I look out. The windshield is shattered in a sunlight burst, a web through which the world is more complicated than I thought, and more peaceful.

I've been up all night and the day stretches long before me, so I decide to sleep where I am. Part of the seat is still wonderfully upholstered, thick and plush, and it reclines now—permanently, but so what? I relax to the softness, my body warm as an animal, my thoughts drifting. It makes no sense, but at this moment I feel rich. Sinking away, it seems like everything worth having is within my grasp. All I have to do is reach my hand into the emptiness.

Chapter Eight

LYMAN'S LUCK

The two men sat across from one another at a scratched plastic table in the palace bar. Lipsha Morrissey hunched over his arms, cradled his hand, rocked forward in his chair. Lyman leaned back slightly, palms placed neatly on the tabletop. Ever since he'd seen the pipe returned from the authorities and put back into the boy's possession, Lyman hadn't been able to get the thought of it from his head. He wanted that pipe with a simple finality that had nothing to do with its worth as a historical artifact. Although he didn't examine all of his motivations, he knew that the desire had something to do with his natural father, for when he imagined himself smoking the pipe that had once belonged to Nector Kashpaw, he saw himself drawing the sacred object solemnly from its bag and also presenting it to friends, to officials, always with the implication that it had, somehow, been passed down to him by right.

The prestige of owning that pipe had dogged

Lyman's thoughts so consistently that he had tried several times to actually buy it from Lipsha. Always, he'd been shyly refused, but now he thought he might reason a little more aggressively. Lyman knotted his square, heavy hands, looked down at his blue class ring. The stone drank deep light. He cocked his head to one side and his wide-spaced eyes figured.

"I'm not trying to persuade you for myself," he said to Lipsha. "Consider it this way—you would be donating the pipe back to your people."

Lipsha licked the end of a straw and shook his head with a distracted smile.

"I'd keep it on permanent display," Lyman continued. "Put it out where the public could look at it, in a glass case maybe, right at the casino entrance. Keep it yourself and you're liable to lose it. Something might happen, just like at the border crossing."

"We got it returned though," Lipsha reminded Lyman. "They took it illegal, they admitted that."

"I'm not saying the loss was your fault." Lyman shook his head, frowning into the steeple of his fingers. "I'm just saying *things happen.*"

"Things do happen," Lipsha agreed.

"To you, they happen all the time."

"I guess." Lipsha crumpled his fingers together in a tight package, and looked down at the little star that shot across the back of his hand. Titus, the bartender, placed a hamburger before him. Titus was dressed in black—black jeans, biker's boots, T-shirt, black plastic diver's watch. His long curls, dry and electric, hung about his shoulders. He gazed at Lyman, then back at Lipsha.

"You ain't got a hangover, do you?" Titus asked Lipsha. "Never deal with Lyman when you're not a hundred percent. He's after that pipe."

"Tell me about it." Lipsha kept on eating. His jaws slowed until he was merely pretending to chew, once, twice. His hair fell out of its band and he suddenly stuffed the rest of the burger into his mouth. He swallowed, staring down at the table, hair flopped across his face, then tossed his head back, hooked the loose strands behind his ears.

"I don't think I better sell."

"Why not?" Lyman's face clouded over as he attempted to control his irritation.

"You ever heard the story about the mess of porridge?"

"What?"

"One brother gives his birthright to the other for some breakfast. It's in the Bible."

Lyman's look eased slightly and he almost started to laugh.

"That hamburger's on the house." He then frowned in deepening suspicion. He began to smooth one hand over the other, back and forth, like he was petting a dog. He worked his hands together faster, faster, and then finally spoke in a quick, dry tone.

"Nector Kashpaw was *my* real father."

"What does that have to do with it?"

"Goddamn it, Lipsha! Think about it once. Everybody could be getting inspiration from this pipe, it's a work of genuine art, it's spiritual. Only you'd rather keep it in your leaky trunk, or stuffed in your footlocker. Somewhere like that. You don't deserve it!"

99

Lipsha stared at his uncle's face, his mouth slightly open, dazed, strangely serene in his contemplation.

Lyman's voice lowered to its most persuasive register. "It belongs to all of us, Lipsha. It especially belongs to me."

"Like Shawnee Ray?"

Lyman tucked his mouth in at the corners, reeled back a little as if at the surprising unfairness of the question. He clenched his jaw, spoke sternly, adopting a minister's logical, reasoning tones.

"Shawnee Ray doesn't 'belong' to me, Lipsha. She goes out with me because she chooses to, because she sees something in me she admires, because she has, I like to think, good taste—she values hard work, intelligence. She goes out with me because of *her*, Lipsha, not because I make her do it."

As Lipsha listened, his stare became wide-eyed, almost frantic, piercing.

"I'll trade you the pipe!" he suddenly cried out.

"For what?"

"Shawnee Ray. Here's the deal: I give you the pipe, and you lay low, step aside."

"You sonofabitch!"

Lipsha raised his hands, palms out, grinning crazily as Lyman jumped up, unable to contain his agitation. He went about the bar, straightening stools, dusting off tables, lifting the chairs and setting them down. He took a grape soda from the glass-door cooler, sat down again with a bowl of popcorn.

100

"You want me to go get the pipe now?" Lipsha asked, his grin stretching huger.

Lyman halted with a handful of popcorn halfway to his mouth, one eye glinting past his fist.

"I'll write the check," he said.

"It's not for *sale*." Lipsha was composed and patient now. "Trade only. You get the pipe, I get to let Shawnee make her own decision."

Lyman drew his head back, sank his chin to his chest in thought. He stared at the counter, his eyes staring blank, then shrewd.

"She's going to love hearing that you tried to do this," he said.

Lipsha turned away, at a loss. For moment after long moment neither man said anything. The only sounds in the bar were a low cloud of conversation around the pool table, the intermittent clocking of balls, Titus in the back room on the phone. The popcorn machine popped over, spilled, and a last kernel exploded, weakly, in the yellow air.

Packing his suitcase for the Indian Gaming Conference, Lyman weighed the pipe for a moment in his hands. Quickly, carefully, he set the pipe, in its pouch, within the inside pocket of his carry-on case and pulled all of the zippers shut. He shuffled through his tickets: Bismarck to Denver, Denver to Reno. His reservations: Sands Regency. The confirmation card was inked in purple with tiny stars flying off the letters of the hotel. He went through everything twice, picked up his bag, and carried it to the spare living room of his government house. He shrugged his arms

101

into his leather suit jacket, brown and supple, made sure all his windows were shut, then locked and triple-locked his front door.

Lyman hadn't been to desert country before. He followed the signs to Ground Transportation, and stood alongside the service way, waiting for the hotel shuttle. The air passing in and out of his lungs tasted of the color of dust, faintly tinged, a dry and melancholy tone. All the buildings he could see were a washed-out yellow margarine color. He strolled to stretch his legs. The buckets of palms, set here and there, smelled of cat piss. He was already sweating in his leather jacket, boiling. His hair fell in limp, damp clumps. Although he had helped to organize the conference, he felt anxious and uncertain, ready to turn around and fly back home. Then the shuttle pulled to the curb and he put his bag inside and tipped his head back and was convinced, suddenly, that something was going to happen to him. His mouth watered, tears formed at the corners of his eyes, his thoughts were eager, and his heart pumped, hot and alert. He tried to contain it but a kick of adrenaline surged up when he walked into the lobby of the Sands and heard the high, manic warble of the slot machines, the controlled shouts of pit bosses, the whine and crash of someone's bad hand sinking, dark, out of view.

He forced himself to get his key at the front desk, and then he made himself go to his room. The decor was jungle bronze, the bed vast and tigerish. Foil and black leopard spots surrounded the mirror and trimmed the desk, table, the chairs of molded plastic. Green shag carpeted the floor, long flows of greasy yarn. He took his wallet out of his pocket, put it in his bag, set the bag down inside his room, backed out, and shut the door.

Crossing the grand floor of the casino, the biggest he'd ever been in, Lyman passed through windows—areas of noise and intensity blocked off from other shapes of smoke and voice. The ceiling was low and mirrored, the cushioned floor spread, the rug endless, the color of good barbecue. The place was dizzyingly lighted, divided by pathways and velvet-roped rotundas into dreamlike parkways. Pleasure soaked into him like resin. He entered caves of darkness where ice cream, chilled in blue polar cases, was sold in a thousand flavors. A doorway crusted in rhinestones. A great orange containing Orange Julius. An elevator dispensing trim hostesses smelling of chlorine from the upstairs swimming pool and offering to spray you with Obsession. Fascinated, awed, he watched a couple of elderly women in identical lime green pantsuits play the quarter slots. He waited, like them, for the glad sound of the payout. He navigated the banks of video poker machines and came out the other side with his hands still clenched in his pockets. A red Camaro. Vintage baby blue Mustang. Lyman ran his fingers over the hoods of the cars that people were playing for in the rear bank of the casino. He passed the five-dollar blackjack tables, passed the ten. He doubled back to show that he could do it. He passed the hundred and then the five-hundred tables. He ambled the entire circle again and as he stood, not watching, looking sideways, breathing carefully, his hands lifted from his pockets in a magical arc.

That was when he whirled, almost ran to the elevators, got on, and rode up to his floor. The attraction and detail of it all was too much, overwhelming, and his eyes fairly ached from straining to see it all. Once inside his room, he reached immediately for the phone, dialed room service, ordered a large fruit salad with cottage cheese. He called back, added a diet soda, called back again, ordered a plate of Super Grande Nachos, then sat in front of the window and willed himself to wait. There was a long blank, a space of time which he knew that he should fill in by focusing on the presentation that he had to deliver the next day. Or he could make a telephone call—surely someone he knew from other, more local tribal gaming conferences had arrived. Surely he was not the only one to book his flight so early, to arrive so soon. He looked at his watch. So slow! He would have done better going out onto the streets, getting directions to a real restaurant, or just walking around to burn away his appetite.

And why not? So what?

He jumped to his feet and searched out his wallet, patted his pockets. Outside the door, he passed the waiter with the cart, making for his room with bored determination, and nearly stopped. But then he saw the salad—large quarter of a pineapple, spiky top still attached, and watermelon, slices of honeydew, red grapes. It looked as though the plastic wrap was molded to the fruit. He kept walking, took the elevator down to the lobby. Just before he went out into the street, he veered around the shining columns, past the churning machines, to the tables where the same people were still tapping and releasing their cards.

People drifted away, the air dimmed and brightened under sizzling marquees. Five hours later, Lyman got up from the blackjack table. He stretched his arms and tipped the dealer. He was seven hundred dollars happier than he was when he sat down. "Now," he said to himself, "*now*." He was advising himself to go, to leave, to find the Italian restaurant recommended to him by the dealer, who clearly wanted to get rid of him. "La Florentine," he said definitively, and stood up. He nodded at the other players, still absorbed in the next hand, counting chips and cards in their heads. Lyman's winnings made a cool package in his hands and he walked to the cashier, but then, as there was a short line, he decided not to wait. He would walk around the slot machines again, uncramp his legs. He passed the ice cream stand and ordered a peanut butter parfait, then put the package under his arms and ate the sundae, standing there, watching people move and shuffle about, jingling their white plastic buckets of quarters.

His features were a mask. His outside expression was fixed, serene, but beneath that, on the real face that was hidden, he could feel his look of bewildered dread. A sudden jittery anxiety coursed through him along with the cold ice cream. His senses dulled. His mouth went numb, he could not taste, couldn't hear above casino clatter, couldn't feel his own hands spooning the peanut sauce between his lips. A certainty clapped

105

down like a wet hand and his brain let go. Fixed hard on the dim comfort of his own surrender he relaxed into it, threw away the rest of his ice cream, and carried the seven hundred dollars in chips back to the high stakes table.

He would have played it, too, but for the accident. An elderly man in a neat white shirt and plaid pants bumped into him halfway across the room, and the jolt sent the chips to the ground. Lyman, ashamed after they were picked up, mumbled that he had been on his way to the cashier. Then, as if a different program had taken over in his brain, he actually did go there, cashed the chips, walked back through the crowd. It was as though he was now surrounded by a force field. He was immune. He got into the elevator and let himself back into his room. Sitting by the window, watching other windows and lights, he peeled off layers of plastic wrap from the tray of food, ate the warm fruit, the corn-chip wedges disintegrating into salsa and sour cream. He ate everything and drank the watery soda. Then he slept, dreamless, the seven hundred curled in an ashtray beside his head.

It was two A.M. when he woke, starting into clarity, his brain on and humming like a machine connected to that money. He dressed quickly and combed his hands through his hair, went downstairs knowing that he couldn't miss. And he couldn't. For the next hour he played perfect games, steadily and easily accumulating chips until he was far ahead. The wins came slower for a while, but the chips kept accumulating. A thousand, then two, then more. Right about there,

106

when he perched just under three thousand, he felt a low wave, a green slide of nausea, and told himself to leave. But he was two people then, split, and could not unstick himself. He started losing his way in a muddy sluice of sloppy plays, and he got desperate. His luck turned unpredictable and he played on, but the momentum had died. The spell was slack. Slowly and unremittingly, things soured. It was for the nostalgia of feeling the luck, wanting it to return, as much as for the money, that he kept playing after he had nothing left.

At four A.M. he stood before the cash machine and punched in his PIN number again and again, unbelieving, but he'd gone beyond his limit.

At four fifteen he cashed the loan from the Bureau of Indian Affairs that had just come in to finance the tribal gaming project. He put half in chips and half in another cashier's check. He started hitting, then the losses dragged him down again and he went bust.

At five he cashed the other check.

At six he brought Nector's pipe to the all-night pawnshop and got a hundred dollars for it.

"I'll be back by noon," he promised the clerk.

At seven in the morning he had nothing left that he could turn to collateral, but he still felt good, drained but on top of things, alert and clean. He walked straight out the double glass doors and stood quietly, hands hanging at his sides, in the cool, dry Nevada dawn. In the Sands parking lot, he watched the sky go from silver to blue and felt the sun's light strengthen. Beyond the railroad tracks, he remembered a bridge, and as though he could smell the water, taste it now, he walked

107

toward it. The trees, the grassy park at its edge, lay only two blocks off and he soon entered the sounds of morning, the click of aspen, a lower murmur. Mild breezes swelled against him, and he smelled the sage in dry flower and the oils of broken cedar twigs. He walked over to the rail beside the river's bank, thought hopefully of jumping in, but the Truckee River was only a foot or so in depth, wandering among gray rocks, too weak to flow, too shallow to run.

Chapter Nine

LIPSHA

INSULATION

What I come up with in my fists when I reached my hand into the nowhere place is insulation. You might call it money, but I know different. If you are poor and you suddenly get bingo rich you'll see money the way I first do. Not so much for what it gets you, but what it keeps away—cold, heat, sore feet, nicotine fits and hungry days, even other people. I debate for a while about just what I should do. I look inside my Gideon's, and chance on a verse from Luke. *Divide the inheritance*, it instructs. I already did that, I figure, sharing Nector's pipe with Lyman Lamartine. In return for not telling Shawnee Ray about my offer to purchase her undivided attention, he borrows the pipe for an undetermined amount of time.

Insulation buys insulation, that's how it goes

108

with me. Every time I play for money using one of June's remaining bingo tickets, I win a small amount. The first time, it's fifty dollars, just gas money, but the trend continues. A week goes by and I win six hundred altogether, the next week two, then six again, nothing for days, then drips and drabs, but always I keep acquiring the insulation. With my mother's bingo tickets, luck is magnetized. She watches over me, at last, in the form of hundreds and twenties. I stuff it all into my pocket. Some blows out into the hands of my buddies, but the greater part collects beneath my mattress.

With money, I notice as time wears on, the spring comes on milder, even those blazing weeks that drop suddenly to freezing. When it is hot, I sleep easy at night beneath the fake breeze in my room. Some would call it a nice new cooling system. I call it insulation. I keep hoping that insulation will impress Zelda Kashpaw so much that she will stop standing in my way, for after that morning when I dozed in the wrecked van and awakened to the shattered window and rattling black spines of last year's sunflowers, I have no thoughts for anyone but Shawnee Ray. Sometimes, falling asleep in the blowing dark, I remember how we tangled together. It was so natural, as if we grew into a single plant. And now I ache for her, now my arms are broken stems. I try to look at other women with serious and measuring anticipation, but it doesn't work. I can't get the feeling right.

I scold my heart for sitting turned over on the table like an empty cup. Still, I can't accept no one else but Shawnee Ray. Even though I tell myself that love is just an image, like the mental picture of your home—which when you get back is full of anxious demands and people, far from perfect—even though I tell myself to go on from where I left off, my heart is stubborn.

I am fixed in the twilight zone of Shawnee Ray's arms. My love is so strong that it busts the barriers and the morals, it whines through padding and steel targets like a bullet, it strikes. It hurts. But the only actual evidence I have of the beautiful things that went on are mental touchtones. Room twenty-two. Twin twos. Inside my mind I erect brass posts and loop thick ropes of wine-colored velvet at the flimsy door. I cordon off that scene, the love tableau, from common touch. I go there the way a person goes to a museum. I close my eyes to get refreshed. Fragrance that clings to my fingers, my skin. Raw cinnamon. Fresh salt. An animal smell that is the taste of actual sensation, of an ache, of joy stuffed into me with each touch so that I grow beyond the boundaries of my own body into one larger, sweeter, more skilled.

I can't get rid of her. My heart keeps beating out her name.

Yet, the more I jump toward love the faster it flees. The more furious I throw my mental life into its capture, the more elusive it becomes, an animal that learns avoiding a trap. Love is hard, loneliness a sure bet. All the songs I listen to and moan over bear this truth. When do you ever hear a song about the fullness and the romance, the dream come into its own? No matter how hard I try, love is just beyond the tips of my fingers,

110

precious as a field of diamonds and elusive, receding fast. The big-bang world is love—we have sex and everything explodes and ever after the pieces are whirling free.

Thanks to the insulation cash, I get my van fixed and then I start lying in wait for Shawnee Ray. I want to talk to her, see her face, put my hand on her knee. The money buys me gas so that I can idle my van in place. I sit outside the grocery store, or on the road to the Kashpaw place, or at the junior college—anywhere that my own Miss Little Shell might pass. It isn't long before I catch her at the entrance to the post office and wave her over to me. She comes eagerly, walking light on her feet, swinging a pack full of schoolbooks. She jumps into the seat next to me and for a minute we don't breathe, just stare into each other's eyes, feasting on the surprising nearness of each other.

"I tried to call you."

"You shouldn't. Zelda, Lyman, they're both—"

"What should I do? I can't stop thinking about you."

She swings her face aside. "I thought I'd marry him—I mean, he thought so too."

"You're still seeing Lyman, then?"

"I never stopped." She looks at me almost defiantly, as if I have a right to feel jealous, a fact I file away to thrill over later. She pauses, gathers herself, and speaks as if she's memorized the lines she has to say. "It was always understood, since Redford. You should probably leave me alone for a while, let me try and get my bearings."

"Do you love me, though?" I speak low, trying to press my voice against her.

She looks at me so long, so tenderly, with such a wistful darkness in her eyes that she really doesn't need to answer my question at all. In the days that follow, I keep that look of hers like a wallet-size photo filed behind clear plastic in my mind. Whenever I find my heart racing after her in longing, in panic at her retreat, I flip to that little picture of her overwhelmed with matching wishes and I somehow convince myself that although harsh time might pass, although we might have explosive troubles, there is no doubt that a loving future together will be ours.

It's not like that's the only pressure on my mind, either, for I've never figured out what Lyman's done with the pipe. About a week after Lyman returns from his conference trip, I ask for it back. With a face like ash, eyes wary, Lyman Lamartine tells me that he hasn't presently got possession of it but he is working on its return.

"Return?" I almost shout.

He won't say from where, and I think maybe a collector has approached from a museum, like they do. He won't talk to me, just fixes control on himself and glares. There is a tone underneath his statement, a pulled string, a fear I never heard in him, a roughness that was never part of his slippery line. I regret about lending the pipe to him, but still, because of the red eyes and outgrown shaggy haircut, he seems less groomed, more human, somebody I can almost trust.

We all got holes in our lives. Nobody dies in a perfect garment. We all got to face the nothingness

112

before us and behind. Call it sleep. We all begin in sleep and that's where we find our end. Even in between, sleep keeps trying to claim us. To stay awake in life as much as possible—that may be the point.

Money helps, though not as much as you think when you don't have it. Anyway, this is temporary bingo-luck money, nothing sure. No matter how I'm tempted to resign as night watchman, I think of Shawnee Ray and do not quit my job. But the fact is, things don't bother me as much at the bar as they did before. New sound system in my room so I can play my songs at any hour. New shirts in my boxes so I don't have to wash the old ones out so often at the Senior Citizens, which means I don't have to listen to so much old-people criticism of me. Insulation. People don't laugh at Lipsha, knowing they might need a loan. Instead of putting on the touch, these days I get touched up, for cash. People don't come around just to visit me and take up my time—except for Lyman Lamartine, who was always insulated, comfortable about money, cool about the changes it can make in a person's life.

Over the weeks, he seems to recover, gains back his old, easy ways, and lands back on top of the reservation heap. He tells me that he has the pipe back, but asks if I mind if he keeps it for a couple more weeks, and although I am suspicious I tell him that it is all right. He says he has to have it exorcised, has to have it reblessed, but no matter how much I prod he will not tell me what has happened. It is strange, the way I feel about him, for our history is a twisted rope and I hold on to

113

it even as I saw against the knots. He is my rival, he is my enemy, and yet I've beat him already by sleeping with Shawnee Ray and I feel guilt even though I never went to church. It's just built into me. In his presence, I'm always mild mannered, eager to help, sorry for him, shamed because it turns out that he does love her. Only not as much as me. Nobody, I am sure, could love another human as much I am starting to love Miss Little Shell.

I do complain to Lyman, though.

"You said if you had the pipe, you wouldn't see her," I remind him.

"I know I said that," Lyman admits, giving me a long look. "But I can't stop—could you?"

The problem is, I understand just how he feels and I know just how much he must need Shawnee Ray, and although a wave of red hatred passes over me, shimmers between us, I can't deny that I approve of his feelings. He was there first, but then, is Shawnee Ray some sort of mining claim? Is she a right-of-occupancy apartment? Is she sunken treasure, found loot? Of course not. My hands itch for Lyman's neck.

"Have you opened up a bank account for all that money you're winning?" he asks me, and I'm grateful that he manages to divert our attention to hard currency.

"Got the cash hid," I tell him.

He shakes his head, lets his mouth form a little smile. "You need financial advice."

I shrug. "I scored big in the college testing, even though I don't talk so perfectly as you do,

114

even though money doesn't make any sense to me."

"You've got the aptitude, but not the latitude," says Lyman. "I can provide the latter."

"Thanks anyway. You helped me enough by giving me this job in the first place."

He has to admit that's true. "You were a risk, Lipsha. But you'll pay off."

"In spades."

"In spades." He allows a laugh, but again his eyes stay on me too long, figuring.

Time draws us into the dead center of the afternoon. We are sitting at an empty table, again, as we often do before the rush is on. The false lights shine on us and upon our hamburger plate specials, which as usual Lyman has thoughtfully ordered. He doesn't make me pay, even though my bingo luck was good that week. He doesn't even mention the bingo, but I know my streak is on his mind. He is anxious to save my money almost as if it were his own, which it is, in a sense. I soon find, to my surprise, that as we talk about the money itself, I am eager to discuss the amounts that are passing through my hands, because I never had the chance before, see, the chance to talk about money. It's no fun to talk about the stuff with poor people—in the first place they don't know what you're talking about, and in the second they can't help but think, *hand it over, asshole*. I find it so pleasant just to discuss dollars and cents in matter-of-fact ways, as though money isn't so unusual a thing to own.

"Money is alive," Lyman tells me. "You don't

115

just stuff it somewhere, leave it. You have to put it in a place where it grows."

"Money's dead stuff, but I like it."

I bite a big hunk from my sandwich. It has everything on it, pickles, mayo, all the works, just like my life now that I am rich.

"Have you ever heard of compound interest, Lipsha?" Now Lyman looks serious. I nod to keep the conversation going, and he continues. "Interest is growth. How can I put this?" He drums his fingers. "You let your money out to work for you, like each dollar is a horse, and you lend the herd out to people who pay you back extra for the privilege. It grows, it accumulates."

"The facts of life," I joke.

Lyman has no humor about this. "The real facts. The sex of money. How it reproduces if you pile it up high enough and put it in the right circumstances."

I put down my tasteless hamburger and all of a sudden lose my humor, too. "Tell me everything you know."

The blood beats in my ears and swirls about inside my head. I keep my mind centered as closely as possible on Lyman's words, but I'm not sure I can swallow all his wisdom. I'm not used to this level of possession, see, and every so often while the Lamartine talks I want to ditch the conversation and break into a maniac frenzy of expensive laughter.

"Success wrecks as many people as failure," he says, "especially Indians. We're not programmed for it."

116

"I had luck from the beginning though, always," I argue. "I'm a lucky guy."

Lyman shakes his head. "You've never had luck you can put your hands on."

"It don't matter."

"You ever hear about the crayfish pots, Lipsha? Listen. There's these three fishermen. An Irishman, a Frenchman, and an Indian. They're picking crayfish from a streambed one day, and they each have a bucket. They're all picking at the same rate, the same number of these crayfish. The Irishman fills his, but he turns his back and the crayfish all get out. The Frenchman fills his, but he turns his back and his crayfish get out too. But when the Indian turns around, though, his bucket's still full. The others can't believe it, they ask how come. The Indian says it's simple. He picked out all Indian crayfish—the minute one of them tries to climb out the others pull him back."

"What's the message?"

"Think about it."

All that comes to me is how Grandma let me take her money for a bus ticket that I needed, how Albertine lent me her own school loan from the U.S. government, how Grandma Lulu put me down for benefits, how people had helped me, how they tried to get me to make something of my life.

"Don't let anybody ever tell you money doesn't make people nicer, kinder, better," says Lyman to gag me.

Maybe he's right, yet all I can think is that the good people I have known so far in life have been cash poor. However, this conversation does make

117

me appreciate them, for their kindness must have come twice as hard. I don't like to say this, I don't like to make a judgment, but I do think that Lyman Lamartine has an ax to grind down to dust ever since his fake tomahawk factory blew up in everybody's face. And yet, the bingo palace that he so recently maneuvered to open is doing bigger business and contributing to the overall economic profile of our reservation, as it says in his brochures. So what was his problem? He should be proud, but you see, here is the thing about Lyman Lamartine. Here's the implicating factor. There is a secret in his face that only someone who formerly possessed the touch can see. A secret.

I watch him as he talks to me and counsels me about which bank in the area is the most stable, how he'll help me open my account. I study him as he asks, point blank, for me to toss in my hand with his next project, which will be a more profitable, a more enormous bingo hall with drawing power that will attract not only surrounding residents but also people from as far away as Grand Forks and Winnipeg. There was a temporary hang-up of his plans, he allows, but he won't give up. He's going forward. He won't be stopped.

The secret is, though, that he doesn't believe what he's doing is completely as simple as making money.

"It's a mixed bag of trouble, like you," he laughs at one point. "There's lots of ways to make money, and gambling is not the nicest, not the best, not the prettiest. It's just the way available right now."

"The easiest."

118

"That's right, too."

I'm lighthearted and secure in my luck. From Lyman's disallowing smile and considering eyes, however, I know he thinks I'm a fool, much too simple for his complicated advice, which he gives me anyway.

"Go after something real," he says in a meaningful tone. I let the sentence gather strength between us, let each word lock onto the next like the muscles in the balanced arms of two wrestlers. It is a challenge, it is an ignorance, for he doesn't know what I'm really after.

Shawnee Ray, Shawnee Ray, my love, *n'gwunajiwi*. I think about her in the shape of clean beer glasses, in their sleek-waisted forms. I think about her in the napkins, which I am sure she uses politely at Zelda's. I think about her as I stock the little rack of pocket combs and beer nuts and I even think about her as I replenish the jars of pickled eggs that sit on the counter. She is everywhere. The band plays slow wailing country love songs each evening and my heart gives, just sinks down, all riddled with holes. I leak love. I grin like a fool when I think of her, wipe too hard on counters and tables as though I am polishing her body—smooth, washed by motel showers, warm to my touch and kiss. I have a picture of her from the newspaper, one of her high school fashion-show triumphs, and I hold the newsprint so often to my lips that the ink smears onto me, indelible, fading to silver her graven image.

A wandering procession of Shawnee Ray pictures trails constant through my brain. I write

119

notes to send her, poems, songs that I compose into my old high school spiral-bound. I place imaginary phone calls, in which I try to hold my breath and speak in a mannerly voice while every moment I am thinking, Please, my baby heart, please, please. I try to keep my promise, let her alone to think, but one morning she answers my desperate call on the first ring. She tells me that the thinking has paid off, that she feels more together, and that I should just keep leaving her alone.

"What?"

"You've been wonderful to me, I can't thank you enough."

"Hey, wait!"

Something doesn't figure in what she's saying, it is all contradictions. At the sudden thought that maybe Lyman has managed to weasel his way back into the front of her affections, my pulse surges ahead and I feel an animal's strength.

"I'm still thinking," she says, sounding a little lame now, her voice halting.

"You've been thinking too much! Stay there, I'm coming over."

I hang the phone up on her loud refusal, and I jump into the van. But I do not entirely lose my head. It is a Sunday, so first I make sure that Zelda is at Holy Mass. Then I bring Shawnee a bundle of flowers from the grocery store in the mall. I purchase these purple daisies and hot red carnations that look like they'll last in a vase. I think of chocolates and I think of a laser stunner or a book or a head of lettuce, something to give to Redford. I don't get these things for fear that Shawnee Ray

120

will think that I am flaunting my money in her face, but I want to buy her a new house, a pet, a car red as the fresh blood she is bleeding from my heart.

I drive over to Zelda's house, get out of the van carrying the flowers. I knock on the door. It is a warm day and a humid breeze is rattling the cottonwood leaves and the lilac brush that grow in the yard. Zelda lives in the original old log house from way back when, a place tucked together by Resounding Sky, added to over years gone by with layer on layer of Sheetrock and plaster, which is why the walls, so thick, keep in the warmed air in winter, and the cool of night all summer. The wood siding is now painted a bright turquoise, and the inside is very close, different now, partitioned off by Zelda into rooms and hallways, so the place has to me a watery slough feeling even though there is no water near except down the hill. It is dim in the house, underwater pleasant.

Shawnee Ray answers the door. I hold out the flowers, almost brushing them into her face. Her warm eyes light before she remembers to give me a suspicious look.

"What do you want?"

"Just to visit with you for a little while."

I hang my head. She knows me as Lipsha, con and fluke rich man. Maybe, like everybody else, she is waiting to see how I'll blow it, lose my money, ditch her, end up back where I belong. Still, as she stands in the door, I thank her in a humble voice for allowing me to enter. She doesn't say a word, just looks at me like what's-he-trying-

121

to-pull and motions at me to carry my flowers through a little hall down to the back of the house.

In spite of her attitude, peace overcomes me as I stand at the entrance to her room. Hopeful thoughts tear at my heart.

"It is an honor to be here," I tell her.

She raises one eyebrow.

"What do you really want?" she asks.

Silence hangs behind her words, and my true feelings surge up through my hands. Her bedroom is bright. Yellow radiance streams through the window that looks out over a brushy little gully. Her bed is crushed against that wall and surrounded very neatly by calendars, drawings, typed sayings, and rows of dried plants. She has a drum hanging from a strap on the wall next to a leather-wrapped beater, the handle decorated with orange and blue cut-glass beads. Her window is protected with not one but three dream catchers, and I remember her saying that Redford sometimes has nightmares. Right now, he's at church with Zelda, but I imagine him sleeping next to Shawnee, curled tight in a little ball, right under that window on a small cot and mattress. I cannot help but see myself there too, my fingers laced above, protecting them both from spirits as they dream together calm as winter bears.

There are also cardboard boxes in the room, half full of folded clothes and books. The drawers are open, I see now, and there is an air of something started that I've interrupted.

"I can't visit long, I'm packing."

"You're moving out?"

"Maybe. Pretty soon, anyway. Right now, I

122

have to go get Zelda and Redford from the Sisters' and finish this."

She puts some things away and picks up a sewing project, trying not to look at me. There is a full concentration in the set of her back, in the arched-over heel of her neck, in her tumbled hair. Then—this hits me with a hammer—she puts the sweetest pair of eyeglasses onto her face. They are just glass, with no rims, like a grandmother or a nun would wear. I can hardly stand it, I get weakened down my thighs and my arm ticks and trembles holding out the flowers. I want at that moment to take off all of her clothes and make important love to her. No, not all she wears. I would leave on those little spectacles, which I would breathe on and smudge and smear and kiss. She has pins in her mouth, and that gets to me too, I mean the danger. I would take them out of her teeth one by one and stick them into her little heart-shaped pincushion before I put my lips on hers.

But she herself removes the pins carefully. "Just about done," she promises when her mouth is empty. "Would you mind trying this on?"

She holds up a leather vest with fringes, lined with calico and piped with satin ribbon.

"It's cool," I say, almost in reverence, taking it from her hands and shrugging my arms into the armholes, which are cut generous. "It fits good, just like you already knew the size."

"Well, naturally." She eases it off me. "I measured Lyman before I cut it out."

I unflex a small aluminum lawn chair propped

against the wall and sit down in it—obviously, it is there for Lyman, too.

Shawnee Ray looks at me, blank and quizzical, then picks up the flowers from my lap and takes the rubber band off and carefully saves it in a drawer. She sticks the stems into a glass of water that she's been drinking from before I came into the room. Then she arranges the stems one by one like a professional. Here's the thing, though. She smiles on them so nice, too nice. In reaction, within my heart, I feel myself rising up with jealousy of those flowers, of how they make her smile but the smile is not for me, of how she gives admiring looks at their beautiful colors.

I put my hand out, between us, and I show her my little tattooed star. It is sinking fast below my knuckles. Although I feel bashful about this I tell her that I got it put onto my hand just for her. She doesn't seem to understand, and lifts her eyebrows at me, all confused and burdened.

"Don't you like stars?"

"Not really."

"Oh."

"I mean, it's fine if you do," she assures me in a polite way. "Tattoos really turn me off."

I bury my hand in my pocket. "Hey!" I exclaim, trying to divert her attention and make a new subject of conversation that might impress her. "Guess who I talked to? Lyman."

She looks wary, so I try to set her mind at ease.

"He gave me money advice. We're like this now." I set my two fingers hard together and hold them up before her.

She does not respond, so I speak louder. "He

124

wants me to throw in with him on a big investment scheme. A project. We even opened a bank account with both of our names on it."

She shakes her head and puts her hands on her hips.

"Don't you even want to know the idea?"

Her eyes are brilliant beams. Of course she does, so I go right ahead and outline the deal. But as I talk, as I get farther into it, make more and more of the details apparent to her, things I should maybe not even reveal, her expression becomes both interested and troubled.

I stop. "What's wrong? What?"

"Where's this land you're talking about, this big resort area that sits on an undeveloped lake? Where is this place?"

"Just a lake," I tell her. "Left wild. The ownership got so fractionated now that the shore has reverted to tribal ownership status, or will when . . ."

Her face takes on a gathering distance as she picks up on the dot-dot-dots of my reluctance to fill her in completely on the information.

I try to divert the subject. "What about going out with me tomorrow? What about the next day and the next day after that?"

"What do you mean, Lipsha, 'tribal'? Does someone live up there now?"

I can't lie, but I can't answer. I look down at my beautiful new shitkickers, the spangled snakehide boots that bingo money bought me, and I get stubborn seeing this magnificence in which I walk. Why should I answer?

She gets pointed.

125

"Why won't you tell me? What are you hiding?"

"I don't want to talk about it."

"You brought it up."

"Yeah, so now I'm dropping it. Let's go out. I miss you."

"Quit dodging around. Where's this land for the bingo palace? What lake?"

"Dancing." I insist more forcibly.

"I want a straight answer."

I don't know what possesses me then or makes my tongue fly. I'm hurt, I suppose, though that's not enough of an excuse. I sling my phrase out so hard it sounds angry.

"You know I'm crazy about you."

Shawnee doesn't react, just frowns and puts her hands to each side of her face.

"Stop it," she says.

"No way."

Now it is like the words that filled me for so long spill right over. "If you're moving out of Zelda's, come live with me. Let's start over, start from nowhere, begin where we left off."

I can't calculate anymore. I know I'm sounding strange, but the words wash out of me like stormy waves.

"Where we left off, Shawnee Ray! Me underneath and your hair swinging over me. Don't be afraid. It's just Lipsha, a short visit, a couple flowers, no drugs. It's true." I pause, seeing her surprised face. I amend myself. "Maybe right now, at this moment, I'm acting unusual, but these are unusual times and things are happening throughout the world that none of us expected. Shawnee!"

I stop cold. She is staring at me in a spell of mystification.

"You listen to the news?" I continue. "Foreign crisis, the crash of stocks and rise of the Japanese. You can't fault me for my feelings for you. You can't take your loving off me like it was a blanket. It's part of me now."

I put my hands to my jeans and start unzipping. Her eyes lose that glazed look, sharpen, and grow deep as a snared doe.

"Don't stare that way, don't let me scare you."

She folds her arms and then gives herself a shake, unclenches her hands, and turns to her sewing machine.

"Sure, turn away, don't look. You might see something that you want. I'm in your power. No matter if you like it or not. I'll do anything for you. Just test me. Anything, at any time, at a minute's notice. Or how's this. You don't need to give me any notice. A bottle of orange pop, a cheap motel, and you. That's all I'm asking for my payment. Eternity was in that room. I don't believe in religions. I don't believe in any gods. I just believe . . ."

I fall silent, for my pants slide so loud to the floor they seem to crash, and I am hobbled until I reach down and kick off my boots. She glares at me and color comes over her face. I watch to see the effect of my words, my dropping clothes, hoping she'll burn and collapse in passion and be mine, but she does none of those things. Her cheeks go hot and a shine of tears comes into her eyes but she gathers control, pushes her rich hair

127

back, and keeps looking at me steady and speculating.

"At least you wear socks."

I feel words rising in me, so many I can't keep my mouth shut.

"You know what I believe in?"

I leave that question and stare at Shawnee until that shine of her emotions returns. I can't help myself. I know I'm making a fool of myself, that this is dangerous, stupid, but I speak softly to her now as I work the tight buttons of my shirt apart one by one.

"Shawnee, I know that you staying with me that night was an impulse move, a great disservice to Zelda, and of course to Lyman. Don't get me wrong. I like Lyman, he's two ways my relative and I understand his feelings for you. You're a perfect accessory to his future. You go with his life, his success, all those ramifications. You'd make a great Senator's wife. Just don't bother doing anything else. Do your duty. Five years time will go by and you'll look at Lyman's face and he'll smile that straight business smile and you'll want my crooked face. He'll say something good, and you'll want me bad. The feel of me will unfreeze in you. Something will grind, come to life, and you'll burn for my eyes looking in your eyes while we—"

She slams her hands down on the table of her sewing machine.

"I'm sorry. I'm going overboard and I know you don't like that kind of talk, but I heard it from you once and you meant it. I know you did. I've made mistakes, and it seems as though nothing's

128

gone right since. But Shawnee, with him, Lyman, sure, he points out your intelligence. But the effect is this: all you do is *about him*. What a good selection *he* made. How interesting *he* was to go back and claim his son, and his son's mother, who luckily turned out smart and beautiful. With me, you'll have to be about yourself. With me, you own who you are. In fact, you'll have to be smarter, stronger, better, 'cause my life ain't gonna shine any light. My deeds won't bounce down on you and give you a halo."

"That's for sure." Shawnee starts the sewing machine up with a foot pedal, feeds a piece of material beneath the needle with a businesslike motion, but her fingers shake.

"Take your foot off that sewing pedal!"

I am losing ground, but I try to contain myself. "You've got to listen to me even though I am making no sense. In fact, because I am making no sense, you should listen harder. We'll get to the truth quicker if we don't worry about logic. You've got feelings for me, hid, and you won't let them out because the world and its big fat woes conquers and prevails on you and you feel you have to serve other people with your life. Your own feelings don't mean shit. You try to road grade and pave them over. Your love for me is just bumps on an icy road. Potholes, honey sweetheart, but they'll bust your suspension. I'll always be there when you think your life is running smooth."

She is shaking with her emotions, and so am I, plus I have no more clothes to shed and I'm feeling foolish. She stands up and throws half a flowered shirt at me.

"You'll do anything for me, anything, you say?"

Her face is wild, her lips stuck in a line.

I nod, blazing my eyes into hers, all want and willingness.

"Put that on," she whispers, intense. "Then get out of here."

I pick up what she's thrown.

"This here is half a shirt," I tell her, just as intense.

"Get out of here!" she shouts.

I don't step back though. The edge is so near. The mournful mirror in that little room beckoned me once to go through, and at this moment I try. I put out my hands, and now the words of grief break from my chest.

"Didn't I give you what you wanted? I gave it to you and I gave it to you like I never did with no one else. Don't you remember how you lay in my arms like a dreamy animal and sighed, and how I made my breath go with yours, perfect in trust, like we were sleeping all winter in a den, you and me? What do you want, what have I done? I was so proud! I got the love medicine!"

Then she speaks, looking at me steady and sad.

"You got the medicine, Lipsha. But you don't got the love."

When she says it, like that, right then, it is as though I am stunned with truth. I can't see for the dazzlement, but I know in one instant that she's right. I stumble backward, but then she sees how I feel and gently takes the shirt from my grip and puts it down on her machine.

"Let me try then," I ask her, in a voice I never heard myself use before. I pry out my words from the heart. "Please, let me have another chance."

So we sink down on the floor, right there in the doorway, and this time it is different than before. You ever seen a couple orange-black butterflies kiss and hover above the ground? This is even more delicate. It is their shadows beneath, that's who the two of us are. Two tender shadows touching in, touching out. Two hungers made out of the dim shade we cast.

But if it was only our shadows moving, loving in that room, what of the other, the heavier and solid-footed selves who stood apart passing judgment, what of us?

Chapter Ten

SHAWNEE'S LUCK

After she shut the door behind Lipsha Morrissey, after she heard him drive out of the yard, Shawnee whirled from the door and walked straight back into her room. She ripped off her shirt, popping a button, chose a different one, her arms jerking the material. She swore impatiently, monotonously, in surprise at herself. She pulled on a clean pair of jeans, then kicked them into a corner. She yanked a purple dress off a hook, then sat on the edge of her bed and crumpled the skirt against her stomach. Her face twisted and she unfolded her

131

hands between her knees, drew her palms up the insides of her thighs. Breathing heavily, she rested her hands at her center, pressing herself back together. She put her arms out suddenly, pounded on the mattress, opened and closed her fists in front of her eyes, and then slapped herself so hard on the cheeks it made her laugh.

She threw herself deliberately, eagerly, down on the floor and started doing push-ups, then she rolled over, hooked her feet underneath the bed frame. Glaring, eyes fixed upon the stitching of her blue cotton star quilt, she continued with sit-ups. She did a hundred, hands across her breasts, and then she lowered herself back into the little oval rag rug and slammed her palms down over her face.

She supposed it was just pure good fortune that you ever loved the person who was right for you. Or who loved you in the way that was most likely to bring happiness, the way that fit the world. Where was that Mister Right all of the magazines talked about? She always saw him as an illustrated profile in her high school history book, or a chapter-end picture and short biography in her English text. Backlighted, smiling, every hair in its place, date and place of birth typed in carefully underneath his studio portrait, that was her picture of the man she would marry.

Lyman fit that studied blank as if the negative had been developed. Lyman Lamartine, Bingo Chief, the subtitle read. In strict opposition to the glossy smile, however, a photograph referring to Mister Wrong now obsessed her. Visiting Marie Kashpaw at Lulu Lamartine's apartment,

132

Shawnee had been unable to turn from the smeared, inky, unshadowed frankness of the framed wanted poster of the father of Lipsha Morrissey. Her gaze was drawn to the shelf, her mind kept scratching for resemblances.

She could see Lipsha whenever she shut her eyes. He was a mess, his shirttails out, hair flapping, mouth sweet in a grin that would change unexpectedly and for reasons that she found interesting. She never knew what he would say. There was a mystery to him, an ease, a calm way that he had with his hands and lips. Now, thinking about how they had just made love, she shivered and in her head a cicada buzz of panic whined. It was unbearable, it made her furious, all her plans were out of whack and useless. She loved him.

Shawnee stood up, went to the table, sat down. She smoothed flat the soft piece of deerskin that her uncle Xavier had given her and cut out a pair of small moccasin soles. The way her uncle would, the Chippewa way instead of the Sioux, she put the tiny gathers in the top, sewed bits of an old flannel blanket inside. Tonight, she decided, she would stitch a tiny bluebird on each toe in order to remember the ones she'd seen, so fierce around their fence-post nests.

As she sewed together two crescents of muskrat fur for each ankle, she grew more calm, but she still wished that she could swear off men altogether. Except for Redford, they were too much trouble. Who would not prefer, after all, to live in a world of women? To need men, to love men, was a great nuisance and a misery. To sit and sew with her sisters in a room was like entering a country where she had always belonged. Shawnee missed Tammy and Mary Fred and her mother so fiercely that she winced at the stab of her longing. Her breathing deepened, she put her work down and restlessly took up the beading needle.

Women made more sense, had their priorities in place, seemed to know just who they were and where they came from, unless they got mixed up with men. Most women, that is, but not Zelda Kashpaw, whose fierce grip made everyone she loved uneasy. Ever since Zelda had insisted on keeping Redford, full-time, if Shawnee Ray decided to dance at the big-money powwows, ever since Zelda had started holding on too tightly, Shawnee Ray had been slowly packing up to move, but she had to be secretive about it and not raise Zelda's suspicions or hurt her feelings. And she couldn't rely on her own mother—here was the fact that proved her point—because her new step-father's needs and attitudes and opinions came first. Shawnee had only herself to depend on. For the past week, she had been checking on a special she had heard about, a memorial dance at a big Montana powwow. Three thousand dollars, winner take all, for women's all-around—traditional, shawl dance, and jingle dress.

Shawnee knew that she could win that prize.

Zelda was a man-woman, Shawnee had decided. Aligned with Lyman Lamartine, the two kept her soldered in their own hopes. Her sisters had no hopes, no reason to manipulate her. The trouble was, every time she made up her mind to go and stay with Tammy and Mary Fred, she would hear that one of them was deep in a binge, or arrested, or maybe worse, converted and spouting Bible verse. She would go to them anyway, she decided now, and stay back in the bush for a while, where she didn't have to worry about pleasing so many people. Where Lyman wouldn't visit her. Where Lipsha might. Where she could sort out her life and make her plans.

Shawnee put down her needle and the butterfly that she was beading onto a clip that would match the pattern on her shawl. Into her hand, she took the little moccasins and cradled her head in her folded arms, in the smoky tanned scent of home-cured hides. Tears dropped onto the edge of her sewing table fast as hard rain, but she soon stopped them, pushing her hands hard across her face.

Zelda's eyes were bright as pointed stars. She was standing in the same doorway where Lipsha Morrissey had argued, begged, pleaded, and thrown off his clothes. Stepping into Shawnee's room, Zelda walked across the rag-braided rug. Shawnee lowered her gaze and looked away as the older woman pivoted with hard assurance. Hands firm on her hips, Zelda was solid as a truck. She absolutely opposed Shawnee Ray's return to Tammy and Mary Fred.

"Who took care of you when you needed it? Who does Redford call his grandma even now?"

"You," said Shawnee.

"It's for your own good," said Zelda, softening. "I just want to stop your wild-goose chasing. That contest—I know the woman . . . she'll never come up with the money."

"She lost her daughter."

135

"Because she left, went to the Cities, never really came home. Just like some."

"You're scared I'll be like Albertine?" Shawnee looked steadily at the older woman, and then spoke coaxingly. "She comes home, she's going to be a doctor. You're lucky with her, you know that."

"I don't call it coming home," said Zelda. "She never stays!"

"Why should she?" Shawnee lost patience. "You drive everyone around you crazy!"

"Oh, I do? I do?" Zelda's voice grew strange, exultant. "Do I drive them so crazy when I take them in, pay their bills, feed them, help them raise their little boys?"

Shawnee turned away, face smarting, confused with guilt.

"No." Her voice small, but then her tone strengthened. "You can't get Albertine back by holding on to me. I'm going to stay with my sisters, just for a little while."

Zelda's features hardened, she firmed her shoulders, settled her hands carefully together to disguise her anxious fears. She reminded Shawnee Ray that people would think that Zelda threw her out, that Lyman would object, that she had no way of raising money for a bus ticket to that Montana powwow, that she owed Zelda her affection, and that, although her sisters had been observed at the end of the previous summer, kneeling on the beaten grass beneath a tent awning and receiving Jesus, they had not attended a single AA or Assembly of God meeting since, and people said

136

that they had backslid powerfully, lost their low-pay jobs.

"You can't go there," reported Zelda once again. Her hair was caught up in a beaded shield, pinned there with a sharp wooden stick; her cheekbones were dusted with magenta blush and her mouth was set firmly into a line of opposition. She stared down at Shawnee Ray, who had never given her a moment's trouble up until this conversation. Zelda expected that the young woman would shrug, gently take out her books, and after the thoughtful lecture, forget the whole idea. Instead, Shawnee met Zelda's eyes with an expression of stubbornness and puzzled fear, and for a long time, neither one of them would look away. Finally, Zelda took a breath, shrugged lightly, and walked out the door.

Shawnee heard Zelda in the kitchen soothing Redford and sifting cereal into a bowl. She heard the rubber seal of the refrigerator unsticking, the coffee sighing through the little white plastic machine on her counter. Hands calm on her knees, Shawnee considered what she would do next. She stared at the little night table, behind which she kept the envelope of money from Lipsha Morrissey. It was her freedom, her train ticket, her camping money, and Zelda didn't know she had it. Shawnee walked to her closet and carefully removed the dress she had been working on late at night. It was velvet, beaded in the old style with fiercely twisting roses and flowers, with thorns and striped leaves. That was one outfit, and she'd almost finished with the dress she was trimming and hemming to match her butterfly shawl. That

137

was two. And three, her jingle dress, hot red, cast light in a corner. Shawnee Ray pushed herself out of her chair and walked into the kitchen.

Redford flung open his arms at the sight of his mother. She cupped his face in her hands and kissed him twice, and when he turned back to his food, she addressed Zelda.

"I'm taking Redford."

"Shawnee Ray!" Zelda spoke loudly, fearfully, too quickly. "I don't want you to go for your own good. They're a bad influence on you."

"I'll come back if things get out of hand," Shawnee said in her most adult, reassuring voice. "I'm just going to visit, and besides, they've been sober for over a year now."

"That's not true!"

"Just because you don't see them much in town these days doesn't mean they're drinking. Mary Fred started going to sweat lodge with Uncle Xavier. He's been studying with an old man up north. He knows a lot about old-time medicine, and he's helping them out, maybe curing them."

"There's no cure for what they've got," said Zelda.

Shawnee's face shaded with an increase of determination. She scooped Redford from his seat at the table and tramped quickly back into her room. He wailed in surprise and then, pleased to be alone with his mother, began to laugh and talk in small and broken words.

Zelda folded her arms across her chest and stood underneath the burning overhead light fixture, staring at the closed back of the door. As she poised that way, unmoving, her expression took

138

on gravity and thought became solid intention. Her face was fixed in lines, rapt and determined, all goodness, from which there was no escape.

CHAPTER ELEVEN

LIPSHA

MINDEMOYA

I walk out of Shawnee Ray's room, and as I go through the dimness of that hibernation household, as I find my way back out into the friendly fixed interior of my bingo van, her love medicine words stick with me. I know I'll never get rid of them, the shock and strangeness of their meaning. I start the van, press down the gas, slowly pull out of the driveway, and I realize I'm different now, changed. Our sex on the floor was not the medicine, not this time, but love. True love. She can't deny it, and I won't let her confuse me with the love ways of Lyman Lamartine.

It's true, I got the medicine, but not the way she thinks. I never made love so you would notice it with anyone but her. I know to touch away hurt, but not touch on pleasure. It's Lyman who learned that skill, I know for a fact from his younger days that he made it happen for women and for girls since the year he was fourteen years old. He always loved girls so he and his brother Henry wanted to be with them all the time, make them go completely open in their arms, drive them wild as dogs to bite their ankles, make their hands into

139

combs, claws, feather mittens. Whatever. I admit I have a medicine that was given to me in my hands, but the fact is until Shawnee Ray I never really used it for sex, never fell in love. I always said I wanted staying power, like my Grandma Kashpaw showed me she possessed. I always bragged that I wished to find the woman who would love me until one of us died or went crazy. The truth is, I've been looking.

Now I fear I have also lost my direction, got so far off the road that, at this moment when I know I have met the one, Shawnee Ray, she does not believe me.

"You really fucked this up," I say to myself. "Lipsha, you got so slick with your hands that you polished off all the rough edges. You ain't believable! And as for Lyman, he has roughed up his style just enough so it looks innocent!"

Even that does not seem right, or enough, and it bothers me that my understanding is so frail. A little portion of sweet heaven is allotted to each of us by our fate.

That was mine, I think as I bounce the gravel road. Sure as hell she'll forget me once Lyman snows her with his brilliant words.

I go back to the bar and sit down to try and get prepared for the experience of losing her even after this last occurrence. I can't. I put on spongy shoes and decide to do something unlike myself, to go out running on the new clay high school track. So I drive over there. I get out of my van in the afternoon wind, so high and brilliant, and I start to move my legs. My jeans are too tight, but I keep going anyway, thinking that the red marks they leave on my skin will remind me of the advice from myself that I hope I'll take. Around the red road I travel, first desperate and stiff jointed, then freer, looser, more myself as I sweat and burn off my anxious hope into beat exhaustion. My chest feels wracked, and very soon I slow to a slog and then walk. I remember back to the days when I tried to doctor my own grandpa with the store-bought love medicine that ended up so tragic and confused. I remember back to my original wish to visit up at the Pillager woman's place, and how my heart quailed and I was too much of a Morrissey coward to do the thing. Maybe all my love medicine was store-bought after all, maybe it was fake, maybe I relied too heavily on the commercial stuff and am only now understanding what it takes to get the real.

"Crazy courage," I shout to the empty bleachers. "Just watch!"

I tip up on my toes and heft my knees and then I take off fast as that shooting star—but about fifty yards along the track I have to throw myself down to earth. I'm half dead, my breath a seared feather in my chest, my weak and half-broke heart thumping. I smell the chemical-sprayed grass, the fertilized dirt underneath. To put my face in the dirt makes me think of lying underneath it. I don't want to die without Shawnee Ray's love, and to get it I'll have to acquire a love medicine that's better than Lyman Lamartine's.

I make my way back to my van through the bleachers. The fact is, I can't afford my own fears anymore. The sky stretches bare and wide, building clouds in the east above me, banks of sleet or rain. I will not let up in my intentions. During the first dry-off of the season, the Old Lady Pillager is always known to come to town. She is by rights my great grandmother, the one who started it all in motion. I will find her, I will follow her, I will make my love request. And I will hope not to die of her darker medicines as a result.

When I finally glimpse the old lady people fear, she is walking down the broad dirt road that leads from deep bush into town. It is a weekday spring morning. The new heat is surprising, and people are taking long and social routes to work—that is, until they see her. As the Pillager passes by, men and women rush indoors to punch their time cards, swing their cars toward parking lots. Some fade back into the bars and shadows of the post office, those who can't cross their breasts or touch the holy medal of a saint. I do none of these things. I am unnoticeable. For in waiting for the Pillager I have become a kind of a fixture, a railing, a piece of carved cement on the Agency steps. Anyway, I happen to glance up from filling out my papers and there she is.

Fleur.

They say that strange things happen when the old lady is around. A dog falls over dead and all of its hair drops out. Gossiping mouths twist to one side and stick that way. Cold winds blow out of nowhere, in places there isn't even a fan system. Yellow jackets build a nest in a loaf of baking bread. And then those drownings: three times she was cast in the lake, and men were taken by the spirits each instance when she came to life, as if she put their name on the list to the death road, replacing hers. These things happened, frightful incidents, but also there is good.

People forget the good, because the bad has more punch. The old lady cures fevers, splints bones, has brought half the old-timers in the Senior's Lounge into this world. That's right. She's older than any of them, so old no one remembers how old. She's a Pillager, the adopted daughter of Old Man Nanapush, this healing doctor witch. She must be a hundred. She's so old that people don't use her name anymore. She's just the Old Lady, Mindemoya. As far as I know, she's just got one surviving child in town, my grandma Lulu, and I watch now to see if she is going to visit the apartment.

Of course, since she walks right by and never notices Lipsha Morrissey, who never amounted to a sack of nothing until the bingo, I am able to get a close look at her. Fleur comes nowhere near the government buildings, she does not let her gaze stray to either side or notice how her path has emptied out. She is a tall woman with a hunch to her shoulders and a face honed and heavy as a sharpened tool. She taps the dust before each step with a stick that looks burnt, made out of twisted diamond willow, a type of slough tree stronger than rebar steel. Her head is knotted in a white scarf and earrings flash, two small green fires at her jawbone. Her feet are big in a pair of old-fashioned men's-type boots. She wears a long dress, an odd style considering her frightful repu-tation, for it is a girl's dress, flounced, covered

143

with rosy flowers, sagging in the front with ruffles. She walks quickly, covers ground so fast that before I think to stand up and maybe talk to her, she is halfway up the hill. In a few minutes she is just an innocent-looking speck of pink and white moving farther on, and then she vanishes between the fat green shrubs and brush around the entrance to the church.

A cousin of mine, a Morrissey girl named Layla, who works in the offices, comes outside and leans against the steel banisters.

"They said Mindemoya was out here."

"Where?" I ask.

I don't know why, but in that moment something closes in me as if to protect the old lady, though she hardly needs me, and though I like this cousin Layla all right and she doesn't mean any harm but is only curious.

"I never saw her," I say. "And I was sitting right here."

Layla stares all around us—at the wide cottonwoods that lean over the clinic, at the school buses pulled up in the big yard across the hill, at the mottled brown brick and thick gray windows of the Senior Citizens apartments, at the road where Fleur has passed. Things look normal. Cars rush or calmly putter back and forth.

"They say she heads there on her feast day," Layla whispers. "Every year."

"I wouldn't know."

Layla frowns toward the hill.

"How come you don't just go and see if she's there?" I ask.

But Layla only scuffs her foot a little, disap-

144

pointed, and then walks back into the offices where she keeps the records of each tribal member filed for her boss—that is, Zelda, who has the record and whereabouts of everyone's ancestors and secret relatives handy to herself. I sit down again. I am waiting for proof-positive self-identification, a complicated thing in Indian Country. I am waiting for a band card, trying out of boredom to prove who I am—the useless son of a criminal father and a mother who died with her hands full of snow—but in trying to prove myself to the authorities, I am having no luck, for Zelda is a solid force to reckon with. I don't have my enrollment and entitlements stabilized, not yet, nor do I have my future figured exactly out. Still, the reason I have been hanging out has just walked down the road.

I stand there on the steps. Duplicates of applications and identification papers weigh down my hands.

"Here." I shove them at Layla. She takes them.

"File it under 'L' for Love Child," I say, walking off.

The way things occur and come together is strange as music. Like I said, the old lady is actually my great grandma, though I never even spoke to her face-to-face before that time. I decide that I will follow her into the church and as I enter I will cross myself with holy water. Then I might be safe enough to go up to her and introduce myself as her descendant, Lipsha, and tell her what I need her to do for me. Of course, the blessed water might not work. She might have medicine to counteract it, she might say something

145

like she said to Flying Nice and I will have to take her place on death's road the next time she is summoned to go. People say that's how she got to live this long. Rumor is, there's no limit to her life. She takes the future of others and makes it her own, sucks it in through a hollow reed, through a straw, a bone.

I get nervous, so instead of tagging the old lady directly into church, I go over to the Senior Citizens, where both of my grandmas keep themselves. Grandma Kashpaw is orderly and always in charge, set up in an apartment decorated with souvenir plates from far-off grandchildren, the walls lined with closets of carefully saved paper sacks and used clothes and brand-new thermal blankets. Grandma Lulu isn't neat like her, and at her place everything is strewn out: papers and Congressional records and magazines. The two live around the corner from one another, down the hall, but I stop first to see my grandma Lulu, on the Pillager side. The old lady is her mother, after all.

"Mindemoya's in town," I inform her without a preview.

Lulu rises from her chair, dusts off her hips, and walks into her kitchen nook to move around some pots and pans on the stove. The smell of browning potatoes and seared meat and onions spreads from that alcove when she lifts a cover. Lulu was once flowery and soft, smelling of perfume, but in her old age she's gotten compact and tensed down. Her arms are hard and brown, as if she does push-ups, and her smell is sharper now—of ink, office products, white erasing fluids.

146

Except for the time she spends at the bingo palace, her pleasure time, she is full speed into politics and each of the spray perfume bottles on her dresser wears a ring of dried unused sweetness. She is out to reclaim the original reservation, no less. It was once six times bigger.

"She comes in on her feast day, gets supplies," I state, when Lulu doesn't answer.

"Not her feast day. My dad's." She speaks briefly and flips the meat, keeps on stirring something with a metal spoon. A purple smell rushes at me. She is cooking a pot of chokecherry jelly.

"Who was he?"

She turns, arches her thin black eyebrows, and gives the pan a sudden, annoyed shake.

That is my cue to quit, I know it, but this time I want more. My father's eyes, shrouded and full of Nanapush light, watch me from my grandma's knickknack shelf. My family people are full of secrets, things they hide from each other and from themselves. Beginnings are lost in time and the ends of things are unpronounceable. I was one of those dark secrets too, according to Zelda, a boy whose mother tried to drown him in a slough but who survived, and whose convict-hero father was silenced by the higher authorities of this country. Grandma Kashpaw raised me, and Grandma Lulu started the ball rolling toward explaining it all. So I count on Lulu, now, to tell me more.

"You don't like to talk about the old lady," I say. "But she's your mother."

"You have an itchy mind." Lulu sets down before me a plate holding venison, limp brown rings of onions, potatoes mashed with a fork, buttered and peppered. She settles herself into a chair across from me. On her plate there is a slice of soft white bread glazed with cooling jelly. Her eyes shoot out tiny points of black light. She is watchful. The fashion-plate wig she wears today is teased in soft spiked waves like beaten egg whites. I pick up the knife and fork and start cutting the meat, eat it, try to think of another approach, the way a wrestler might circle, arms out to grapple. But I miss my opening. She dives in first and takes me down.

"Even if I told you what you want to know, it wouldn't do you any good."

"Why not?"

"You're too simple. You think you got things figured out. But you young Indians today are living on a different planet."

"Maybe I'm ignorant," I say, putting down my fork, both mad and reasonable. "But if I had a mother here alive, at least I wouldn't hate her."

"I don't hate the old lady," Lulu says, pausing for a moment, evening her voice. "I understand her."

Which leaves me something to think over.

Outside the Senior Citizens, the air is dry and still unnaturally hot for spring. Wheels of fine gray dirt hang lazy over the road. The new leaf buds click and the church seems to yawn before me, a big, empty, white, board building with long colored windows and a square steeple topped by a little painted roof of dark green shingles. The reservation spreads downhill, and I have a good view of the town, its gas station, its tree-shaded

148

bar, and the small box houses built by government administration. Some sag, gray and unpainted, and others seem alert, bright pink, lime, blue, bristling with stovepipes, antennas, little windmills, for it is popular these days to make lawn ornaments out of long poles and twirling plastic milk jugs cut in various surprising shapes. Screen doors snap. Children swirl their tin trucks in the dirt. Women lean down the steps to frown at their dead plots of grass. The houses are all built helter-skelter, streets put in later. They dribble away onto flat prairie to the south and trees take them over to the north and begin to enfold them in quick-growing bush.

To that side, out of the leathery green trees, a road of coarse tan gravel floats in the morning heat. I follow it to the first of the church steps. At the top, I reach forward and open the heavy brown door, then I step inside. The air is dark and heavy with the scent of spent incense. The pews are dim furrows of empty quiet. As I enter, I can hear the wind rush up suddenly outside, in the trees, and my heart taps quickly. In the center of the church, Fleur Pillager sits straight, suspended. I kneel down beside her. She ignores me. I cough.

"Booshoo." I offer a hello.

"What do you want?"

She booms this out, echoing, using the old Chippewa language that I can barely understand or much less answer. I hardly even know the French mix and so I speak English and say that I am her great grandson, right out, just like that. She only nods as an answer so that I wonder if she places me. After a while she says, *"Geget na?"*,

149

"Is that right?", like a question, pulling down her mouth. I don't know where to go from there, so we just sit side by side.

She doesn't do anything that I can see from the corner of my eye. Her hand doesn't move to toss a pinch of powder or make some sign that will hang over me. She carries no purse where she could keep, say, her medicine charm, a child's finger wrapped in a strip of doehide like people say. I already looked at the dirt to make sure she left the footprints of the big men's boots, not tracks of the bear. Just thinking about those objects freezes my voice box, and I can't answer when she finally does.

"I've got to go to the store."

She clips her words off in English perfect as a nun. We stand. She is not the type to genuflect before the altar, she just turns heel and walks toward the door. I open it and step out. She has leaned her stick against the building and I hand it back.

"Could I carry your groceries home for you?" I ask.

When she smiles at me, unblinking, showing her sharp old teeth, I gulp air, feel a flutter of black wings in my heart. It is her grin that can kill, I've heard, the slow spread of fierce pleasure on her face. But nothing happens to me.

"It's a long walk, grandson," is all that she says, and she is right.

Maybe I have smoked too much into my lungs so far in life, or maybe I have weakened myself with sugar, I don't know, except I can't keep up

150

with her. She can't be a hundred, more like ninety years at most, she moves along so fast. I carry the bag, just a few things—flour, oatmeal, a number ten can of coffee, and some potatoes. I am glad I wore my running shoes in which I gathered strength, yet she is shaming me, this old-time, maybe *djessikid* woman.

I do tell her my name halfway there, not that she asks for it. She frowns at the Morrissey part and says that she doesn't agree that she is related to any of that clan. I hesitate to remind her that my grandmother is her daughter, Lulu, but I do sense Fleur Pillager is being polite, not saying to me that the Morrisseys are no-goods, a family that for bad give the Lazarres a run.

"I'm not a Morrissey by blood though," I say, "or not hardly." I explain how my mother left me off with Grandma Kashpaw because I was the son of a Nanapush man related through the Pillagers. It is then that she nods her head, in time to her walking. The name Kashpaw means something to her.

"If you're a Pillager then claim so. Don't say Morrissey."

"Would the Pillagers claim me back?"

She looks over at me, turns her mouth down. "Why not? There's none of us left."

We walk on in quiet, the sun traveling down lower and lower into the windless trees. I have had my imagination turned on full volume at the time, but I do think that the woods go all silent as she passes, the birds choke on their own songs, the rabbits stop skipping, trees go stiff, deer freeze in their huddled bush. Cars pass at first—none

151

stopping to offer us a ride—then fewer, and even fewer as we go down roads and gravel turnoffs that get us closer to earth, narrow, sift to dirt, then peter out in unused and nearly grown-over ruts and go on, still after that, in trackless scrub and finally stop in sheer grass and sage surrounded by bush. She must have got up in the middle of the night to walk into town from all of this distance. I knew the reservation inside out, I thought, but it turns out I knew it by car, not foot. Now it feels like we're lost, off the radar, and at this a weakness grips my legs.

We have come around to the far end of Matchimanito Lake, which is right where Lyman Lamartine intends to erect his gambler's paradise.

I am not now, and nor have I ever been, interested in visiting here. It is a spirit place, good if you are good and bad if you have done bad things, like me. I am relieved that there is no sign of the water itself yet, no opening through the brush, no gleam of dark waves catching the sky. There is also no way further into the bush that I can see, no path, and yet the old lady points forward with her black stick and before I know it she walks straight into a clump of sumac. Vanishes.

I follow as best I can. The trunks are dense, twisting against me, and the leaves seem to wrap around me so I can't keep the springtime flash of her dress in my line of vision. I keep edging forward, easing under dead falls and squeezing through crossed tangles. The air grows dense, buzzing, and smells of ripped green wood and heavy sunlight. I try backing up once but the twigs and leaves have closed behind me in sharp knots.

152

This is a one-way woods. She has me. She is drawing me forward on a magic string coughed up from her insides. She is an owl waiting on the other end with her claws out, with her tongue like a meat fork. I crouch down, shaking, and try to get my bearings, but then I think I feel the wood ticks crawling eagerly into my socks and I jump, lunging, and run straight through a singed burn-out filled with raspberry brush, out into a small grassy rise. Her house sits on top, bleak but normal, in the shadows of a denser olden growth beyond which the lake winks, fine and blue surfaced, all postcard perfect and false. She is there, too, bent over, her elbow sawing up and down, working the curved iron handle of a pump.

"You made it," she says without turning. She picks the bucket up and walks into her house. It is an old-time place, a low, long house of sawed beams tamped smoothly between with yellow gumbo clay, dug up from underneath the top soil. The roof has a little tin chimney and I stand there long enough to see it puff smoke. Her windows are small, polished clean, empty, not hung at the sides with curtains. I gulp down my fear to remember that Fleur Pillager has cured diseases, brought children into the world. I am her own blood. But I still wish I had some medicine to protect me.

"You're thirsty," she says when I finally step through the door.

Her house reminds me of Lulu's apartment, for it is stacked to the low ceiling with papers, with folders, with bundled envelopes and boxes of rippled cardboard that seem to hold still more files

153

and newspapers and clippings. The place smells of paper, mildewed, dried, leaked on, but carefully saved. For there is care in the arrangement of these stacks against the old, whitewashed inside walls that are covered everywhere with hairline cracks and patterns of tangled thready lines.

"I'm making tea."

I sit, and my gaze naturally drops down on the rubbed and faded pattern of her oilcloth on the table. It is covered with pen lines, rushing on straight, sloping, doubling back.

"Somebody wrote on your tablecloth," I say, and then I shut my mouth, for it isn't probably a good idea to be so observant. But she doesn't mind.

"You're thirsty," she repeats.

"No, I'm not," I say, weakening and dizzy. "Maybe a little."

She gets up, hands me a dipper of water from her metal pail, then takes the kettle off her stove and throws a handful of dried, crushed leaves into a stew pot with the hot water. After a moment, she pours two cups and puts one in front of me. She spoons out a blob of honey that looks like it was raked from a tree. Her hand is brown and bony, long fingered and dry like it has been baked in the sun. I take a hot, sweet, fragrant gulp, and my vision clears, yet all the rest of me is fuzzy, dense, too heavy to move. I look at the strange lines on her walls, between the neat stacks of letters, and pick out familiar patterns.

"Someone wrote there, too," I point out stupidly, leaning forward and instantly realizing that I am reading a set of words, a sentence, some-

154

thing that loops toward the window, which makes no sense to me and which I can't understand. I open my mouth, but can't think of anything to add, so shut it and examine my folded hands while Fleur gets up again and begins to stir something in a black iron pot. She has an old woodstove maybe from the thirties, a big thing with winged nickel handles on the doors. Her bed sags beneath a bearskin that doesn't look dead but shines like live fur. A red trader's blanket is folded at the foot. The bed is held up not by legs but by more files and books. Above it there is a shelf, and on that, a shallow round drum. Beaver and ermine and otter skins hang there, a bandolier-type tobacco bag, beaded all over, braids of sweet grass, sage bundles, and other things, too, in pouches, things that I try very hard not to look at too close. There is a bowl on the floor that holds stones, completely round stones that the water from the lake has washed smooth. The sight of them makes my mouth go dry again, for I know that they are not just rocks but spirit rocks, full of existence, and that she probably talks to them at night and tells them what to do for her, who to visit, who to bother.

It's getting dark now, and before me she sets a plate of bean soup which I dig into so as not to offend her, though as I eat, the taste of smoke and grease and heavy comfort soothes me into an almost ordinary mind frame. One plate, another, and now my tongue feels thick and swollen. I drink more water from the dipper. The air is dark and full. The old lady lights a glass kerosene lamp and goes outside. I stand up, splash my face from

155

the basin of water she's left, afraid that I have fallen under some sort of spell, drunk a sleeping powder in the hot tea, eaten herbs disguised by salt in the bean soup. But as soon as the water touches my face I feel all right. I wash myself a little better with a slab of harsh yellow lye soap, the kind I remember from my first years of life. No pink Camay here like at Lulu's, no towels either. I dry my hands and face on my shirt and then stand at the door to be ready when she comes back.

It is cool out, now, and she wears a long green sagging sweater. She eases past me and pours hot water from her kettle into a basin, starts washing the bowls and spoon. Her back is turned. Her elbows move rhythmically, her hands scour, the lamp flares golden, and I calm myself, knowing this is my chance.

"I need a love medicine."

My words drop in a well. She does not answer, but continues at her task, and then, unexpectedly, too quickly for an old lady, she whirls around and catches me in the dim light, looks steadily into my eyes until I blink, once, twice. When I open my eyes again, she broadens, blurs beyond my reach, beyond belief. Her face spreads out on the bones and goes on darkening and darkening. Her nose tilts up into a black snout and her eyes sink. I struggle to move from my place, but my legs are numb, my arms, my face, and then the lamp goes out. Blackness. I sit there motionless and my head fills with the hot rasp of her voice.

CHAPTER TWELVE

FLEUR'S LUCK

The fourth and last time she came back to the reservation, Fleur Pillager was dressed in stark white. Her padded-shoulder suit, pinched at the waist, caught the spring sun. She moved in a glare, a shield of new light. She carried gloves, wore spotless high heels. A short-brimmed hat tipped a spotted veil across her face. Those of us who dared to notice saw that her braids had grown thick as tails and hung long down her back, bound together with a red strip of cloth. The oldest people frowned when they heard that detail, remembering how in the old days the warriors arranged their hair, tied back when they prepared to meet an enemy.

Fleur's car was also white and it was large, a Pierce-Arrow with a Minnesota license plate. Inside, sulking in the passenger's seat, a boy raised and lowered hand to chewing mouth, methodically drawing one licorice whip after another from a crisp red-and-white-striped bag of candy he had insisted on buying at the trader's store.

Everyone knew and did not know her. There were no cries of greeting, no hands held admiringly to the face and smiles. No one smoothed Fleur's hair down on each side of her forehead and said *Daughter, daughter, we've missed you.* Peendigaen. *Sit and eat some of this good soup.* No one offered her bread and tea. Only sharp-eyed gossipers already hurried to build story onto story, jumped to wonder at the white suit of foreign cut, the luxury car, the boy.

It was reported that he held his candy in his fist at the trader's store, and ate it looking straight into the faces of the Migwans girls, who watched each dark twist as it passed before them. Sugar-hypnotized, mouths watering, they swallowed and looked down as he continued to chew, staring at them with no curiosity.

Like her clothes, her hat, her purse and car, the boy, too, was white. No trace, the old ladies bent close to the problem agreed, no trace, no sign of Fleur Pillager in him. Perhaps she was just caring for the boy, son of a rich *zhaginash*, perhaps she was—and there was no word to use as description but one was quickly invented—hired milk.

And yet the car and clothes were troubling. Stolen perhaps, though the Pillager acted as though she owned them. But then, she'd always acted as though she owned everything and nothing: sky, earth, those who crossed her path, road, and Pillager land. It was because she owned herself, they said, because she was a four-souled woman. Like her grandmother, Fleur Pillager possessed more souls than she had a right to. It was not proper. Even now, who knew how many she had left to use? She could not be killed, that fact was now proved once more. For here she was again, a presence that did not stand to reason. She should have been dead, but perhaps, knowing death was near, she had thrown a soul out into the world, a decoy, and lived on without harm.

And here, too, was another worrisome detail, a

source of argument, for where did they go, those souls? Whom did they inhabit, haunt? Why, after she survived the sickness, did the fox bark under Two Hat's window and why, after she did not drown yet again, did that owl sit at the entrance to the church, just over the doorway on the pine branch, blinking with pale eyes at the Sunday worshipers, of whom only Josette Bizhieu was brave enough to offer tobacco and speak these words—"Grandfather, I see that you are watching us, but go. Do not bother us. We were good to you. Do not be lonely for us where you are."

And after that, why did it happen that although Josette Bizhieu had been polite and the grandfather lifted soundlessly into the air, it did no good. Josette's mother and her sister's small daughter died together, same day, same hour. Sometime later, in the road, the black dog stood guarding air. Why did these things happen when Fleur Pillager was around? Or did they happen all of the time, perhaps, and was her presence a way of putting order to the random way death struck?

Whatever it was, soon darker rumors were afloat.

The boy and Fleur went to the house of Nanapush. The car sat nightlong in the yard and all the next day and the next day no one drove it, a nuisance, for it meant all those interested had to find an excuse to pass by the old man's place if they wanted to see for themselves the thing Fleur drove, or catch a glimpse of her young boy.

He had a blue rubber ball, which he threw in the yard but never very high, and caught in his hands. He had an orange, which he peeled, tossing

159

down the brilliant skin. He had a black umbrella, which he raised and stood beneath when the sky opened and it rained. It was a small umbrella, just right for a child. This caused great interest. Even more than the car, it struck the envious full on. Since when did children carry umbrellas? And was this a fact now to be expected, that children would not get wet from rain, and if so, how were they to become vulnerable to knowledge? For it was well known that the rain must fall occasionally upon that soft place on the skull of a child in order for that child to understand the language of adults. From that source, they then learned both the ways of animals and, these days, to please teachers in the schools of the nuns and United States government.

If children were to stand beneath umbrellas, what next? And anyway, what child besides this white boy of Fleur's ever would consent to remain so motionless?

For he hardly moved at all, it was true. He stood in the yard as rain drove down, returning stare for glance, watching all who dared approach until they grew uneasy, lost their curiosity. Those light eyes! That pale hair! Then the sun came out, and someone noticed, as well, that he did not cast a shadow. This, at last, answered many questions.

He must be a soul Fleur had tossed out in the face of death. An argument. Bait. He was a piece of her own fate used to divert attention from her real business, which was something now thrown open for speculation.

Since old Nanapush had saved her from death, since he was her only friend on the reservation, her visiting the man stood to reason. Yet, to stay

160

so long indoors? To talk endlessly together in the yard? To allow the mud of spring to come over their feet and ruin that white suit as, together, they went out every day to check his traplines in the woods? Or were they up to something else? Marking out certain boundaries? Old lines, old places, old grounds of the long dead Pillagers?

And still, that white car. And still, that pale boy in the yard. And soon, very soon, eventually and as expected, the Agent.

After the Pillager land around the lake was stripped bare by the lumber company and of no more use, as the logging companies moved on west, it was put up for sale and bought by the former Indian Agent, Jewett Parker Tatro, a man now wealthy in land but in little else. He still lived in government housing, clung to a place just at the edge of town. He longed for the great yellow barns and brick house of his New England childhood, a dairy farm broken up among his brothers, sold piece by piece from under them, and he wanted to return. But no one was interested in purchasing the land for which he had cheated so carefully and persistently. And he was restless. Since his retirement, he showed up anywhere two people gathered. Now he stood carefully aside, gaunt and lean, his beard a tough gray horn jutting off his chin, his eyes as black as any full-blood's, watching.

The white Pierce-Arrow. His look glittered and intensified when Fleur stepped from Nanapush's door. His eyes became the beacons of his wishes. He walked alongside the machine, stepping with the eager reverence of a prospective owner. Once

161

or twice he smoothed his hand across the hood, kicked the tires, jiggled the grille, and tugged the chromed bumpers. He put his hand to the window to make a shadow through which he could see inside, where, that morning, the boy sat, this time eating nothing, but dressed in a fine, fawn-colored suit, and wherefrom he emerged. Jewett Parker Tatro had in his life managed with such thorough ease to acquire anything that pleased him—beaded moccasins, tobacco bags, clothing, drums, rare baskets, property of course—that when he saw the car he made an immediate assumption. He could get it from Fleur, just like he had acquired her land, and he would. He had not yet determined the method, but there was no question that this would happen. There was only time between him and the capture of his desire.

Even the boy did not deflect his attention, though if Tatro had not been preoccupied, he would have asked questions enough to form an explanation. The automobile, the clarity of his own greed, concentrated him. He looked at the car, he looked at Fleur, and that is when we realized that the decoy was not the boy, as we previously believed, but the car. Large parcels and belongings would soon change owners. From wherever she had been Fleur had studied the situation and kept track of time, calculated justice, assessed possibilities. That was not a white woman's powder in her purse. Gamblers in the old days kept a powder of human bones—dried, crushed, pounded fine—to rub on their hands. So did she. So we were not surprised when, casually and unimportantly, with no reference to anything

162

else or anyone, even though plenty of those who had the time to watch had gathered, Fleur and Nanapush sat down in front of the house and then, with no ceremony, took out a new deck of cards.

The two of them began to play. Jewett Parker Tatro was riveted with interest. He caught his breath. Deepened lights shown in the pits of his eyes, but even he knew better than to play cards with Fleur Pillager, and so he did not approach. However, as if in his stead, the boy joined the game, and there were those who counted the tipped balance that became the rocking vertigo that culminated in the Agent's undoing as the instant he saw the boy sit down to play, and at the same time, did not truly see him.

The boy leaned to the rough little table in the trampled yard, twisted his spoiled face at the watchers, and made himself at home with Nanapush and Fleur. Jewett Tatro approached, struck ground with his hand-carved cane. He came near enough to see everything and yet did not although he squinted his eyes. And then, according to those who were there, in paying strict attention to Fleur the Agent watched the wrong person, for those who really knew how to observe kept their eyes on the boy as he took his place between his elders. They saw the smoothness of his face, the shut innocence, the vacant look that absorbed without interest. They saw his smile gleam, once, knew that dullness was a veil. They saw the smallness of him, the childish candy fat, the tightness of his rich-boy suit. And then, unfurling from his cuffs and wrists, they saw his hands. His wrists appeared, his palms, and then

163

the fingers—long and pale, strong, spidery, and rough. The boy shuffled with an organist's blur and the breath of the little crowd held. He dealt. There were those who found slim shade to watch, those who rolled cigarettes of pouch tobacco, those who smoothly stroked their chins or grinned with excitement, and those who turned and walked silently back down the road. Once the Agent sat down, it didn't matter who stayed or who left. For to all, the outcome was obvious.

Fleur was never one to take an uncalculated piece of revenge. She was never one to answer injustice with a fair exchange. She gave back twofold. When the Agent got up from his chair she would have what he owned, or the boy would, the two one and the same. As for the Agent, the car, you do not feed bait to a gasping fish. What does it matter? You simply extract the hook.

CHAPTER THIRTEEN

LYMAN'S DREAM

From the outside, staring into the lighted face of the video slot machine, he looked like anyone. His jaw hung slightly open, his hands worked the levers, the buttons, he watched the bars reel over in a whirl and fashion themselves into regular shapes before him. He was playing Caribbean Gold, working for the treasure chest. Knives spun. Brown pirates and ladies. Skulls, flags, and golden coins. The mystery intensified. The quiet of the hushed air surrounded him. Slowly, with

164

an endless burst, the tension vaulted over him but Lyman dipped into an automatically refilling bucket of quarters and continued, and continued, until he had pushed so many coins into the heavy slot that his hands were raw, stiff as wax.

The microprocessors inside the machine were starting to question, to hum, to whine with the weight of self-importance. Lyman was even money, then he was gaining, when all of a sudden Shawnee's face flashed in the little video square. Once. Twice. Three times. Then Redford clanked down beside her. He played a quarter, another, then a whole handful, but his own face did not appear in the magic line along with theirs. Sometimes Zelda's, sometimes Lipsha's. Sometimes the face of the old Pillager woman leapt glaring from nowhere. But never his own.

His own reflection was lodged at the bottom of the river where his brother Henry had jumped in and drowned. His face was composed of Kashpaw's face. Shawnee's wishes moved him, her religious interests sent him into the woods. Her hopes were his. Lyman's hands were strung with his mother's clever nerves. His feet were the size of his father's tracks—ambitions, chances, progress reports, and hope. He was everybody else's creature but his own. And yet, as quarter after quarter fed off his fingers, he began to receive a hint of himself, an ID picture composed of his economic tribulations and triumphs, a personal glimpse from the outside. He was drive. He was necessity. If not him, there was no one who would plan his plans, lift his voice, scheme, and bring the possibilities into existence.

165

The face of Fleur Pillager appeared before him and the walls melted into leaves and standing poplar, then into brush, into darkness so intense his eyes strained miserably before he shut them. He was sitting face-to-face with the old lady, listening, as Lipsha had described, to the hot rasp of her bear voice.

Land is the only thing that lasts life to life. Money burns like tinder, flows off like water, and as for the government's promises, the wind is steadier.

She spoke to him, and her tone was not the quiet blessing of other elders he knew, but a hungry voice, still fierce, disdainful and impatient.

This time, don't sell out for a barrel of weevil-shot flour and a mossy pork.

Blinking, back to himself, part of the world again, Lyman smoothed his dirty hair off his face and lay back on his blankets in the backyard of his house. The air was light and cool. Over him, in a twisting and muscular arch, the veined brawn of an old oak tree clasped at and released patches of sky. The towering air was colored such a sweet blue he could not stop looking. Perhaps he had dreamed and perhaps she had really come to him. Maybe during his sleep she had sat by him and spoken those words into his ear. *Put your winnings and earnings in a land-acquiring account. Take the quick new money. Use it to purchase the fast old ground.* He almost laughed at the certainty and possibility. Use a patch of federal trust land somewhere, anywhere near his employee base. Add to

166

it, diversify, recycle what money came in immediately into land-based operations.

He saw wheatland accumulating, a pasta plant, then sunflowers. Acres of sunflowers turning with the day. He saw a possible big-time resort. A marina. Boats, pleasure-seekers. He saw Shawnee Ray painting and sewing and making beautiful things in a little studio with a wide glass window looking out into the stillness, the depth, the unforced beauty of the woods and lakes. He saw Redford, from time to time, accompanying him to his office and tapping out requests for information on accounts on his computer. Whatever else happened, he would be a good father, that is, he would be himself—instead of trucks, he would play store. Teach value for value, pound for pound. Already, he was sure, Redford had an investor's eye.

Lyman's secret in life was that he had never, not ever, not in any part of himself, ever given up. His boots also had filled with water on the evening he dove into the gray swell of icy water after his brother. Lyman wasn't a good swimmer, he didn't know how to stroke and kick, and he felt in one moment during the struggle exhausted. His body had loosened fearfully, another movement seemed impossible. And then from somewhere, he couldn't tell where, because it wasn't in him but outside him, the pull, one inch, the next inch, the tiny article of faith.

167

CHAPTER FOURTEEN

LIPSHA

RELIGIOUS WARS

Love won't be tampered with, love won't go away. Push it to one side and it creeps to the other. Throw it in the garbage and it springs up clean. Try to root it out and it only flourishes. Love is a weed, a dandelion that you poison from your heart. The taproots wait. The seeds blow off, ticklish, into a part of the yard you didn't spray. And one day, though you worked, though you prodded out each spiky leaf, you lift your eyes and dozens of fat golden faces bob in the grass.

After I get clear of the old lady's house, I never am quite sure about all the things that she told me, for it seems as though the important ones have entered my understanding from the inside. Scenes without words appeared that night. Dreams. I saw Fleur Pillager when she was young, heard her speak in low voices, telling me her bear thoughts, laughing in tongues. For although she took pity on me, accepted me as her relation, she gave me nothing I could use outright—no love teas, no dried frog hearts, no hints or special charms. *Admit your love*, I think she said, *take it in although it tears you up*. I don't have a choice about it, anyway, for I am lost. Everything that I take in about Shawnee Ray mixes me up bad, but I let it happen. She makes my heart seize like an over-

168

heated engine. I think of her and feel myself melt down to a metal sludge. From that molten mess, I still hope she'll fix my heart into the shape she wants, like she does the patterns of her original designs. And then one day I hear the rumor that she's got a different plan in mind.

"That girl's got ambition," they all say, for Shawnee Ray has gone over to the All Red Road Powwow in Montana to dance the jingle dress and sell her designed clothes. College money, she tells everyone. She is going to get schooled in the arts. On the phone, she had said that she will soon pay me back the money that I gave her for fabric. Now I know where she's going to get it. Odds are she'll beat her competitors and come home in a week with big prize money. Knowing Shawnee Ray, she won't bingo that money away, either. She will put her money down on an apartment, get a baby-sitter, take classes, embark upon some kind of major, acquire two initials, three, then four behind her name, all of which will cause her to be hired by an art gallery, or maybe she'll go political, into a law firm, a lobby group, an Indian gaming agency in Washington, where she will be swallowed in the brilliance of a successful life and I will never be able to follow.

I can hardly lift the mop. I throw it across the bar like a messy javelin, and then I go back into my room and lie down on the rocking plastic waves of my bed thinking that my heart will explode with spirals of love and confusion and fear of what comes next. I believe Shawnee loves me, I trust in my vision, but in deference to Lyman's fatherhood she is deflecting her sights once again from me. I

169

am doing what I can do, trying to be irresistible by being responsible. I counsel myself that I should stay away from Shawnee Ray and not try to change her decision, but over and over in my mind's sight I see her foot press the sewing pedal, I see her little round glasses fog. I see back, to before that scene, and I am caught. Again, I watch her emerge from the rushing water in the motel room.

She lies down beside me, takes my hand, moves over me, her breasts both full and pointed, her waist a band of flexible emotion, and between her legs a rough and stirring sweetness. Again, with Shawnee Ray, I enter the trailless forest. I never slept all that long-ago motel night. As dawn spilled, I watched the ice blue radiance stray over the flimsy mutton-colored curtains and my heart quailed in me. I know it wasn't long before we had to check out. That was when the mirror in that small room spoke to me, dim, calling me right through its shadowy door. All night Shawnee Ray had tossed and grumbled at me, kicking and rolling and touching my hand. I knew it was just the way people don't fit the first time they are together, and I longed to change that, to make our love habit.

Hopeless, as I've said. Breathing hard, listening to Titus open up the bar, curled around my lonely pillow, I remember her saying those fatal words.

You got the medicine, but you don't got the love.

Does she believe that even now? Did she argue me out of her heart? I get so downcast after time that I begin to open the book too much, the plastic Bible which is still my only souvenir of that long-

170

ago night. In the beginning pages there is a section for the desperate. Big problems, all of which I personally suffer, are given neat reference points, conveniently labeled. Adultery, Adversity, Anxiety, Conceit, Confidence (False), Covetousness, Crime, Death, Deceit, Depravity, Divorce, Doubt, Drunkenness, Enemies, Excuses, Extravagance, Falsehood, Fault finding, Fear, Flesh, Greed, Hatred, Intemperance, Judging, Lip service, Lust, Pride, Revenge, Self-exultation, Sin, Submission, Swearing, Temptation, Tribulation, and Worldliness. There is also Backsliding, Bitterness, Defeat, Depression, Loneliness (Overcoming), Trouble (In), and Weariness.

Weariness gets it about right for me and so I find the chapter in Matthew about the yoke being easy, the burden light, and I fix on the words *gentle* and *lowly in heart*. Lowly in heart describes me so perfect and describes what I can't be, also—humble and contented with what I got. A job. Money. People who don't hate me. I get to wondering if the Son of Man had any mad-green love affairs. Unless He did, He could never understand us humans, I am sure.

I page through, wondering: Where does it come from, this beautiful sickness of the heart? Why would I choose the feeling it over the not feeling it? Why, although she doesn't even love me back the same, do I feel thankful to Shawnee Ray Toose? It comes to me, in time, that part of my emotion for her is all mixed up with the love that she has for her little boy. I love her the more as she resists me in favor of her son's father.

171

Somehow, I'm proud she loves her little boy enough to stay away from bad risks like Lipsha Morrissey.

I am getting riskier with every day, too, like something in my brain has sunk out of sight. Darker thoughts inhabit me. I think of Stan Mahng, this guy I used to know who got a crush on a girl from off-reservation and ran away with her to Colorado. They were heard from once, twice, and then she returned alone and soon married a completely different person. Only thing was, she had Stan's baby one month into that sudden union, and when Stan returned from the mountains and he heard about that, he went over to their house in the hope of getting to see his child. They let Stan in the door and anyway, real polite, he visited with them, and held his little baby. Then he left without hardly saying anything, for he was a quiet kind of guy, and went off to ice-fish on Matchimanito Lake, where his cousin's house was set.

Well, they saw Stan go in the icehouse door, but they never saw him come out. He carried in his ice auger, used a pruning saw to enlarge the fishing hole big enough so that he could slide through with rocks tied on his feet. There he sat, on the bottom of the lake until spring thaw.

I get to thinking of others. Stacy Cuthbert, who killed her rival with a shovel. Of Martha May Davis, who held up a Stamart and used the money next day to buy herself a thousand-dollar white lace wedding dress. I think of my own grandmother Lulu with all her towering love of men, of how Nector Kashpaw set her house on fire from

172

the heat of his attraction. Naturally, I think of the frozen hand of Xavier Toose, and the long-running gossip that has followed Fleur Pillager into her old age, about how she loved men outside, against trees, in the water, between the dangerous crystal-set tables in the high society of Saint Paul, Minnesota. I think of the other Pillager named Moses whose *windigo* love howl still rings across the lake from his island of stone, where he died of desire. I wonder how it was my grandmother Marie stayed so calm in love, or why it was that Zelda lost her love-luck after Xavier and never married a Chippewa.

And after all that, I keep coming back to Stan Mahng. It is as though I see him down there all winter, on the lake bottom. At last he was in a place that ran deep as his own feelings. I almost felt glad for how he finally found that spot. The cold might have been unpleasant, but it drove out the heat of sorrow. Sometimes a light beam shot through the ice, a slash of raving silver, but most often, I think, only the resolving dark.

One early morning night, before I rise to my daily job, I decide that I have a problem that the good little book must help me deal with and I turn the beginning list of pages for a reference to the thought of Suicide. But there is nothing there. I look through twice, and then a third time, thinking maybe it will be under another heading like Contemplating, suicide, or Feeling like, suicide, or Committed, suicide, but there is no mention of this area at all. I'm just curious, it's not like I have a noose in my hands, a pistol, a garment bag, or pills. I'm just thinking that it would be nice to have a verse handy just in case scriptures come up short.

I get furious at the absence. So mad that I throw the book across the room with all my force. And it hits my stereo, it turns my stereo on, and through the speakers, through the system, through the electronic noodles, at that moment my life or death answer comes, top volume.

. . . life is but a joke . . .

Cold air flows up my spine to the roots of my hair as the man himself, Jimi Hendrix, speaks to me, breathes at me past death, drags me out of my cave to flat turquoise spaces where the wildcats announce themselves and towers crumble into sand and mountains fall against karate chops and I am not to worry. If life only is a joke then I'll get lost in it. Leave behind all the serious shit. Live like he did with a big smile of crazed pain and genius upon his face. Get religious, for want of anything more ridiculous.

For I have to admit the book knocked on the power. If life's a joke, then suicide's a bad punch line, I guess. I reach in the corner for the Bible, smooth the fluttered pages, and ease myself cautiously onto my bed again to ponder.

We never ask for all this heat and silence in the first place, it's true. This package deal. It's like a million-dollar worthless letter in the mail. You're chosen from the nothingness, but you don't know for what. You open the confusing ad and you think, Shall I send it in or should I just let the possibilities ripen? You don't know shit! You are left on your own doorstep! You are set there in a basket, and one day you hear the knock and open the door and reach down and there is your life.

I relax deeper into my bed, and as I lie there a peculiar thing happens. I feel time pass. Or more rightly, since it is always ticking by, I become aware of its passage. I sense it running through my hands, my fingers touching the hem, my mouth catching at the flavor, just a fleeting change upon my lips. The music beats onward, the guitar licks like holy fire, burning time like paper, like a match to alcohol. My thoughts enlarge. Outside, trees are sieving air and seeding and whipping through the black gates of clockwork. All around us, time. Time over us. The sky never twice, the river once. No moment the same. Time glimpsed like a mighty book, swift pages turning fast in us and slow in stone. Time gathering, a muscle of space, a rhythmical flex of darkness curving like a cat, and me, Lipsha Morrissey, one hair on its ass.

Why fight the joke, why rush the moment? Who the hell knows how it all turns out?

After this, my day proceeds in the usual manner. Nothing seems so terribly different, and yet, those big spaces that collide in my room set me on a further linkage of considerations. Thoughts of God bother me and will not quit. I wonder whether I should start reciting Bible quotes to Shawnee Ray, whether my becoming a witness of some kind, a Christian martyr, might press a button in her heart.

For the fact is, you can think big, but your real concerns are little. Schemes and hopes. I would go down-dirty, I would do anything to get Shawnee Ray. It occurs to me that she is also

175

involved in some of our more traditional religious pursuits, and I can maybe get to her through her own uncle, Xavier Toose. I know that Lyman is involved as well, and now I wonder to myself whether getting the real old-time traditional religion wouldn't help my case.

With religion there is always that personal impossibility, a barrier which stops me, of believing in a God in the first place. Where and who? No spirit ever was revealed to me, I got no message through a burning bush. I never heard words spoken in my head unless I did a garbage lid of drugs. First of all, I think about the Catholics, maybe signing up with them somehow. I am attracted to their ritual motions, although when the nuns tell you straight-faced that you are eating the real true and precious body and the blood of Christ, you have to wonder. How come the Catholics make such a big deal out of converting cannibals? Drinking blood, eating flesh, it goes on every Mass. Also Confession is a thing I can't agree with. I say it's cheap. You kneel down in that box and say what you done. And then, basically, you get off scot-free, only cranking out a few Hail Marys or some Our Fathers. No restitution demanded, no community service.

I suppose it is natural, too, after all my thinking, and after my experience with Old Lady Pillager, that I should also take an interest in the Chippewa religion. Not that I am about to go crawling after illusions. No, my main motive in getting traditional is the hope of attracting Shawnee Ray's attention to my staying power.

176

So I go looking for a home to rest in Shawnee Ray's heart. I want a place where I can belong, but I end up as part of a surprising configuration. I go looking for a god I cannot resist, try to get to heaven through the ozone hole, land on any old star. I look for peace, I look for love. I end up in a religious war.

I go to Lyman in order to scope out the possibilities, to get the angle, and to check out his religious technique along with his love strategies. It is a sweet, new summer weekday at his government house, and I find him inside with the telephone in his hand, clouds of smoke around his head, the television laugh track slashing air, radio chiming in the other room. There is a worried look on his face and excitement in the intense way he mouths his words. He gestures at me, points at a chair that is set among his exercise machines, all pulleys, weights, and dials. I make myself at home and overhear his business talk. Casino talk, state compact talk, blackjack equipment talk, which goes on and on until I pour myself a coffee, sit down, and watch him so steadily that finally he catches my eye once, twice, and then hangs up.

"Your mother is my grandmother, you're my half uncle and half brother and my boss," I say, quickly, before the phone rings again. "So I am going to ask a favor of you."

"Shoot."

"My favor is religious," I go on. "I haven't ever done an official sort of spiritual quest, just the kind of grab-you-by-the-collar stumble, you know the type of thing. So I'm in the market for a more

177

high-type vision, and I don't know where to go for it, who to ask."

At that, Lyman takes the phone off the hook, a thing I've never seen him do before. He walks into his small living room, hits the television power button. Sit-com characters are blipped into the vacuum, and Lyman sits down across from me in a stiff, low plaid chair. I see that his grass dance outfit and his accessories—strings of yarn, fluff and feathers, ankle bells and moccasins—are spread all across the room, on the coffee table and the plastic end tables. He has been chewing for his own moccasins, I see, softening some hide in the traditional and ancient way. To my mind, this is both a touching and an awful thing, Lyman repairing his brother's grass dance outfit, a thing most unusual for a big shot like him. I know he's doing it in order to impress Shawnee Ray. I am jealous to see that they have the use of a needle and thread in common. I am uneasy at the evidence of the depth of Lyman's love design.

"It so happens I'm going to go see Xavier Toose. Bring him some tobacco. You know why?"

Of course I don't.

Lyman picks up a wristband, squints at his needle in concentration, running at it with a bit of waxed thread. He tells me that he needs to debate a few things and ask advice. He is trying to think whether to include me in some plan that he has in mind. I can tell that he is going through an inside struggle. He finally bests himself.

"You gave me the pipe. I can't refuse you." He sighs. "I'll ask Toose to put you out for a fast, for a quest, the same time as me."

178

"With you?"

"We won't be together or anything, just be waiting for a vision at the same time."

Things are moving quicker than I hoped, maybe even than I wanted. I had in mind something a little less radical than four or maybe six days alone in the bush with no food.

"Sure you never had a vision?" asked Lyman.

I think back. I was cracked on the head by an old vet with a wine bottle. That was by accident, but I decided then and there I would not join the army. I was visited by the form of my mother in the Northern Lights. I talked to her sitting in a bar so close we could have clasped fingers. I saw dandelions, me in the grass, picking handfuls, gathering up the yellow pollen in a ditch and putting those tart flowers to my face when I thought of Shawnee Ray. I had those kind of visions. I saw blank-outs of my own past, like the time when Zelda swore how she found me in the slough or when Jimi spoke. I saw things here and there and everywhere but lost my powers of the touch nonetheless.

"Sure," I say, "I had plenty of visions, but I ain't satisfied with them."

I honestly admire Lyman's ease in the larger world, and I appreciate his taking me in his hand like this with the money, now the religion, his basic good nature. Of course, he doesn't get the whole picture, doesn't know that despite denying all rumors I am planning to slowly zero in upon Shawnee Ray. He doesn't know I am a spy, a thief scoping out his love medicines. I keep on trying

179

to convince myself that if he has genuine love for Shawnee, it is lodged in his heart so deep the point has disappeared from view like a fine-point needle. But seeing his devoted work on that grass dance clothing makes me pause before I think of the moving strands of fringe and ribbon, at which thought I shiver and grow weak with longing at the memory of the swing of Shawnee's hair.

There it is, soft morals, but how can you argue? Lyman is trying to do his duty. Shawnee Ray is full of noble attitude. I am a creature of the same old underhanded shit. Not only that, but I am up against the heavens themself. The supernatural world. If there does happen in the scheme of the universe to be a prime creator, a God who takes our actions personal, my plan to grab some spirit power just in order to impress a woman might be construed as low, as not in keeping with the big dedications of others, like Lyman.

But that's how much I love Shawnee Ray. Heaven is a dangerous place, I already know that from lying in her arms. How much worse than to live without her could it be to live in hell? For some reason, as if God was up there, I look out Lyman's window. It is one of those wide unvariable days when the sky is like the inside of a big, white opal shell. Streaks of dim pale reflections hang windless on one side of the horizon. On the other, darker shades cast fuming shadows.

No, I don't hate Lyman the way I probably should, since he is my rival for the woman I adore down to her heels. I can't get behind inventing faults, he's just another guy. I don't even dislike him, and in fact, I actually enjoy hanging around with my uncle, beating him at pool, drinking a beer or two, talking business. That morning, I make my report on my bingo winnings and hand over my bank account, which is mounting with comfortable persistence. The numbers put Lyman into such a good mood that he makes a new pot of coffee, spoons some flavored nondairy creamer into mine, a treat he bought at his own convenience store. He all but invites me to stay. So I decide to help him out a little since he's helping me, to string beads or whatever he has in mind. He offers me a piece of leather to chew, but I politely refuse. The smoky taste helps him cut down on cigarettes, he says, and then he starts biting the leather, chomping it in a sad way, a hungry way, until I begin to feel a space yawn inside me.

We get to talking. I can't help asking, since the subject is so unavoidable, and I'm nervous, and since after all we are related, about his brother Henry, the one who died, a relative I never knew. Lyman sits back in his couch chair for a minute, relaxed as I've never seen him, and suddenly he breaks out into a smile. Not even a sad smile. He's looking at the dark cloth of the fringe-trimmed shirt that Henry once wore.

"I can see him," he says, "that time we traveled on the pow-wow trail. We brought our things along in a suitcase and sometimes we just sat underneath the arbor, in that dry heat, listening to the popple leaves curl when the drum stopped. There was that silence between the songs, when all the talk seems so far away, when the announcer

181

starts teasing the dancers back to the arena—it's like your heart is waiting to beat. You take a breath, another breath, and then you're laughing at something, or you're hungry again, ready to go snagging, to walk by that camp full of beautiful sisters.

"We both danced sometimes, when the mood came upon us, and those times, oh well, my brother Henry, he was the best, they'd all say it. The most promising grass dancer, though he didn't always win because that wasn't the point with Henry—he danced to move within his own thoughts. We were different. I danced for prize money."

Lyman leans forward now and laughs low and hard at himself, but then he softens, sips his coffee, and after a while he starts in again, not even looking at me.

"Once we sat on the side of a hill in August when the grass had grown long, tasseled out and feathered in a lush and rainy summer. We watched the opposite side of an ungrazed hill where the grass was moving, going, rushing, as if a great hand was pushing it from underneath. You know how that is, how it makes you reach to understand it—that grass changing. Sometimes it was as if a different hand from above pressed down, fingers spread, showing the silver underside of fur. Coursing, streaming, that grass fled. Then changed direction. At lower currents it was rising up, green smoke.

"And Henry says to me, not drunk, just speaking from the heart, 'Little Brother, I see the earth breathing, coming at me, almost like it's playing with me.'

"In return, I was almost going to make a joke. But then I saw he was right in what he said, so I did not speak. We were both of us in the grip of something, then. Modest power, but unrelenting power. The grass will cover him, I thought. For the grass was running in the dried sloughs and in the ditches. Wind, earth, water—all of it flowed together as the lick of green flames, as the grass.

"And I said, 'Henry, *don't go.*'

"That's all I said to him. He'd enlisted in the Marines. Still, he never heard me, I don't think. By then, he was far away in his thoughts, already gone.

"Just like you are, Little Brother," says Lyman, looking close at me, "just like you always were. Just like you'll always be."

And I have to look away, almost afraid to think, to feel the way he's just called me his little brother. Because I love his girl, I cannot meet his gaze. We could have maybe gotten more in tune somehow, right then, in the quiet of his house, but we are set up to fail by the sight of Shawnee Ray in both our minds. Shawnee Ray at the center pole, behind the eagle staff, before the loudspeakers, dancing in the arbor, all flashing light of cut beads and jingles.

I take a deep breath. I take another. It stabs, full of sorrow. We are so related I can hardly find the knot. I feel all embarrassed by these lost emotions and I can't open up my heart, except finally to make a lame comment and then suggest that we go someplace and eat.

"Eat," says Lyman.

He looks down at the dance shirt he has picked up and holds in his hands. I see, as we regard the cloth together, how the light shines through the worn-out places where the weave has thinned and pulled. The shirt is old, frail, of a Kleenex softness, faded; all through it the threads look ready to part.

Almost immediately, as we pull out onto the road, I can't help but go on to try to change the subject. I ask, in a casual voice, how Lyman and Shawnee are doing these days.

"Okay," he says, distracted.

We ride awhile longer, and I still can't hold back.

"What do you mean, okay?" I ask.

"Just okay," he says. "Well, not so good."

My heart leaps up at my throat, but he won't say anything else more specific about their troubles.

"She's so smart, that Shawnee Ray," I sigh, attempting to draw him out as we drive along.

"She's got a good head on her shoulders," he responds, almost suspiciously, as we leave the dusty gravel and enter the highway to town. "She could amount to something, but she's got two Achilles' heels named Mary Fred and Tammy."

"Her sisters."

"One's the ball and the other's the chain. It wouldn't be so bad, but she left Redford with them."

"Why not with you?" I ask.

Lyman shrugs. "She's not thinking, or I backed her into a corner. She says I'm in too thick with

184

Zelda, trying to block her, keep her down on the farm so to speak. She says she does not intend to spend her whole life as a bingo caller, but hey, who said that was the deal? I'm grooming her."

"Oh."

Lyman's back to his business self, done with the memories and the spiritual side of life, and I try to be quick to follow.

"She's going to be my manager," he goes on. "Shawnee's good with people."

"That's true."

"Except for this thing with Redford. Talk about a lack of judgment! Of course, I've got a court order going through and by tomorrow I should have him back."

I think this is strange, all of a sudden him going to court, and I am filled with a carbonating heat.

"You can't take Redford—I mean, you're not even on the records as his dad."

"How would you know?" Lyman shakes his head. "You're unbelievable. Zelda's in that office, remember, and I do have some rights even if Shawnee Ray won't marry me."

"Lyman, she's a good mother," I now say.

"Good? Oh yes, too good a mother, up until now."

The way he says this, mouth turned down, ironical, it seems to me like he is happy that she made a mistake at last, if that's even what it is. He talks like he doesn't place particular value on her uplifting ways, or is making them into something negative, like he's tried, in fact, to take her down. I don't answer for a minute, for it occurs to me that being a smart woman and a good mother are

185

two things I never valued quite enough in Shawnee Ray either. What I think about more than anything else is the sex—day in and day out those thoughts preoccupy my brain. But now, I put my mind onto her other qualities: I picture the way she holds Redford in her strong arms, and how she brings him walking in the woods to show him a bird, a leaf. I have watched her unbeknown, seen her hugging him so close as they walk the supermarket aisle together to pick up a jug of milk. She gets all fierce when her boy is threatened, so I know now that she must have been unhinged by our love on the floor, desperate to escape, half crazy to leave him with her sisters.

I get a piercing pain right beneath the hollow of my heart. I see her rocking Redford, kissing him, touching his face with her finger, and it presses a panic jolt. First off, there is no way I can imagine June Morrissey doing that to me, and my thoughts veer away in longing. The subject makes my throat choke up with envy. I try to swallow. Even left for a week with Tammy and Mary Fred, I wish I was that little boy, I wish that I was Redford.

I make an attempt to control myself, for I see now that Lyman sees himself as Redford's father and I see myself as Redford's competition. That is not right. I want everything about Shawnee Ray, even her motherhood. Only, I want her to mother me, to heal me. I've helped stand in the way of her future just as much as Lyman. Between the three of us, including Redford, we've all but torn her into equal pieces. I roust myself from these thoughts, new thoughts, things I cannot tell Lyman. I don't trust him and I'm angry at how

186

he's forced her to his will. The two of us have now reached the Dairy Queen. I try to shake my shoulders free, but they're loaded with heavy chips of resentment. I don't like knowing the deeper Lyman, the side of him that loved his brother. It makes it so much harder to do him dirt. We get out of the car and stroll into the air-conditioned area where customers are spooning cold mush-wax into their mouths.

"What do you want?" I ask Lyman. I take out my wallet, full of bingo money I'm determined to use.

"Hot dog. Large Diet Pepsi. I'll pay."

"No," I say. "I've got my money out. I'll pay."

Lyman, used to always footing the bill, is almost shocked.

We get our food and sit down at a little plastic table. We unwrap the hot dogs and I try to take a bite, to stuff my mouth, before I speak, but it is like I have no further resistance to my angers.

"You don't know her!" I suddenly throw down my hot dog on the table. "You don't understand her. You don't know who she is! And here you are, trying to discredit her!"

"Who?"

Lyman doesn't take my meaning at all, he just looks at me all quizzical and then, after a while of watching me, when I don't answer, just glare at him, Lyman considers. He cocks his head to the side, opens his mouth, shuts it, then sits back with his pop and puts the straw between his teeth.

"Shawnee Ray," he mumbles, making sure.

I almost knock my pop over on the table, because I lean so suddenly right into his face.

"I know her," I say. "I know her better than you do."

"Really?" He is still not even threatened. It is frustrating, because I don't want to overplay my hand. I get so upset looking at the strong arms and winning bone structure of Lyman Lamartine that my teeth clench on the plastic straw. I raise the straw up, and then I spray pop onto our reservation's biggest tamale. His face goes numb. He looks down at his shirt.

"Stupid little punk."

"Motherfucker!"

That gets him and he dives, like from the high board, right over the little tabletop where I am waiting with all the rage I have tempered in my heart. Our fight is about the biggest mess I've ever started, for that's the way you get when related friends turn to sudden enemies—you hate worse than any strangers. You have to pound out the old affection along with all the new aggravation. But unfortunately a few other folks get involved, too. Doing a flying drop kick, I knock into an entire large-size family who are carefully turning from the ice cream counter and balancing five-topping sundaes with whipped cream and cherries. The cherries explode into the air, the walnut bits zing sideways, the ice cream blobs collide at super speed.

The father sluices pineapple and chocolate down some lady's bosom front, and there begins an immediate and deadly argument about who will pay the bill for the dry cleaning. Lyman's arm, in the meantime, goes haywire as he staggers backward groping for purchase. I have delivered a near knockout connecting punch. His hand goes down in a super nacho plate. The random eater, annoyed, throws the remains at me but I see it coming, duck, and it happens to catch a customer who has just entered from a construction site and is pulling off his hard hat. From there on, until I grab Lyman from the grip of someone big who is massaging a banana split into his growing-out-traditional hair, I can't really describe or explain. It is just one big explosion.

Then we are back in the car. We are driving. We are licking all flavors of creamy substances off of our arms and hands.

"I never fought you before," says Lyman, excited and almost joyful.

"I never fought you before, either," I admit, but I'm not happy.

"Hey," he says, holding a hand out, dripping strawberry topping.

"Hey." I clasp it. "No hard feelings."

But the truth is, lying low after that incident the next two days, I do have harder feelings to deal with than I ever thought. For then we have this conversation in which Lyman says things that complicate my simple hatred of the thing he is doing.

"Lipsha, I have this confession to make," says Lyman. "I'm probably messed up these days because of Shawnee. Something's going on with her, but I don't know what. It's not just this trip, it's something deeper."

My heart sings so hard in a sudden key I have trouble quieting it. I take my breath deep.

"You just got to know this," he blurts out, his

189

voice a strained cry. "I'm so crazy for her I could die, real easy, and Redford's my boy. Would you leave him with those unstable sisters of hers, now would you? Think about it. Shawnee Ray, she's in my head every minute, and I know she's not the same about me. She never forgave me after the things I did. . . . Once, I broke up with her. She was pregnant, but that's history. I'm loving her so hard I think she'll crack, let her feelings well up inside, you know? I just don't know how to go much farther, and I was thinking, see, just wondering if you had any advice. I'm drinking my pride, here. You, a young guy, you might have a way with girls, Lipsha. Things you can tell me. Maybe you could let me in on your secrets."

He gets red in the face after that, bashful, like any moment he could break down and wail. I feel like some low form of life. What am I supposed to say? I cast about in my mind, come up empty of everything but guilt. Here I thought he had the love ways, the smooth ways that I could imitate, but it turns out he's just as confused and oppressed by love as me. Lyman's such a complicated guy there's something uncanny about him, scary, like it's a disease of the spirit, a kind of sainthood that's out of control.

It is tempting to confess everything. I've got to be wary though. For some reason an adage I never knew comes into my mind. *Lie down with dogs, get up with fleas. Lie down with saints, get up with holes in your hands and feet.* I mutter something hopeless about my clumsiness and fears that I hope reassures him, and then I put a hand on his hard

190

shoulder just a moment to let him know that I understand the depth.

As it happens, mixing it up with Lyman doesn't unwedge either my friendship feelings for him or my love for Shawnee Ray, and that last gets worse than ever, so bad that I wake up in the morning and moan and whine before I can slosh out of bed. I know I should quit thinking about her, but I don't exactly have a choice for she's just *there* wherever I turn, *there* when I let my guard down, *there* when I want her and *there* when I don't. Each day, I try to put her out of my mind. For an hour or two I'm in the struggle, I'm talking and arguing, for a while I'm in the fight, resisting all thoughts of Shawnee Ray Toose. And then I weary of it. I get bored of my own resistance. I think of her hand where I want it or her smile flashing, sweet, over her left shoulder. I cannot win out against myself. I just poop out and say, "I'm bad, I have evil tendencies." I accept it, accept myself, and taste her nipple in my mouth. Of course, it's not that I see my love for Shawnee Ray as evil. It's the part where I want to steal her away from my uncle Lyman that is hard to defend against my conscience.

I work late and turn in later, pretend that I have a reason to sleep. I try to step aside, knowing of the reality of Lyman's feelings. But Shawnee gets in the way of my resolution so easily, my heart is all sprung doors and busted windows when it comes to her. I keep recalling our first shocking kiss. I eat, but only strange things, the snacks that Shawnee Ray and I shared at our one meal at the Coin-Op—a Polish sausage sandwich and a

191

chocolate chip cookie. I begin to wish that we'd included a fruit or two, something fresh at least. I drink tea, which she likes, instead of my thick black coffee, and I imagine her soft and slippery touch at any hour when my mind is temporarily unoccupied. It is as though my out-of-the-body sex with Shawnee those two times has increased my longing to an unbearable degree. I can't turn it off. I can't live with it. This uncooked and useless desire with no hope that lives inside me seems like some sort of curse. A net of burning threads. A snare trap that hangs loose around my neck waiting for her hands to jerk me dead.

So it is a relief when Lyman comes into the bar a few nights later. He orders the usual diet pop and suggests tomorrow is a good time to visit Xavier Toose. He says that Redford and Shawnee are now back with Zelda, where they belong. He says he's fixed things, that all is under control. I should take off a week. I am more than ready. I clasp my arms so brotherly around him that he startles in surprise. My face is wide and pure, a shining sun, and I am prepared to see a vision that will fix my mind higher, above the belt.

CHAPTER FIFTEEN

REDFORD'S LUCK

Redford was awake, watching out for his mother. She would come back for him soon with the money she'd win at the big powwow dancing jingle dress. First place and nothing less, she had said. He knew he had to wait for her, and he had to be as good as possible, but Mary Fred was hard to sleep with. Her feet, limp and brown as two trout, hung over the edge of the cot in the shed. Her round arms reached out and slapped at things she saw in her dreams. Redford had been knocked awake out of his own dream where he was hiding in a washing machine.

"*Tss*," his aunt mumbled, half awake, "wasn't nothing." But Redford sat up after her breathing went deep again, and he watched.

There was something coming and he knew it.

It was coming from far off but he had a picture of it in his mind. It was a large thing made of metal with many barbed hooks, points, and drag chains on it, something like Grandma Zelda's potato peeler, only a giant one that rolled out of the sky, scraping clouds down with it and jabbing or crushing everything that lay in its path on the ground.

Redford watched Mary Fred carefully, trying to figure. If he woke her up, maybe she would know what to do about the thing, but he thought he'd wait until he saw it for sure before he shook her. He liked that he could look at a grown-up woman for as long and close up as he wanted, but something about Mary Fred's face scared him. He took a strand of her crackly, curled hair and held it in his hands as if it was the rein to a horse. She had a salty, half-sour, almost puppy smell that wasn't a comfort. He wanted to touch the satin roses sewed on her pink sweater, but he knew he shouldn't do that even in her sleep. If she woke up and found him touching the roses, she would tell him to quit.

He felt drowsy, slumped down, and put his legs beneath the blanket. He closed his eyes and dreamed that the cot was lifting up beneath him, that it was arching its canvas back and then traveling very fast and in the wrong direction, for when he looked up he saw they were advancing to meet the great metal thing with hooks and barbs and all sorts of sharp equipment to catch their bodies and draw their blood. He heard its insides as it rushed toward them, purring softly like a powerful motor, and then they were right in its shadow. He pulled the reins as hard as he could and the horse reared, lifting him. His aunt clapped her hand across his mouth.

"Okay," she said. "Lay low. They're outside and they're gonna hunt."

Her voice was a whine, high and thin, another child's. She touched his shoulder and Redford leaned over with her to look through a crack in the boards.

They were out there all right. Mary Fred saw them. One tribal police officer, a social worker, and Zelda Kashpaw. There had been no whistle, no dream, no voice to warn her that they were coming. There was only the crunching sound of cinders in the yard, the engine throbbing, the dust sifting off their car in a fine light-brownish cloud and settling around them.

"We'll wait, see what they do." She took Redford in her lap and pressed her soft arms around him. "Don't you worry," she whispered

194

against his ear. "Mary Fred knows how to talk to them."

Redford didn't want to look at the car and the police. If he saw Grandma Zelda, he would feel like crying to her, even though Mary Fred had explained she was trying to steal him away. He'd heard the sisters talking, worrying late at night over Lyman's case. Suitcase. He thought it was a kind of carrying box. His aunt's heart beat so fast beside his ear that it seemed to push the satin roses in and out. He put his face to them carefully and breathed the deep, powdery air of her, and the lower smell, the yeast and ferment, the beer. Flower smells were in her little face cream bottles, in her brushes, and around the washbowl after she used it. The petals felt so smooth against his cheek that he had to press closer. She hugged him still tighter. Within the smells of her soft skin and her roses, he closed his eyes then, and took his breaths softly and quickly with her heart.

The three didn't dare get out of the car yet because of Mary Fred's big, ragged dogs loping up the dirt driveway. They were rangy, alert, and bounced up and down on their cushioned paws, like wolves, like they were dancing on hot tar. They didn't waste their energy barking, but quietly positioned themselves on every side of the car and in front of the bellied-out screen door to the Toose house. It was six in the morning, but the wind was up already, blowing dust, ruffling their heavy coyote coats. The big brownish dog on Zelda's side had unusual black and white mark-

195

ings, stripes almost, like a hyena, and he grinned at her, tongue out and teeth showing.

"Shoo!" Zelda opened her door with a quick jerk.

The brown dog sidestepped the door and jumped before her, tiptoeing. Its dirty white muzzle curled and its eyes crossed suddenly as if it was zeroing its crosshair sights in on the exact place it would bite her. She ducked back and slammed the door.

"It's mean," she told Officer Leo Pukwan, a slow man. The son of the son of tribal police, he was carrying on the family occupation. He sat solidly and now, with no change in expression, rolled down his window, unsnapped his holster, drew his pistol out, and pointed it at the dog's head. The dog smacked down, threw itself under the car, and was out and around the back of the house before Pukwan drew his gun back. The other dogs vanished, and from wherever they had disappeared to, they began to howl and the door to the low shoebox-style house slammed open.

"You've got no business here." Tammy was ready for them, tousled but calm, a wide short woman in a boxy haircut, man's sweatshirt and worn-out jeans. "You've got no warrant."

"We do have a warrant," said Pukwan evenly.

"And the court papers?"

"We've got those too," said Zelda.

Tammy's rough raw-looking features were bitter and belligerent. Her swollen eyes took Zelda in and she looked ready to spit with disgust. Standing outside the car, Officer Pukwan stood firm, but watched her warily.

196

"*Booshoo*, Tammy."

"Get the fuck out of here."

"We have *papers*." Zelda spoke emphatically.

"We're doing this for the protection of your nephew," said the social worker, Vicki Koob, holding a manila envelope in the air.

"Protection from who? Where's Lyman? Scared to show his fat face?"

"Just let us take Redford and we'll go." Zelda stood firm, commanding.

"Redford loves me, loves us," Tammy said. "His mother's our fucking sister."

At first glance, Vicki Koob could see that Redford and Mary Fred were not in the house, but she pushed past Tammy and took out her notebook to describe it anyway, for the files, to back up this questionable action. The house consisted of just one rectangular room with white-washed walls and a little gas stove in the middle. She had already come through the cooking lean-to with the other stove and a washstand and rusty refrigerator. That refrigerator contained nothing but some wrinkled potatoes and a package of turkey necks. Vicki Koob noted that fact in her bound notebook. The beds along the walls of the big room were covered with tattered quilts and cheap, pilled dime-store blankets bearing faded American Indian geometric designs. There was no one hiding underneath the beds. She felt the scored, brown, wooden chairs. Touched the top of the little aluminum dinette table covered with a yellowed oilcloth. One wall was filled with neatly stacked crates—old tools and springs and small

197

half-dismantled appliances. Five or six television sets were arranged in a kind of pyramid. Their control panels spewed colored wires and on at least one the screen was cracked all the way across. Only the topmost set, with coat-hanger antenna angled sensitively to catch the bounding signals across the reservation, looked as though it could possibly work.

Not one detail escaped Vicki Koob's trained and cataloging gaze. She noticed the cupboard that held only commodity flour and coffee. The unsanitary tin oil-drum beneath the kitchen window, full of empty surplus pork cans and beer bottles, caught her eye, as did Tammy's serious physical and mental deteriorations. She quickly described these "benchmarks of alcoholic dependency within the extended family of Redford Toose" as she transferred the room to paper.

"Twice the maximum allowable space between door and threshold," she wrote. "Probably no insulation. 2–3 inch cracks in walls inadequately sealed with whitewashed mud." She made a mental note but could see no point in describing the burst reclining chair, the shadeless lamp with its plastic orchid in the bubble-glass base, or the three-dimensional picture of Jesus. When plugged in, lights rolled behind the water under the Lord so that He seemed to be strolling although he never actually went forward, of course, but only pushed the glowing waves behind Him forever, like a tame rat in a treadmill.

When Mary Fred saw Pukwan ambling across the yard with his big brown thumbs in his belt, his placid smile, his tiny black eyes moving back and forth, she put Redford under the cot. Pukwan stopped at the shed and stood quietly. He spread his arms wide to show her he hadn't drawn his revolver.

"Mon petite niece," he said in the mixed voyageur's language, in the soft way people used if they were relatives or sometimes if they needed gas or a couple of dollars. "Why don't you come out here and stop this foolishness?"

"I'm not your goddamn niece," yelled Mary Fred.

She bit her lip, pushed her permanent-burned hair off her face, and watched him through the cracks, circling, a big, tan punching dummy with his boots full of sand so he never stayed down once he fell. He was empty inside, all stale air. But he knew how to get to her. And now he was circling because he wasn't sure she didn't have a weapon, maybe a knife. Pukwan knew that Mary Fred was big and strong and would be hard to subdue if he got her mad. She had broad shoulders, dirty tricks, and stood solid like her father, the Toose who was killed threshing in Belle Prairie.

"I feel bad to have to do this," Pukwan called to Mary Fred. "But for god sakes let's nobody get hurt. Come on out with the boy, why don't you? I know you got him in there."

Mary Fred did not give herself away this time, but let him wonder. Slowly and quietly she pulled her belt through its loops and wrapped it around and around her hand until only the big oval buckle with fake turquoise chunks shaped into a butterfly stuck out over her knuckles. Pukwan was talking but she wasn't listening to what he said. She was listening to the pitch of his voice, the tone of it that would tighten or tremble at a certain moment when he decided to rush the shed. He kept talking slowly and reasonably, flexing the dialect from time to time, even mentioning her father.

"He was a damn good man. I don't care what they say, Mary Fred, I knew him."

Mary Fred looked at the stone butterfly that spread its wings across her fist. The wings were light and cool, not heavy. It was ready to fly. Pukwan wanted to get to Mary Fred through her father, but she would not think about him. Instead, she concentrated on the sky blue stone.

"He was a damn good man," Pukwan said again.

Mary Fred heard his starched uniform gathering before his boots hit the ground. Once, twice, three times. It took him four solid bounds to get right where she wanted him. She kicked the plank door open when he reached for the handle and the corner caught him on the jaw. He faltered, and Mary Fred hit him flat on the chin with the butterfly buckle. She hit him so hard the shock of it went up her arm like a string pulled taut. Her fist opened, numb, and she let the belt unloop before she closed her hand on the tip end of it and sent the stone butterfly swooping out in a wide circle around her as if it was on the end of a leash. Pukwan reeled backward as she walked toward him swinging the belt. She expected him to fall but he just stumbled. And then he took the gun from his hip.

Mary Fred let the belt go limp. She and Pukwan

stood within feet of each other, breathing. Each heard the human sound of air going in and out of the other person's chest. Each read the face of the other. Mary Fred saw the patterns of tiny capillaries that age, drink, and hard living had blown to the corners of his eyes. She saw the spoked wheels of his iris and the arteries like tangled thread.

She took a quick shallow breath and did not move. She saw black trails, roads burned into a map, and then she was located somewhere in the net of veins and sinew that was the complexity of her world, so she did not see Zelda and Vicki Koob and her sister Tammy running toward her, but felt them instead like flies caught in the same web, rocking it.

"Mary Fred!" Zelda had stopped in the grass. Her voice was tight as a string. "It's better this way, Mary Fred. We're going to help you."

Mary Fred straightened, threw her shoulders back, then lifted into the air, and flew toward the others. The light, powerful feeling swept her up. She floated higher, seeing the grass below. Her arms opened for bullets but no bullets came. Pukwan did not shoot. Instead, he raised his fist and brought the gun down hard on her head.

Mary Fred did not fall immediately, but stood in his arms a moment. Perhaps she gazed still farther back behind the covering of his face. Perhaps she was completely stunned and did not think as she sagged and fell. Her head rolled forward and hair covered her features, so it was impossible for Pukwan to see with what particular

201

expression she gazed into the head-splitting wheel of light, or blackness, that overcame her.

Pukwan turned the vehicle onto the gravel road that led back to town. Redford sat between Zelda and the social worker. Vicki Koob remembered the emergency chocolate bar she kept in her purse, fished it out, and offered it to Redford. He did not react, so she closed his fingers over the package and peeled the paper off one end.

The car accelerated. Redford felt the road and wheels pummeling each other and the rush of the heavy motor purring in high gear. He knew that what he'd seen in his mind that morning, the thing coming out of the sky with barbs and chains, had hooked him. Somehow he was caught and held in the bleak tin smell of the pale woman's armpit. Somehow he was pinned between their pounds of breathless flesh. He looked at the chocolate in his hand. He was squeezing the bar so hard that a thin brown trickle had melted down his arm. Automatically, he put the candy into his mouth.

As he bit down, he saw his aunt very clearly, just as she had been when they had carried him from the shed. She was stretched flat on the ground, on her stomach, and her arms were curled around her head as if in sleep. One leg was drawn up and it looked for all the world like she was running full tilt into the ground, as though she had been trying to pass into the earth, to bury herself.

There was no blood on Mary Fred, but Redford tasted blood now at the sight of her, for he bit down hard and cut his own lip. He ate the chocolate, every bit of it, tasting his aunt's blood. And when he had the chocolate down inside him and all licked off his hands, he opened his mouth to say thank you to the woman, as his mother had taught him. But instead of a thank you coming out, he was astonished to hear a great rattling scream, and then another, rip out like pieces of his own body and whirl onto the sharp things all around him.

CHAPTER SIXTEEN

SHAWNEE DANCING

An early morning rain freshened the grass and high winds blew off the clouds, but over and over that day the dust thickened, a slow haze that choked the dancers. A water truck bounced around the arena in low gear and a boy slouched on the back end, spraying slow arcs. Rainbows sprang from side to side as he gestured with the water, and Shawnee focused on the shifting colors, slowed her heart, tried to calm her mind during the endless memorial giveaway.

So many poplar branches wrapped in money! So many blankets, so many shawls, so many pillows and headscarves and kerchiefs and wash-cloths passed before her that she began to tire of objects and things. So much *stuff* in the world. She grew hungry, mentally counted her change, listened hopefully for another feast to be announced. So far, she'd been in every line of

203

guests fed to honor every relative who'd died in the past year.

Corn soup, fry bread, Juneberry pie, and bangs with jelly. Tripe soup, boiled meat, plates of sliced cantaloupe and watermelon. Shawnee Ray remembered a heavy white bakery bun stowed in her canvas carryall. She reached in and removed it gratefully, ate standing so she wouldn't crush the jingles on the type of dress her father had called a snoose dress, because the shiny clackers were made from the tops of Copenhagen tins. She brushed the crumbs carefully away from her hips, smoothed the fringes on her sleeves, and thought of Redford's thick hair. The jingle dress was original to Chippewas, given to a Mille Lacs man by women who appeared to him in a dream, moving to their own music. Shawnee loved dancing the jingle dress dance best because her father had so often helped her with the steps—hard to do because the skirt was straight and tight, but when she danced right, it was as though she were stepping down upon a springy cushion of air.

She had danced hard at each Grand Entry, earning every last point, and she'd been led by the hand by the judges and placed among the final four in the traditional women's and the shawl dance. Her chances for the last, the jingle dress, were good, and she had actually slept peacefully and deep in her bedroll the night before. She'd rubbed her feet raw in places, but she'd brought a roll of duct tape and a tiny scissors. Back in her tent, she'd cut pieces off and stuck them onto the places were she'd stepped hard on pebbles

204

or blistered. Nothing hurt, nothing pained her anymore.

The last of her corn bread eaten, she watched the woman who sponsored the special memorial dance for her daughter. That young woman's staged portrait, head tipped, smiling in a pretty, dreamy way, was carried around the circle along with her dead brother's army photograph. The woman, who held both of the pictures, was solid and thick with muscle, but her feet tapped underneath her powerful body with a fastidious deer's grace. Shawnee watched her—a judge for these dances, she had laid a heavy pawlike hand on Shawnee's shoulder, choosing her, motioning her to the line, and Shawnee had smiled. But the woman, Ida, registered nothing and walked almost rudely away, slow, swaying, implacable in her long grief.

Shawnee was ashamed to realize she almost resented that slowness, for she was grateful for the sponsored prize and desperate to win it. The old woman had her own time and everybody else's too—sometimes when the sun shone hot she put up an umbrella, a white one bearing a portrait of Daffy Duck. Sometimes she set a giveaway washcloth upon her head. She spoke with only a few relatives, seemed mostly content to preside over all she saw like a monument or feature of the landscape.

A cool wind flowed down, reaching from the shadows of the low belt of olive-pale mountains to the north. Dusk fell for hours in violet bands. Over the encampment a great blue night cloud spread, slowly unfurling like a cape, and then, from underneath, as the announcer called in the dancers, a low barge of red fire moved.

Black light jabbed the stillness. The air came tremendously alive. As the jingle-dress dancers walked into the center of the grass arena, their clothing trembled sweetly. The women arranged themselves in a circle and stood composed, elbows tucked to their sides, chins set, eagle fans, macaw feathers, bead purses, and dream catchers held stiff. Shawnee Ray was positioned at the eastern door, facing the west, country of the spirits. Lifting her face to the band of red light, the cloud, as she waited for the first throb of the drum, the push up, for the long-winded announcer to cease, for her last chance, her vision suddenly focused on one incident from her childhood, snapshot clear: she saw her father, in her mind's eye, bent by the curved grille of their old gray car.

Wings of sweat, dark blue, spread across the back of his work shirt—he always wore washed-blue shirts the color of cloudy shade. His black-bird hair had grown out of its haircut and flopped over his forehead. When he stood up and turned away from the car, Shawnee Ray saw that he had a butterfly in his hands.

She must have been eight or nine, wearing one of the boys' T-shirts Mama bleached in Hilex water. Her father held in his toughened hands the butterfly, brittle and long dead, but still perfect. It was black and yellow-orange, all charred lines and fire. He put his hands out, told Shawnee Ray to stand still, and then, glancing once into her serious eyes, he smiled and rubbed the butterfly

206

wings onto her collarbone and across her shoulders, down her arms, until the color and the powder of it were blended into her skin.

"Ask the butterfly," he whispered, "for help, for grace."

Shawnee had felt a strange lightening in her arms, in her chest, when he did this. The way he said it, she had understood everything about the butterfly. The sharp, delicate wings, the way it floated over grass, the way it seemed to breathe fanning in the sun, the wisdom of how it blended into flowers or changed into a leaf. In herself, Shawnee knew the same kind of possibilities and closed her eyes almost in shock, she was so light and powerful at that moment. Then her father caught her up and threw her high into the air. She could not remember landing in his arms or landing at all. She only remembered the last sun filling her eyes and the world tipping crazily behind her, out of sight.

CHAPTER SEVENTEEN

LIPSHA

GETTING NOWHERE FAST

I believe in the wandering son, the missing father, and the naked spirit of the Holy Ghost. I believe in the crush of night, the ragged holes in the feet of the plaster Jesus, through which you see the wires cross. I believe in the single malt whiskey if you're rich, the bottle of white port if you're

207

broke. I believe in the peace of worms. I believe in the extension ladder and the angel with the torn mouth at the bottom, waiting to wrestle. I believe in the one on one, in the hands and voice of Jimi Hendrix, and that I will always love Shawnee Ray, even though I come to know a side to her that's fearful.

Before I go on out with Lyman to my vision fast I feel it is important for me to have just a word, a normal conversation, with Shawnee Ray Toose. After all, she is the one I hope will be there with the feasting food when we return. She is the reason I am going off on what seems, the more I think about it, a desperate and foolish mission. And I am worried, too, about the way Zelda Kashpaw and Lyman have managed to get Shawnee under their control although she did what she said, earned some money, made a college hunt.

Zelda took Redford from the Toose house, using the system, and now that Shawnee Ray is back from her nearly big-time second-place jingle-dress finish, there is no sign of her. She lives again with Zelda. But no one sees her, no one hears what she's up to, no one reports on her the way they used to. She has dropped out of my line of vision, or maybe she is a prisoner fed scraps in Zelda's house. In Lyman's company, however, we will be admitted for a visit.

We swirl into Zelda's driveway, get out of the car, and immediately, looking so anxious and tense my heart cranks over, Shawnee Ray walks slowly down the steps with a cookie-smeared Redford in her arms. She hesitates. There is a sadness about the way she looks at us and her

208

movements seem quiet and shocked. In a dazed way, she hands Redford over to his father, who holds him with a sort of neat authority and starts fussing with and dusting up the little boy right off. I think they look natural together, Lyman and his son, and in my heart I feel a plucked string.

"Hey," I greet Shawnee Ray.

She nods. I look very serious and searching into the unknowns of her face.

Suddenly Redford lets out a belly shriek at nothing in particular. To prove the efficiency of his fatherhood status, then, Lyman is forced to resist tossing him back to his mother, and begins to try all sorts of methods to divert the boy's attention. He jiggles, he prances, he hops and changes his voice to high, odd, coos, but nothing works. At last he turns away from me and Shawnee Ray and walks around the back of the house, where there is a little sandbox set up, and a couple plastic trucks.

I take my chance, turn to Shawnee Ray again, with urgent haste. There is an eager look in her face for me, I am sure of it. I think she is about to bloom toward me like the flowers in my dreams. In spite of knowing Lyman is just around the corner, my lips part and my whole face yearns for her face and I have to jerk my arms around my back to keep them from winding around her waist, from gliding down the fountains of her soft, thick hair, from holding the delicate seashell structure of her chin, her cheeks, from smoothing the lids of her eyes and the sweet, short eyebrows. I stand there with my mouth open, waiting for inspiration.

"Would you marry me?"

At first Shawnee Ray draws back like she is insulted at my request, as though she maybe thinks it is a joke. The edges of her mouth go down and she starts to turn away, and then, giving me one slight glance, she sees the something in my face. The ravaged something. The diet of Polish sausage and old cookies, the dreams, the anguish and the tea, the sacrifice of half my sanity, the religion. She stares hard at me, and I cleave tenderly toward what I anticipate as the equal longing in her look. I hold out my arms, but she bats at the air, leaning backwards, her face changing, moving.

"Get real." Her voice is high-pitched, strained, and her eyes are shining too bright.

"I am real."

I say these words so desperate that my knees buckle. I go down before her on my knees, and then I put out my arms and tenderly clasp the worn blue spots on the knees of her jeans. It is like I never saw a thing so beautiful as those two lovely pieces of fabric, rubbed smooth. She tries to move away but my arms tighten in spite of myself and she's hobbled. She almost loses her balance. She stands still a moment, and then she bends over and she pushes at me in a panic. I loosen my grip of her knees in surprise and then her foot plants itself under my chin with such force I go tumbling backwards.

"Get out of my way. . . ." Her voice is too even, too low, trembling underneath the tone with a kind of threat I've never heard. I scuttle back-

210

wards like a crab, out of reach of her hard leather toes, away from that scorching voice.

"What'd I do?"

"What'd he do?"

It is Lyman, returning with a now sand-over-cookie-caked Redford round the side of the yard. The two make their way evenly toward us, but Shawnee abruptly strides over to Lyman and grabs Redford from his arms. Too shocked to wail, Redford looks at us with big eyes, back and forth.

"What'd he do?" Shawnee's voice is a ripped screen. She is not my sweet Shawnee, not my tender airbrush picture. Suddenly she shows the undertone, the strokes of which she is created. Her hair flows like snakes, shaking down, and in her cornered anger she is jiggling Redford so fast that his cheeks bounce.

"He asked me to *marry* him!" She says these lovely words in an intense and awful voice of scorn.

"And I mean it," I say humbly, falling back onto my knees, dazed and addled as a sheep.

"Oh, shut up," says Shawnee Ray. "And you," she addresses Lyman as he starts for me, "stay away from him. I won't marry you either. Get that idea out of your bingo brain."

Lyman stands in paralyzed surprise like he was frozen with a laser gun.

"Shawnee Ray," he says gently. "You don't know what you're saying."

There is a silence, and then, taking one deep breath, she screams loudly—an incoherent, strange cry, like a baboon in the desert. The air vibrates. I put my hands over my ears. She does

211

that same robbed and naked scream again, a sound that makes my neck crawl. Her face is working, witchy, so frightful that Redford buries his face in her shirt, hanging on like a frightened little monkey as she whirls. She seems to grow larger, her shirt billows, her hair is dark leaves in a storm.

"Get out of here! I won't marry either of you. Period. You . . ." she looks down at me, her mouth twisting, "you talk so big about your feelings and you can't even make it back to school."

Lyman steps toward her.

"Don't you come near me, don't you even try. If you ever go to court again, if you ever get in my way . . ."

"I'm Redford's father," says Lyman gently.

Shawnee turns. She walks back to the house with Redford, talking to him in a soothing and familiar voice. She opens the door, goes inside, and we hear a cupboard slam. A short wail, more calm talk. Lyman shuffles around, and I back toward the car, both of us uncertain, hoping that the scene is over. But no, just as we are tentatively confident in our leave-taking Shawnee Ray comes back down the steps and stands in front of Lyman. She puts her hands on her waist. She is like that tough lady in "The Big Valley," hips thrust out in tight pants, heeled shoes, mouth held in a bold sneer.

"You're Redford's father? Says who? You weren't there when it counted. You're too late. I'm Redford's mother."

Her voice becomes musical and horrible, for it is falsely charming with a loathing current underneath. "Think back, Lyman," she warbles. "You

212

weren't my only boyfriend, remember? I had three other guys and I only made a birth control mistake with one of them."

She leans close to Lyman, chin jutting, and pushes her face into his face.

"Want to take a blood test?"

Lyman is smiling foolishly now, with a look of glazed wonder. I put my hands on his shoulders, guide him backwards, open the car door, and put him in still with that amused and quizzical indulgent expression on his face. It's like an expression made of china, one that can easily shatter to its opposite, and I know it's time to get moving, get out of there.

The funny thing is that as we drive along no silence grows between us, and we have no reaction to what just happened. Not two miles onward, we begin to talk about inconsequential things. We wonder about the sky, if it looks rainy or the day will hold. We anticipate the road and what comes next. We have a lot to think about, but we can't talk. We can't make the past half hour real. It is as if neither one of us can take in the Shawnee Ray we both saw. We can't understand, can't absorb, can't admit, and will not let that woman be her.

We drive the small roads, the back roads, leading surely and slowly farther on toward the house that belongs to Xavier Toose. He lives at the edge of an allotment that blends into the land around Matchimanito, the land that belongs to Fleur Pillager. I can't figure Lyman here. We are nearing the very same rolling, sweet, wooded hills that he wants to use for the big casino that he plans, the luck place, the money-maker scheme that will build day cares, endow scholarships, cure the ills of addiction of which it is a cause. I know that Lyman has thought out the consequences and the big-time benefits, but I believe, now, that he hasn't really examined the personal. Maybe that's what his quest is about, the bigger picture of an operating genius. Or maybe Lyman Lamartine is deep down religious. And then again, maybe given what we've just been through, we have a lot of things to think about regarding Shawnee Ray.

We take a turnoff, and the brush closes. I am still stunned by Shawnee's knees so close, her ankles so perfect to grip. Luckily, by this time, Lyman is concentrating on the world beyond this one, and has let go of that final scene. As we bounce down the last, long drive, just wheel ruts, to Xavier's, he is trying to instruct me about a sweat lodge, the proper way you enter it and crawl around in it, but I am dizzy. There was a moment back there when I felt that Shawnee Ray wasn't really angry, that she was screaming hard to cover up the true feeling that she has for me. I try to recast the whole scene in my thoughts. I wonder if she wasn't putting on her tantrum for the benefit of Lyman, and planning to wink at me as we left. I never turned around! I never looked in the rearview! If I had, what would I have seen? If I had only stayed, I think now, ditched Lyman, let her rage herself into my arms, maybe she might have bent to my life. I fear I may have blown it, may have lost my narrow chance. I still can't admit that she really might be furious. For one thing, there is no reason, is there? How could she? I have done nothing but overadore her.

We come to a halt in the yard of Xavier Toose's place, and we get out of the car. Xavier walks lightly toward us, easily, like his joints were new oiled. He's wearing a light green shirt and blue jeans. He is a kind of medium-looking man all around. You wouldn't pick him out in any crowd as holy, that's for sure. He has no blessed airs about him, he is not like a priest, and not spooky like Fleur. He has no manner of the Touch Me and I'll Strike You Dead. He is sort of round, just tall enough, not fat in the face or thin, and cheerful. He is not like Russell Kashpaw, who works with him, a Mount Rushmore-looking Indian. No, Xavier has a kind of big, arched nose, extremely black and shining eyes, thin and surprised-looking eyebrows, and a humorous mouth. The one different thing besides his hand with the fingers gone is that he wears an earring, one little shell. We touch his arms and right away, from the warm current in his presence, I am reassured. Here is not a man who will allow me to waste away and die or be eaten by wild animals in either the spirit or the natural realm. I am encouraged by the kind gaze upon my face, the joking forbearance.

"I almost chickened out," I tell him.

His only answer is, "Some do."

He motions for us to walk out in back of his small, brown house and down a trail. I take deep breaths, for at any moment I expect a flash to hit, some kind of electric power to jolt on, a message to seep into my feet through this holy land that

215

stretches from Xavier's backyard all the way to the shore I don't want to think about, the waters of Matchimanito Lake. I expect some unearthly voice to blare on with each footstep, worry that I might be smote from the days of old. What happens, however, is that Xavier Toose puts us to work.

"Heavy labor's good for body sculpting," says Lyman, an hour into what we're accomplishing.

"I thought we were coming here to get enlightened," I complain. It has turned into a muggy, hot, scratchy day and we are in deep and windless bush searching out nice-size and bendable willow poles, slogging through the steaming, spongy grass near a slough. I have a small hatchet, not near sharp enough, with which I am chipping at the base of a tough sapling. Lyman, lucking out as always, has a keen bow-shaped Swedish saw with which he dispatches three times as many trees.

When we have enough leaf-stripped poles, we drag them back, and then there is the careful twine-tying with tight lodge knots, the posthole digging, the gathering of the stones that pass muster. And for the last, standing at the shores of the lake I don't want to think about, there is a lot of argument over which kind of rock heats up the best. Not that I know enough to argue—it is just that by then I am in all respects pissed off at Lyman.

"Who cares?" I pick up one that I hope Fleur has cursed. "I mean, take this smooth black one here. Hot's hot."

216

"Hot's not just hot," he answers. "There's qualities of heat. Take this speckled one."

"That looks like an egg, like it would explode."

"Rocks don't blow up."

"If they get hot enough and if there's any water in their seams, they do." I make this up.

Lyman bites his lip, tries to control himself.

"I'm worried about this idea of superheating stones," I continue, annoyed he doesn't believe my scientific theories. "The physics of it sounds dangerous."

"I'm sick of babying you."

"Who asked you?"

Lyman sighs, and hefts another big rock in his weight lifter's arms. For him, the heavier the better-heating.

"Wouldn't a banana split taste good about now?"

Lyman kind of laughs.

"How hot could it really get?" I wonder after a few minutes.

"Real hot," Lyman answers in a relishing voice.

Later on, I find out. The lodge looks too little for us all to enter and I wish we'd made it three times as big. There is this person attending to the fire, a big Terminator-muscled convict type with a lot of tattoos—probably free, courtesy of Russell Kashpaw. The whites of his eyes show and he grins too much. A red bandanna is tied onto his head, and he is getting the instructions, too, even as he prepares the fire for us and then keeps heating up the rocks fiery red. They're placed in a little half circle next to an altar made of earth, sprinkled in a line with cedar. A bowl of tobacco,

217

just a small wood bowl, is set to one side. When Xavier says he is ready, the guy, Joe, puts the rocks in the fire pit with a shovel. Xavier goes inside the sweat lodge. Lyman and I take our clothes off and get in too. The big guy closes the flap. Xavier throws a dipperful of water down on the stones, and then it starts getting hot.

Xavier prays and talks to us and instructs us. Out of the blue, Lyman comes up with a very insightful, long, and meaningful prayer that sounds like it could be used to open up a conference. I am worrying about what I'll say, since I don't believe exactly in who- or whatever I am talking to, but when the turn is mine I find that heat adds to my praying ability. My words flow, as if my syllables are thinned honey. Amazingly hot, surprisingly hot. So hot I can't take it. But then I do take it, and I get hotter yet. I try to cool off by talking faster, praying louder, as if my tongue is a little fan, but then I give up and fall quiet. Xavier has given us this teaching that the sweat lodge is female, like a womb, like our mother we have to crawl on the earth to re-enter. He has encouraged us to let ourselves feel that connection we must have forgot, and I think I do without trying, for as I am getting hot, as I am praying, I find myself slipping away from the present, into a dark dream that hasn't a forwards or a backwards. I stop talking, or thinking, or even feeling the blasting heat that sizzles out of the rocks every time Xavier splashes them with water. I just exist, float, my ears stopped, my mind doused. After a while the heat feels bearable, then it feels like the most perfect embrace there ever was. Then Lyman says he wants it hotter, and splashes more water on the stones.

I could kill Lyman. I'm a cooked steak. My breath feels cold on my hands, and I know that I'll never leave the place alive. Panic grabs me. I begin to pray in a maniac's voice, desperate and pure, until I slip from the present in which Xavier Toose's voice is wide and soothing as the sky. I don't get the gist of his instructions, but I feel the comfort. Again, I want to stay there, and stay, but it's all over. We emerge into the normal sunlight, the day which before had been low and humid but now seems fragile, fresh and cool. I should be a newborn baby but instead I feel strange, unrocked. A roar of disappointment builds inside my head.

I look around for June, through the trees, toward the road, as if I'd see the flash of the blue car speeding into the mint-conditioned day. But there's no sign of her, no return.

I mope around half listening to Xavier tell us what we must do, but I'm only there in the flesh. We walk down to the lake, dive in to wash ourselves entirely clean. The water doesn't thrill me, doesn't want me. I close my eyes against the darkness and get out as quickly as I can without looking either at the annoying perfection of Lyman's muscle-toned wrestling star's build, or at the beefy collisions of scars and tattoos of snakes and women in eventful positions that round the thighs of the helpful convict. Xavier douses himself, too, and he teases Joe about his snakes and women. But I can't get into the tone of the day, for sadness inhabits me.

"What's wrong?" Lyman whispers to me once, impatient, probably thinking I am hurt by Shawnee Ray.

I considered. What is wrong? What is my problem?

"I miss my mother," I say.

Lyman snorts, puts his hand before his face, and I know at that moment he is sorry that he ever asked me to go with him on this spiritual journey. I try to whip myself back into mental shape. I am hardly managing to do the least thing that is required, just go along with what is happening, truck off into the woods behind Xavier's house. In the long shadows of that afternoon I find myself wandering alone looking for a place where I can spend as long as it takes for a vision to come my way. The choices are numerous, but I am supposed to pick a personal spot to gather power.

I try, but I just stumble around for the longest time until I lose track of where I am, but nothing matters. By that time, being lost is a trivial detail.

I lower myself onto a hard, cold rock, and get depressed still worse when I look up and see that I am in eyeshot of the damn old lake where bad things happen, where I visited the old woman, where in deep fear I listened to her bear talk. In Matchimanito Fleur Pillager drowned and came back to life, and her cousin Moses haunts the island with the howls of cats. I don't care though. If the horned thing, the grappling black thing that lives down there, bellies after me, I won't run. What's the point? There is no good book to help me and once again I have no motive, no reason for staying alive.

220

"This is great," I say out loud, building myself a little nest out of pine needles and wood moss and leaves. "If I was feeling like myself, I'd be so fucking scared I'd never sleep."

I have only three pieces of equipment—my sleeping bag with the blue elks in rut pictured on the inside flannel, a plastic bottle of water, and a garbage bag. That last, my supposed tarp for rain, I fill with more leaves to make a mattress. That is probably cheating. Oh yes, I have some tobacco too, and a little cedar that Xavier pressed into my hand. Beyond that, nothing. Although it is still daytime, and the light is falling dappled through the twigs and leaves, I crawl into my sleeping bag.

I don't know what time it is when I wake. In sleep, my dragging down feeling vanished and is now replaced with the normal instinct for self-preservation, only crazed beyond sense. I can't believe I've gotten myself into this situation. The wind picks up, the dark is pure and intense, and I hear the terrible rustles of surrounding animals, and even the monster hoot of *Ko ko ko*, the owl, sounding in my ears.

From all sides, fears grab and shake me. I put my head in my hands, rock back and forth, wish at least I'd built a little place for myself up in the trees. Deer could step on me down here on the ground. I think of their pointed hooves. Then I think of teeth. Fangs, tusks, rabbit incisors. Jaws for tearing. Sharks. Forget sharks. Bears. Raccoons. In this overbearing dark, I won't see it coming. Slashing death. Of course, I know there have been no bear attacks, no packs of wolves descending on lone campers, no owl or squirrel flocks reported tearing up a human, not in all the time I have ever been around here, and yet, and yet there is always a first for a freak occurrence. That's what makes the news.

I groan out loud and curl into myself and for the rest of the night whenever some noise startles me I jump up, shout, then settle back again to wait for the next advance of nature. In this way, with frequent yells, I fend off the invisible intruders. I keep peering and staring into the faceless dark that is not even lit by the glow of wild eyes.

Morning. Morning. Night. Night. Morning. I go through two cycles and then I lose track. The first day I am hungry and all my visions consist of Big Macs. The next day nothing matters again. I drink water from the lake and wait to die of an old paralyzing curse, but nothing happens. Upon waking, sometime after, I begin to take an interest in my surroundings. I watch an ant kill a bug of some kind and saw it into pieces and carry it away. A small brown bird hops from one branch to another. Then it hops back to the first branch again. A weasel flashes through once, looks straight at me, curious, and vanishes. A blue jay lands, squawks, and disappears. I try to interpret these things as signs of something bigger, but I can't jack up their meanings.

I sleep, becoming weaker, and when I wake my head feels light and fat as a balloon. I fall into a dreamy and unpleasant mood and all of a sudden I am annoyed that I turned out as an Indian. If I were something else, maybe all French, maybe nothing, or say, a Norwegian, I'd be sitting in comfort, eating pancakes. Or Chinese. Longingly, I shut my eyes and imagine the snap of fried wontons between my teeth at Ho Wun's. I taste sweet-and-sour fried batter. Hot crispy noodles. No fair. I resent the lengths that I am driven by the blood. I take mental revenge, then, by imagining what would happen if all the Indians in the country suddenly disappeared, went back where they came from.

In my mind's eye I see us Chippewas jumping back into the big shell that spawned us, the Mandan sliding down their gourd vine, Navajos climbing underground and covering themselves up, the Earthmaker accepting Winnebagos back into primal clay, the Senecas hoisting themselves into the sky, the Hopis following their reed to the Underworld.

And then what? I study on that only for a moment before I know the answer. Lyman Lamartine would somehow wangle his way out of the great Native apocalypse. Lyman would finally, and entirely, be in charge. Policies and programs would flow from his desk, examining this problem. He'd issue directives with a calm born of disaster, marshal all his forces. Even if no Indian returned to this world, Lyman Lamartine's paperwork would live on, even flourish, for the types like him are snarled so deeply into the system that they can't be pulled without unraveling the bones and guts. Cabinets of files would shift priorities, regenerate in twice-as-thick reports.

Yet, in that same daydream, I get even with Lyman too. He sheds his turquoise and inlay

223

rings, his Hush Puppies shoes, his go-to-Washington two-hundred-dollar suit and bolo tie, and he stands along with everybody else. I make Lyman run for the shell along with all the other Chippewas, but too late. The shell claps shut around me and Shawnee Ray and Redford and it sails off, leaving Lyman on the shore. He's left to watch until it's just a pearl in the distance, until it winks over the edge of the world.

Of course, this is just a dream. It won't be so easy to get rid of him.

By throwing my lot in with Lyman I've gotten to be part of something very big, very muddy, and very slow. A megalith of mediocrity, somebody said, but he was a dropout from the Bureau, fired, and Lyman and I have our fates intertwined, mixed up like the roots of two plants. I kept on seizing in my mind on that comfortable feeling we once had together, when Lyman said he remembered the day he and his brother Henry lay and dozed under the powwow trees, the pine arbor, listening to dancers pound dirt.

Nowadays, they put a rug of Astroturf down on the arena and there is no dust, no grit to chew on. Still, I fall asleep imagining those good food-filled days and more like them, before us, with the bingo money I've accumulated. I wake, wishing that I had a book to read, my Walkman. I play back all the Hendrix in my memory, then heavy metal and around the time the sun goes down I make a surprising discovery that I don't really need a stereo cassette. I am hooked up to my own brain. This is not a major vision, but it helps pass the time. Movies come back. Books. I rewatch all the

Godfather series, then reread the *Dune* trilogy and my Kashpaw dad's favorite, *Moby-Dick*. I go on and on back below the surface of my mind. Of course, Shawnee Ray is there at each bend. The thought of her is so troubling, every time I look out toward the lake, especially, that I have to try and stow it. I imagine a little cardboard box, and then I wrap her up tenderly, even though she fights me, and I put her inside. I mail her to myself. Open on arrival. I feel better once she is temporarily contained.

I have gotten used to the rustlings and squeaks and calls by then. I have given up on getting scared. I am just bored, and now I realize I've never been that way before. Something was always happening in my real life, at every minute, compared to out here in the woods. What is so great, what is so wonderful, what is so outrageously fantastic about the woods? I ask this of myself as I sit there. There's not a goddamn thing to do but think. From time to time, I get disgusted. I start talking to myself, mutter a curse on all I see.

"Let Lyman build his old casino here, what's the difference? What does it matter where he puts the thing? At least there would be other human voices. I wouldn't mind a little slot machine right here, by this rock, with a big dollar lunch and free Pepsi. That would be fine with me."

For the purposes of his plan, this is a spot like none other: lake view, perfect for a large-scale resort. And now, as I sit here, my mind a blank for long hours, I have to agree.

Morning. Night. Night. Morning. I have no

225

idea what is passing, time or space. I am still falling in and out of deep despairs, plus I am still not getting what I define as a vision. Where is it? I think that after I have dealt with the hunger, which gets so bad sometimes I put leaves in my mouth and chew them and spit them back out, some bright picture will approach me. I now settle into the frame of mind where nothing frightens me, or surprises me, where I would welcome a bear walking into my little camp and saying something conversational.

That's another thing: I am getting lonelier and lonelier. After a while, it is a toss-up between the loneliness and the hunger. Shawnee arrives during one of my periods of wakefulness, and I can't help untie the package and take out her memory. From then on, her face before she flew into the rage is on a line with the image of the hot dog I so regret not having eaten back at the Dairy Queen. I taste mustard, sweet relish, and most agonizingly, the light salt sweat on Shawnee's neck. How I regret the waste of all the ice cream that smashed on people and the floor. Towering concoctions rise in my mind. Walnut toppings. Shawnee Ray spoons large quantities of frozen slush into my open mouth, or drops in loaded nachos, one by one. I try to heighten this, to make it into something like a vision to light my path, but I know that it isn't the real thing. I get stubborn. I am positive that Lyman is having by-the-book visions right and left, and that I will be completely smoked if I don't have something deep and amazing to balance him off. But nothing happens, nothing happens, and

226

still nothing more happens, until I began to call this my getting nowhere fast.

Then early in the morning something does occur. Not the thing that should have, of course. The light is gray in the trees when I wake, like old silver, and the sleeping bag feels snug, warmer than usual. I drift in and out of sleep twice more before I surface to the consciousness that there is *something else warming me up*. I feel the weight suddenly, the other presence, and as I uncover my head and peer out of the bag the smell hits me before the sight of the shaggy round ball of fur nestled at my hips. Black fur, white stripes. The mother of all skunks. I don't know why but I think it's a she. Maybe it's the self-assurance, the way she continues to sleep heavily on the most comfortable part of my body. I begin to ease myself back from her, carefully intending not to drop her or damage or even wake her with my movements, but of course, there is no hope of that. All of a sudden, her black eyes open gleaming bright, her mouth yawns, full of pointy teeth.

This ain't real estate.

I hear a crabby, drowsy voice in my head. Now is it the skunk who says this, or is it that my mind has finally sprung a leak? I panic at the thought that I've finally flipped, and scramble backwards, dumping her, rude and sudden. She rises on her tiptoes, this skunk. She stiffens. And then I swear, frozen as I am in place, that she pats down with her front paws, drumming a little tune. Then, just before she lifts her plumed tail, she glances over her shoulder at me and gives me a smile of satisfaction.

227

This ain't real estate, I think, and then I am surrounded and inhabited by a thing so powerful I don't even recognize it as a smell.

There is no before, no after, no breathing or getting around the drastic moment that practically lifts me off my feet. I stand, drenched, but not alone, for the skunk odor is a kind of presence all of itself. It is a live cloud in which I move. It is a thing I can feel and touch—and then Xavier Toose appears. He is there so suddenly and looks so real that I just gape. I think at first he's been shot, had a heart attack, that he's finally bought it, for he collapses on the ground and begins to roll this way, that, over and over so quick it looks like he's in agony. But now, as I run to him, as I try to help, his arms flap helplessly, his face is screwed up but not with suffering. He's laughing, and laughing so hard there is no use talking to him, no use at all.

I walk back in silence, without my spiritual guide. I enter the area set up for us underneath a tarp near Xavier's house. Well ahead of me, Joe the convict dives for cover. I see that there is food underneath clean white and blue dish cloths, all centered on the picnic table. But the skunk has shut off all of my senses. I have to imagine from a long distance. Wild rice cooked with mushrooms, Juneberry jelly on fresh bannock and bangs. I have to imagine the taste of Kool-Aid and iced tea and picture steam rising in the sealed thermoses of coffee. Sliced melon and the cake. Angel cake. I dig in and no one stops me. The skunk smell rings in my head so loud I can't hear, can't face them.

I just know they're somewhere else, around me, howling at the outcome. I swallow down a hot dish thick with hamburger and tomatoes. I chew jerky—beef and buffalo.

No one dares to approach me. They make a circle, call to me from the edges of Xavier's yard. But that's too far away and I don't answer, just keep eating, though I'm full sooner than I can believe. I see the smoke that rises from the little fire, but I don't go there to sit. They're all weeping with laughter now, heady with my story.

I am completely shamed out by Lyman.

Eventually, I creep close to the circle around the low flames.

"I was begging for a vision," Lyman begins quietly, his voice low but very pleased with what is coming. "I was begging for a vision." He sets his preface out again.

The drama of it! I look unhappily from side to side, and everyone's eyes are fixed with solemn satisfaction upon Lyman, even as they discreetly hold their noses because of me. Lyman it is, and will always be. Never Lipsha. I settle into the bones of my defeat, sit there quiet with my hands in my lap. In my heart, I hate Lyman, but on my face a look of expecting love is pressed.

CHAPTER EIGHTEEN

LYMAN DANCING

On the third day he rose and in the clearing, where the sun shone down, on the edge of the dried

229

slough, in long sharp yellow-green spears of grass, Lyman began to dance. It was the first time since Henry had died that he had not danced in his brother's clothes. It was the first time, ever, that he didn't dance for money. The air was cool, the sun a mild radiance. In places the dried mud was baked into an even floor of shaley cracks, and although his bare feet made no impression, the packed silt was powdery and soft. Among the clumps of grass, he moved with the wind, side to side, swaying in the old northern style. He trembled with the grass, did the shake dance, shoulders loose as rags. He felt no hunger and no thirst, and he wasn't tired, although he'd hardly slept. As the wind came up, as he stepped and twirled, he began to hear the singing that had begun at dawn as a murmur and complaint in his head take shape and form.

The song advanced, grew round, came closer, closer, always in fours, slowing and then picking up, until just beyond the frame of thick scrub he knew that someone—he didn't recognize who—had set down a drum. That person was joined by the other voices—one deep as a frog's bark, another hollow, an owl's request, a woman with a hawk's *keer*, an old-style victory trill, high and shattering, and then he could not distinguish one from the next—there was a whole crowd out there, singing.

Everybody thought that when Lyman danced, he was dancing for Shawnee. But no, every dance, he was dancing for Henry. In younger days there had been times he resented dancing in the shadow of his brother, always hearing those words from

230

the announcer. *We have here our most promising grass dancer, Henry Lamartine Junior. And his brother there, Lyman, he's pretty good too.* There were times he almost thought he wouldn't shake his brother's hand coming through the line to congratulate the winners, except that he never did succeed because Henry always reached out eagerly and hugged him to his chest.

As the sun rose, heating the ground, as he continued to dance, Lyman began to wish for that shadow. For Henry not only danced before him and blocked out the sun but the glare, too. He had absorbed it and folded his brother back into his friendly shade.

When you dance, Lyman Jr., you are dancing with my ghost.

That day, as the light went down in the hills and the breeze came up, cool, Lyman once more felt his brother's shadow fall. He kept on dancing as the shadow lengthened and spread into dusk. The sun vanished and then, very clearly, from just beyond the trees, he heard Henry tell him that he should put those old dance clothes to rest.

They look beat, man, and so do you.

Then they both laughed, for when Lyman danced in those clothes, it was to keep Henry alive, to give him heart, for his drowned ghost was restless and low in spirit. Now the song came up, the words strengthened, and Lyman bent with the reeds, back and forth, side to side. His dance was all about the dusk Henry had jumped into the river, went down with his boots full of cold spring runoff, drowned. Lyman danced the water closing over, running, going and running and running,

231

and he danced his brother losing resistance, slumping, his body feeding into the current. Then Lyman danced his own rough struggle from the freezing muscle of water where he had jumped in to grab Henry back, and failed. Leaving the water, Lyman wiped his feet along the slough bed, along the grass, wiped the mud of that river bottom off over, over again, and once again, carefully, gracefully, with completeness, hour after hour, until finally, from the drum and with the singers just past the clearing, he heard Henry's voice ride the sky.

It is calm, so calm
In that place where I am
My little brother

CHAPTER NINETEEN

ALBERTINE'S LUCK

Albertine woke dizzily in the small room that her mother always kept for visitors, and turned over again, pushing her face into the animal-warm pillows. Browning toast, coffee, the scent of sizzling butter, juice of berries boiling down and thickening on the stove, drew her out of sleep. She pushed her hands over her face and kicked her mother's quilts down her knees, then stumbled across the cold linoleum and dragged on socks, jeans, a sweatshirt. She had a short vacation break and her car had died twice on the way home. Much later than she was expected, almost halfway through the night, she'd pulled into her mother's

232

driveway. Now the buzz of exhaustion and spent adrenaline surged over her. Her ears burned from the cold wind and her temples pinched and throbbed.

"Want some?"

It was Shawnee, a mug in her hands lettered in red Yes, there is a Kalamazoo! Albertine accepted it in both hands and breathed lightly on the steaming coffee. The thin, acid stuff went down leaving a burn like a hot thread in her chest.

"Where's Mom?"

"She went to church."

"Where's Redford?"

"With her."

The two young women could have been sisters, though Albertine was older and tired-looking, her eyes circled in dark violet stains. Her hair, a shade lighter, fell in a long sweep and sun through the window picked out streaks of red blond. She glanced at Shawnee, dropped her eyes, wondered what to say and if she had the strength to say anything at all. Her own relationship with her mother was one of careful and mutually calibrated distance. They had faced off long ago and then reached an agreement. Albertine would reveal nothing troubling or damaging to the image that her mother wished to keep of her, and for her part, Zelda would not pry for details about Albertine's life. The unstated pact had made things so much easier between them that it was hard, almost impossible, to strike a deeper chord in their conversations now.

It was enough for Zelda to know that Albertine was in medical school. That fact relieved Albertine

233

of every other explanation. It had been enough for Albertine to know her mother had a job. Their work had given them both safe topics and easy complaints. Even Shawnee's presence had been helpful at first, removing the pressure that Zelda had often brought to bear on Albertine in the past regarding marriage, a grandchild, a larger picture for Zelda to compose around herself, its center.

"Are things any better?" Albertine was slightly more alert, knowing that once Zelda returned they wouldn't have a chance for honesty. "Have you got any plans?"

Shawnee tucked a strand of hair behind her ear. She looked down at her knees, rubbed her hands across the faded material of her jeans. She was wearing a belt with a turquoise stone butterfly buckle.

"I'm leaving here," she said, into Albertine's silence.

"Really leaving," she said to Albertine, again.

Albertine felt herself sliding, tumbling, falling back into the soft-grained emotions of her childhood. She used to crawl beneath the quilts on the bed where her mother slept on her back—rigid, alone, untouchable, like a carved statue—and she used to breathe in her mother's warmth, the smoky human closeness, the coffee, and the stale spice of her clove gum and cigarettes.

Zelda had once entered and left rooms in drifting clouds and the mousy menthol vapor was part of the whole of Albertine's love. No matter that, now, she knew all about the effects of second-hand nicotine, no matter that she didn't smoke and helped counsel patients not to, she thought of the odor as safe. She never dared fold herself against her mother, never dared to grab her tight, but only swept her lips against the porous, fine skin of her cheek, touched her work-tough fingers. Even that hurt, and once, in bed with a man she hated, paralyzed with what she'd done, Albertine had realized that the desperation with which she gave in to his touch had been no more than a child's wish to crawl closer to the side of her mother. And never mind her father, a picture in a frame.

There would be no end to what she needed from a husband, a lover. Albertine knew this at the time and understood that the only answer to her need would be realized in healing others the exact way she herself needed to be helped. It was what she saw in so many doctors, even the best ones, the most obsessed—something missing at the core, something they filled in themselves, mysteriously, by giving it entirely away.

Now, in the tiny sun-struck room, with Shawnee Ray sitting in front of her, Albertine leaned back and tried to gather all of the strings. There seemed no way at first to break the sinew of her mother's need. The tighter you pulled the tighter it held.

There was an empty place sawed out of Albertine where a child should have fit, and when Redford ran into the house her arms shot open with an ache even though he was probably not going to greet her the way she hoped. It was true, as Shawnee had said, that he had become more

235

suspicious and watchful since the incident with the tribal police. Zelda picked him up, let him down again, and he struck the floor with sturdy quickness. With only a lowered glance in Albertine's direction he ran to his mother and welded himself to her, crawled up her legs with his hands gripping her pockets, her belt loops, until she swung him to her chest. He wrapped his legs around her waist and hung there for several moments before he turned and only then, relief breaking from inside of him, he shouted hello to Albertine. He would go to her from Shawnee, swinging his arms to meet hers, but he had to assure himself first that his mother would stay in the same room. Once, when Shawnee walked into the entryway to put away his puffy red jacket, Redford clawed his way down and wrestled from Zelda's quick snatching grip to make sure that his mother returned.

All that day, as she watched the boy and the two women, Albertine saw patterns developing in the air. A cat's cradle. Twine pulled, relaxed, made telling shapes. Later on that night, falling into sleep, she remembered her uncle Eli's hands pulling and dropping the slender designs. Lightning. Frog. Bat. Twin stars. Turtle. Chicken foot. Arrow. Women's belt and butterfly. The figures moved against the dark like trails of light.

Zelda sewed everything too tight, pulled her thread until it broke, became impatient with the way her work turned out before she halfway finished, but when the three women were working together on Redford's dance outfit, Albertine could see that Shawnee Ray bent her strength like a bow to the older women's need, that there was force in the calm way she took the needle from Zelda and pulled out stitches while Zelda fumed, threw up her hands, and went to the stove. The food that Zelda loved to make was all contained in one pan—browned rice, butter, chicken gravy, and a box of frozen peas. Shawnee Ray turned to look at what Zelda was stirring and then caught Albertine's eye.

"You two think it's so funny," Zelda remarked. "So what if I can't sew—I can type for days. That's just the way I am."

"One-pot dinner?"

Zelda turned to the side, opened her mouth, and shifted her hip. She was in a good mood, ready to be teased, happy for all of the attention directed at her.

"You complaining? After hospital food, in that cafeteria?"

"It's just that you used to be so particular, get everything just so, like Grandma. It's just that I'm used to you being so particular."

"I don't do that anymore, not since our little boy."

Shawnee's lips stiffened and although she bent to the needle, quickly bit the end off a knotted thread, Albertine saw the design.

"What do you mean 'our boy,' Mom? What about when Shawnee decides she's ready to go back to school?"

"I'll be right here to keep Redford." Zelda's voice was too firm, her eyes opened too wide,

237

fixed, her spoon banging down too hard in the pot. "He deserves full-time care."

Albertine looked at Shawnee, leaving her the opening and the silence. But the younger woman couldn't make the words fill her mouth. She kept biting the string, looking at her hands now, shaking one finger free of the prick of her needle.

"Whether Redford goes with her or not is really Shawnee's choice, isn't it?"

Albertine strove for a cheerful tone, a coaxing normalcy, an open-ended lightness.

"Not if she's going to fool with a no-good Morrissey."

Shawnee put down the cloth and almost tipped the little plastic tubs of beads over as she violently began to straighten and put away the project that they'd all been working on. Albertine pressed her fingers to her eyes, suddenly exhausted, as if she'd been reading reports through the night and morning and was now expected to make decisions on the basis of details she'd not quite absorbed. The practice seemed to have improved her ability to reason unstated futures quickly, because now, cutting through the mess of emotions and unknown facts, she was able to state the impossible quite clearly.

"Let me get this straight. You're talking about Lipsha?"

"Should be Lyman," Zelda said tersely, plunging her spoon into the stew. "He's around here all the time, asking for her, talking to me about it. He's always asking me how come Shawnee's so furious with him, asking me what's wrong with him, how come she's changed? After all, he's Redford's natural father."

Shawnee turned a yellow tub of beads over onto the floor and the sudden spill diverted all of them. Albertine crawled after the beads, and Redford and Shawnee did too. Chasing them back and forth across the floor, they made a game of capturing the tiny glass specks and brushing them off their fingers. Zelda continued to stand at the stove and at last, when Shawnee had left the room to wash Redford, she spoke to her daughter.

"You think I'm standing in her way."

"Maybe she feels something for Lipsha."

"She'll get over it."

Albertine paused, thought a moment, and then spoke of something that had never been raised between the two of them before.

"Did you? Ever get over it?"

Zelda stopped, poised the spoon, then turned slowly to regard Albertine.

"Did I ever get over who, your father?"

"No. Him. The one before."

Zelda gave a sharp, almost hysterical croak of laughter and then turned back to the stove and busied herself, salting, peppering, finding and tasting the ingredients to her stew. She made no acknowledgment of the question and spoke of nothing related to their conversation for the rest of the evening, but kept up a stream of talk that fell between the two of them, a mild rain of inconsequences that extinguished any topic of serious regard but also signaled to Albertine the extent of the blow she had dealt her mother, the shock of recognition.

CHAPTER TWENTY

LIPSHA

A LITTLE VISION

My cousin Albertine, back from med school, uses a careful touch to divert me from the congregation around Lyman and leads me to her car. Each leaf springs clear to me as we leave Xavier's place, each blade of quack grass and each thorny stick. You ever seen a coyote pick his way across a field? He doesn't just walk, but wends himself careful among unseen menaces and small attractions that we have no way to sense from our dimmer world. That is how my thoughts move as we drift along the gravel that has been freshened by a sprinkling of rain. We get into the car, pull onto the pitted road, and I try not to brush too hard against my sorrows. Instead, I ask Albertine about hers. Not that she has many. Albertine is doing what she wants, and I can see that although she is tired she is also sure of her path.

The window is open and the air is rushing in, probably sweet with hay and pollens though I can't smell this air, the last breeze with any summer warmth left. From now on there will be all heavier and clouded evenings awash in rain, and then the snow, which will begin early in the year and drag on without end until we're all of us worn out and gray as foiled ghosts.

240

"I can't think ahead," I say to Albertine. "I don't want to live."

"Take a bath in tomato juice," she suggests.

"This ain't related to my getting sprayed," I tell her. "It's an emotional thing."

"To do with Shawnee Ray?"

"That's right."

There's a long and rushing silence, trees blurring, sloughs beside us.

"Let her go to school," Albertine says. "Leave her alone until you get your own self together, Lipsha."

Her voice is low, but it easily carries within the wind that fills the front seat of the car.

"You're a hard-ass like your mother," I tell her, but my voice doesn't penetrate like hers and slides right out into the breeze that booms and sings all around us.

I mean to at least thank Albertine for the ride and all she has done to support me, and also to tell her that I do not mean to give up on Shawnee Ray, not ever, even if my battle is useless. I intend to express my regret for letting down all of those who cared about me, by not coming up with a proper vision, and on, and on, but as I start to make this speech I find my tongue has rusted from lack of use. All that I can muster is a wave from my weakened hand, a gesture.

The day is quiet, and I creep around the back way to my room without seeing anyone, just sneak in and open the door and let myself in. I put my things down and without turning on a light, even, without doing anything besides shower long and uselessly, drinking nothing more than a glass of water, I fall into the comforting wash of my bed and drift into embarrassed sleep. I just go into it, boom, and I am out of commission.

Deep in the night, I wake.

With that waking, something happens to me which I attempt to resist. I try to go back to sleep, to let the green fuzz overtake me, but instead, my thoughts connect one onto the next and I begin to remember things I do not even want to think about. I remember back through the days of my youth and then my childhood until I reach the time when I was a baby. The feelings I had then are very clear to me. For the first time, I realize what happened the moment after I was placed onto my first cradle of water, after I sank down. A darkness like the darkness that now covers me swarms up, and I drift lower. I feel the hand from which I've fallen. I feel the cool shock. I rest on the mud bottom with the stones in the sack. I open my mouth to cry and water gushes into my chest.

Gone! Gone! I am alone, the same as dead, and then I am dead. The water crushes out my life.

I lie there on the bottom of the slough all the rest of the night and the next day too, crying. It is like my whole body has been filling all of these years with a secret aquifer, a sorrow. I remember the sensation I spent my whole life trying to forget. The quick tug, the stones that tumbled, the deep of dark. I hear my mother's voice, feel her touch, and by that I know the truth. I know that she did the same that was done to her—a young girl left out to live on the woods and survive on pine sap and leaves and buried roots.

Pain comes to us from deep back, from where it grew in the human body. Pain sucks more pain into it, we don't know why. It lives, and we harbor its weight. When the worst comes, we will not act the opposite. We will do what we were taught, we who learnt our lessons in the dead light. We pass them on. We hurt, and hurt others, in a circular motion.

I am weak and small, shut in my tiny room, but I am safe. No one to hinder, no one to find, no one remembering, even my buddy Titus, who thinks I am still at Xavier's house. No one calls for Lipsha, no one knocks. It is as if I stayed down at the bottom of that slough.

And I go into it, and I kept going, for I have no strength to pull myself out.

You heard what Zelda said to me from her barstool. *So why weren't you drowned?* I never thought about it either, since, but a long ways into the night I realize one thing: no way I could have made it alone. I was saved. And not by Zelda, not at first, but by something else, something that was down there with me. I don't know who or how, and then sometime in the night I look up into dark air and see the face.

Darkened and drenched, coming toward me from the other side of drowning—it presses its mouth on mine and holds me with its fins and horns and rocks me with its long and shining plant arms. Its face is lion-jawed, a thing of beach foam, resembling the jack of clubs. Its face has the shock of the unburied goodness, the saving tones. Its face is the cloud fate that will some day surround me when I am ready to die. What it is I don't know, I can't tell. I never will. But I do know I am rocked and saved and cradled.

No wonder, as Zelda reports it, I smiled.

Now that I have unwillingly remembered all the past, I counsel myself that I should get up and live my life a new and normal person, but like I said, I am so weak that I just lie in my waterbed. The pictures and stories and sights do not relent. I go farther, see more. I unroll my whole childhood and go on into the present, until I pass myself up and I get the future. It is so ordinary and so demanding all at once that at first I can't understand it. There is no punch to it, no great convening dramas, and it makes me all dismayed, it is so small.

Here is the gist of what I see and hear. There is a voice all right, but it is coming out of that damn skunk. That creature is a nuisance! Even here, in my room, I am not safe from that animal. It putters over, slick and determined, and it jumps back onto my chest. I see it through the dark.

This ain't real estate, it nags at me.

I'm tired of waiting for a vision and just getting this unpleasant refrain, so I lash out.

"Go back where you came from," I order it. "Shut up and quit bothering me. I got enough to think about."

The animal blinks its brilliant black marble eyes at me, all curious.

"I'm not kidding," I threaten.

You're a slow learner like they all said, despite your A.C.T.s.

"You must have sneaked in the back way," I say. "Or did you get here in my sleeping bag?"

244

There's no answer.

"Okay." I finally give up. "Tell me something I don't know."

And that's when I get the vision.

The new casino starts out promising. I see the construction, the bulldozers scraping off wild growth from the land like a skin, raising mounds of dirt and twisted roots. Roads are built, trees shaved, tar laid onto the new and winding roads. Stones and cement blocks and wood are hauled into the woods, which is no longer a woods, as the building is set up and raised. It starts out as revenue falling out of the sky. I see clouds raining money into the open mouths of the tribal bank accounts. Easy money, easy flow. No sweat. No bother. I see money shining down like sunshine into Lyman Lamartine's life. It comes thick and fast and furious.

This ain't real estate, the skunk says again.

Of course, that skunk is right, for the complex is slated to develop Pillager land, partly Fleur's land and partly old allotments that the tribe holds in common, and which is fractionated through the dead and scattered holdouts who have never signed the treaties that gave away so much of what we called ours.

Where Fleur's cabin stands, a parking lot will be rolled out of asphalt. Over Pillager grave markers, sawed by wind and softened, blackjack tables. Where the trees that shelter brown birds rise, bright banks of slot machines. Out upon the lake that the lion man inhabits, where Pillagers drowned and lived, where black stones still roll round to the surface, the great gaming room will

245

face with picture windows. Twenty-four-hour bingo. I see the large-scale beauty of it all, the thirty-foot screens on which a pleasant-voiced young girl reads the numbers of balls, day in and day out. Auditorium seats, catered coffee, free lunch. State-of-the-art markers, electronic boards. I see the peach and lime interior, the obedient lines of humans all intent on the letters and the numbers that flash on the twin screens telling how near, how far, how close to the perfect dreamstuff they're coming.

I try to be polite, then, even gentle.

"Excuse me," I say, "I got the wrong vision. Could you change the channel?"

To what?

"I don't know. Maybe to some horses who split the sky with their hooves. Or a bear, an eagle with a bald head and long brown wings to carry me a saying to mess with Lyman's mind.".

There's more.

And I argue out loud.

"I see it another way!" I cry. "I see the casino dome, the rounded shape, maybe of a great stone turtle. I see it winking and glittering under all those lights! The old ones used to say you eat turtle heart, you win at cards. I hear the hush of bells, continual, a high and ringing money-mutter, and the slick sigh of bills changing hands. I feel the cash in my fingers. New twenties so fine they stick to one another. I hear the dinging and the silvery chatter of coins sliding down the chutes, quarters upon quarters upon tokens upon lovely silver dollars. And oh, here's the best part. I see the dealer dealing me face up, and I am hitting on

246

each hand, yes, hitting once and hitting twice, and the other customers are saying *Good hit, Lipsha*, putting their money down with mine, more and more of it in piles and drifts. Because I'm lucky, don't you get it, don't you see?"

And these words come next, and last.

Luck don't stick when you sell it.

"Mine does," I insist, but inside me, I know that damn skunk is right.

Then I sleep for a long while and when I wake it is bright, it is morning, and I am new and ready to begin the day that dawns. There is a small strip of field between the littered parking lot of the bar, which I must clean, and the housing area of small windblown trailers and prefabs where Lyman Lamartine lives. I walk out there and with a mind full of hard thoughts I stand by popple scrub, in tall grass, blown over and harsh, green and dry. From my low vantage, I consider the modest huddle of human development. The thing is, I already know the outcome, and it's more or less a gray area of tense negotiations. It's not completely one way or another, traditional against the bingo. You have to stay alive to keep your tradition alive and working. Everybody knows bingo money is not based on solid ground. The Mindemoya's took to Lyman, though, even appeared to him somehow in a dream, or so he said. People used to say she was waiting for me to visit in order to pass on her knowledge, but that's not true. Fleur Pillager is a poker sharp, along with her other medicines. She wants a bigger catch, a fish that knows how to steal the bait, a clever operator who can use the luck that temporary loopholes in the

247

law bring to Indians for higher causes, steady advances.

And yet I can't help wonder, now that I know the high and the low of bingo life, if we're going in the wrong direction, arms flung wide, too eager. The money life has got no substance, there's nothing left when the day is done but a pack of receipts. Money gets money, but little else, nothing sensible to look at or touch or feel in yourself down to your bones. I can't help think that Fleur Pillager has made the best of what gives here by tapping Lyman for the long term. As for the short, what the skunk said is right. Our reservation is not real estate, luck fades when sold. Attraction has no staying power, no weight, no heart.

CHAPTER TWENTY-ONE

GERRY'S LUCK

Months went by and he lived only for the dreams—bright, monotonous, unwinking dreams in which he led a thoroughly boring everyday life. To sleep in a bed wider than himself, to shit behind a closed door, to walk a curved road, a straight road, a ditch, to make love, to make love, he would never stop making love, eating steak, eating hash browned potatoes. Fried potatoes. Bangs. Fry bread. To watch his last wife, Dot, knit solemnly and fiercely, frowning at each stitch. To see his children. To stand still as a doe detached from a screen of brush, to put aside the rifle, forget

248

venison with mustard, to watch the animal swivel her intelligent ears, watch ducks land, watch light gather blue dark in the eyes of a woman, his daughter, his son, to walk inside of a house, out, in, to open a door with your own hands.

In solitary, he stared at his foot until it changed to a paw. He chewed his paws and wept and let his hair grow long, coursing down his back. He said the name of his wife a thousand times every morning. Dot, Dot, Dot. A mantra. Morse code. She called him every week, even after the divorce. Remarried, she kept on calling him but still, after a time, it was another woman who began to obsess Gerry. He drew June's face on notebook paper, a woman of leaves, rain, snow, clouds. She was a storm in his dreams and her teeth were lightning. She was a little brown mink stealing bait on his trapline, a curve in air, a comma, winking and unwinking. All day he stared at the crack beside the door and thought *windigo, windigo*, because he had a flu, a fever that made the cell bloom and collapse, and he remembered the stories of Old Man Nanapush.

In a voice like a wind-strummed reed, Nanapush spoke from his bed, where he sat all day that winter, falling over into sleep at night. He told of the ice giant shoving cracked floes between drifts of his lips, chewing ice bones with ice teeth, sinking frozen into view from frozen clouds. For two days Gerry's cell breathed to life, walls disappeared, and then the world shrunk back to itself again and his mind hid underneath a black cloth. His mind was deepest sky, dreamless and pure, his thoughts black earth. He smelled dirt and new rain. Prison smells were chemical, or sweat, milky disinfectant, piss, old piss, metallic breath, the aftershave on guards. His own smell was of a dog. The dog his mother kept—tick-bit, rangy and half feral.

His intuition told him there would be a low whistle when it happened, a warning, but there was nothing. Just papers. Tribal council papers with his mother's name obscure. The tribe had taken an interest, and under the Indian Religious Freedom Act brought him near his medicine advisors. Lulu Lamartine's name was merely set down with the rest of them but her forceful wrangling was behind every single other signature, he knew. Minnesota prisons were renting cells. There was one available in Minnesota's new maximum-security facility and he would be transferred there. Fine! Fine! Oh fuck! Something surged in him like true love at the prospect of being somewhere, anywhere else, and he looked forward to the ride like a child, impatient for the power of different clouds, the brush of a different wind.

He was issued a jacket, boots, a hat, army mittens. The hat had earflaps that tied on top like a lumberjack's. Not only would he have to wait in deep cold for the plane, but once there he'd have time to walk around outdoors. Minnesota, land of changing seasons! Land of 10,000 Lakes and happy Vikings. Land of Chippewas, land of Sioux, land of weak coffee and fiberglass walleyes. Kind and righteous Minnesota, land of weight machines, real eggs, deep-fried doughnuts, iced Long Johns, and for some reason birthday cakes galore. Why did he see, all night in his mind, big square sheets of pink-frosted birthday cakes, sugar heavy, lettered in white, dimpled, fluted. Land of 10,000 Birthday Cakes. Land of mushy sloughs, wheeling honkers, ranging wolves, and pleasant women, earnest Swedish women, staunch political support.

When he woke in the white blast of light at four thirty they did it all—packed his things into a duffel bag, locked his hands in front of him, walked him out to the federal marshals who politely asked him please to stand still as they attached leg irons and a transport belt. The cuff and chain hobble around his ankles allowed him to walk like a man with his pants down around his feet. His arms fit snugly, buckled to his waist. He hugged himself. And it was better, as the car moved, as the view began to change—so much view, so many trees—better than he could have fucking dreamed.

Fucking dreamed! His thoughts, on fire, wheeled in bright array. To see the trees in changing rows, fields, the curious white suburban ranches, farms, huddled trailers, too much going by all at once. Too much! And from the hangar, wanging like a cracked radiator, laughter and an argument he didn't catch the drift of, back and forth, between the marshals and the pilot.

As they lifted off and gravity pressed him back into the vinyl seat, he felt his luck coming back, floating down on him like a nylon net to drag him to the top. He shut his eyes. He could feel the weight of his body, smell burnt plastic, acid coffee. Pleasure wrapped him so suddenly that he thought his bones would crack. Then they were

251

out of the steep ascent, leveling off, and he saw raw pink light, the sunrise twist and burn.

He knew from sitting in the still eye of chance that fate was not random. Chance was full of runs and soft noise, pardons and betrayals and double-backs. Chance was patterns of a stranger complexity than we could name, but predictable. There was no such thing as a complete lack of order, only a design so vast it seemed unrepetitive up close, that is, until you sat doing nothing for so long that your brain ached and, one day, just maybe, you caught a wider glimpse.

Some people, lightning struck twice. Some people attracted accidents. Fate bunched up and gathered like a blanket. Some people were born on the smooth parts and some got folded into the pucker. When the engine skipped and chattered and burped back into its drawl, Gerry opened his eyes, alert, and asked if there wasn't some way to remove the bar from his legs while airborne.

"Can't do it."

The marshals were firm, professional, both slim and tall, though with opposite coloring and a difference of twenty years or so in age. One was all shades of sand, tan hair and thick eyelashes too, and the other was black haired with pale green eyes and a lumped-out jutting chin. The sand-colored one leaned back into his seat to doze, and the dark one by agreement kept his eyes fixed upon the prisoner. They were well trained, confi-dent, with nothing to prove, and Gerry felt safe with them.

The sky went dark again.

"We're moving through a storm system," the

pilot called back into the cabin, then all they heard was the sound of his effort as he strove to guide the small craft into wind. There was a long period of turbulence, and several times the air seemed to have been yanked out from under them like a magic carpet, so that they quickly dropped altitude.

"Ah, shit."

It was the pilot. His voice registered a thrill of regret. Gerry looked out of the window and saw the white earth, the branches of bare trees, rush so quickly up from below that he scarcely had time in his surprise to roll into a cannonball. Crash position. But the landing wasn't so much a crash as a peculiar distortion of time and space in which things moved soundlessly, and afterward, what he remembered of it was an almost liquid passion of disruption and then silence. Quiet snow. One eye was banged shut like a cupboard. The sun was up all around him and the white world glowed like the inside of a giant coffee cup.

The sandy-haired marshal hung still. The other—he couldn't see the other, or the pilot. Smoke puffed from the mangled tail and Gerry squeezed himself tighter, rolled off the split seat and through a gap torn into the fabric of the cabin. Once outside the plane in a litter of wreckage, in falling snow, he knelt to recover his balance and slowly stood on his feet and then began to hobble-hop, the prisoner's two-step. He drove himself through crossed brush, skirted stands of cattails and reeds and kept hopping. And all the while, as he moved, not cold in the least because of the effort, his life kept surging up between his feet,

253

his bound wrists, welling up like black water when you step on thin ice, spreading up through his arms, choking him, practically killing him with the accumulated joy.

CHAPTER TWENTY-TWO

LIPSHA

ESCAPE

I turn deep into myself after Albertine's advice that I should let Shawnee go while I retrieve myself and better my position in life. As it turns out, I don't have any choice. Shawnee leaves the reservation after gaining back the custody of Redford, and for a while I hear nothing of her, then learn she is enrolling at the university. "In the arts, in the arts," people say, with a rhythm in their voices that means although dubious at least there is a name to her future. I put my hand on the phone, draw it back, and then finally call information. I carry Shawnee's number around in my shirt pocket like a lucky sweepstakes and occasionally read it out fondly. Sometimes I even dial, let the phone ring just once, and hang up. In that act I see myself as her guardian angel, announcing my presence, my faraway affections, but not demanding so much as the complication of a friendly hello.

For my love is larger than it was before she blasted it with fire. It was a single plant, a lovely pine, but now seeds, released from their cones

254

at high temperatures, are floating everyplace and taking root on every scraped bare piece of ground. My love before she got so mad was all about what was best for Lipsha Morrissey. Since those endless moments of truth and rage in Zelda's yard, I have reconsidered. If my love is worth anything, it will be larger than myself. Which is not to say I don't dream about motels, her body moving, and read sex books and thrillers and my Gideon's for more inspiration.

One night, I am at the dizzying bloody part, all of the ways in which King David smites right and left, and I am trying to get a handle on what lesson I might learn. All I keep seeing is a ninja dressed up in old-time robes. You read Samuel and see if you don't see the same. I page forward to Chapter 17 of Kings where Elijah lays himself over a child three times and prays for the kid's soul to return to its body. He finally brings this child to life, and then he delivers the revived boy back to his mother. This is more my type of scenery and I build up a picture of myself as Elijah, saving Shawnee Ray's son for her. The concept is so rewarding that I douse my light and lie down on my bed, in the dark, and I begin to project a career of doing this sort of savior work, which makes Shawnee Ray so grateful that she doesn't just apologize, she anoints my head with oil and washes my feet with her hair like those long-ago women did to show their appreciation for a kindness.

I can feel her hair coil around my feet, my ankles. I can feel her tears of regret and thankfulness upon my legs, her face gently touching my knee, and then leaning in her sorrow on my thighs

255

and then by accident, just by sheer accident at first, losing her balance a slight bit and grasping at my belt loop and then trying to right herself but slipping on that water and oil and putting her warm face to me. Like magic, then, my robes part. God, how the Red Sea burns! I rewind the tape to play it again, go back to the beginning where I am just dragging Shawnee Ray's son from water, say, and using the CPR ability that I learned in high school, when I suddenly sit up in my bed in a dizzy rush.

I am sure she sees me, sure I see her, and I know that we will be together in the way most ultimate. We can't vision what the future harbors, and we are blind to our approaching fate. I have to hope that my long and faithful trudge toward heaven will not be ignored. I have to believe that surely we will be together in some subdivision of the higher ground.

Cheerfully, saving for the future, I go off to bingo. Though dark rumors abound, my winnings are now taken for granted. I am considered lucky, that simple. People envy, people grumble, but nobody challenges the assumption. I am the only one who can see the mounting figures in my joint account.

Night after night, I let the numbers accumulate until it just so happens that I go to the bank. There, I chance to find the actual amount in the book is zero, not closed by a stranger, but by Lyman Lamartine, joint account signer. I say nothing to him, although the steady pattern on the ground is tossed directly into focus: through my winnings, my uncle has paid up on loan moneys, questionable and necessary transactions. He has made the bottom line. I was the conduit, the easy mark, my name the temporary storage. I was the pool in an indoor-plumbed wishing well. Lyman kept his money going round and round, recycled his dollars through me. And yet, I don't get upset and I don't get overbearing or complain. I just stop going to the bingo.

For my luck has turned uncertain. My luck is pollen and chaff. Sprinkled onto me by Lyman's schemes, it was merely sucker's fortune.

Drifts of bright leaves collect around me, and then the driving snow. For the whole autumn season into winter, I do nothing but work at a slow driving pace. Christmas comes, I ignore the jolly caverns and parties, and New Year's Eve, too, with its blast of booze and sound. I don't want to make predictions, and have no reason for taking on any self-improving vows. I go into one of my mental hibernations to think and figure. I am laid up alone in January, then, staring at the ceiling above me when I hear the news. I don't even have a radio or television going in my room. I don't even have my phone hooked up after I ripped it from the plug one night spent willing it with reddened eyes to ring.

I am thinking of nothing in particular when the screen in my head goes all irrational, buzzes with noise and static, then blanks out.

What's happening? I wonder to myself.

And before you know it I am sleeping, and not only that but dreaming a bad dream that I am in a jail, in the night that never is a night but always

257

full of sighs and noises and hollers, full of clanking and never wholly dark, either, so that confusion of the senses overtakes judgment. I resent the gray fuzz, that fake night, and know I'll wake meaner than when I slept.

This is my father's night, and all of a sudden I am beside him, there in the all-night workroom of the laundry where he washes and folds. I see him working with billows of clothes, of pillowcases and such, simple jumpsuits, underwear, socks. He is surrounded by heavy machinery and he keeps on folding, drying, dragging twisted wet laundry from big tumblers. I wake with that square of prison light still shining in my head. I have dreamed my father real on many occasions, but I never had a picture like this one, so authentic and full of the assurance of him, so perfect in its knowledge.

I wait, to find out what it means, and by noon of the next day word filters through the bar. People entering for quick lunches tell me of the startling event. I hear it first from Titus, who knows my blood connection with the escapee. In previous breakouts, Gerry Nanapush has foiled guards, shrunk himself through an opening no larger than a pie box, somehow managed to torque himself into the body of a truck that drives through the gates with him clinging underneath. He has hid in the trunk of June's car when I was at the wheel. He has climbed drainpipes and appeared within public spaces. This time, it seems, he flew. He was in transit—nobody knows where for sure, but the rumors congregate around the efforts of Grandma Lulu to get him transferred. Yes, that

258

is Gerry No-shit-barn-built-can-hold-a-Chippewa Nanapush. Same as ever, running free.

I race back to my room, where the phone is still ripped from its little jack, and I reconnect myself back to the outside world. I hope a wavelength will now summon me. My number is in the book, the marked bone is in the left hand, the sinner's hand, the gambler's hand. I know I'll get a call.

Midnight.

"Hey."

"You."

"Yeah."

"Phone booth?"

"Fargo."

I want to ask where in Fargo and for a long moment I ponder how, in case the line is tapped. But he takes care of that for me and into the yawn of space between us says some words in the old-time language. The syllables bunch and go by fast, but I catch at them before the phone buzzes smooth. I memorize what I heard, but as I scope out his intention for the next hour, I become confused. My father is either playing Star Wars games at Art's Arcade, or he is holed up at the Fargo library, or he is hiding curled up in the lodge dumpster of the Sons of Norway.

Here's the thing. Except for that evening at Fleur Pillager's, when terror caused me to understand every word that came through, loud and clear, I don't know our traditional language all that well. Now the lack catches up with me. To my horror, I'm not sure what my father revealed to me on the phone. I work out each word with a pencil, then erase it. I fix on each syllable, slippery as a minnow.

259

In the end, however, all I can make out are these three strange possibilities. It occurs to me, though, that I'd better get to Fargo before the library closes tomorrow or before Dad runs out of quarters or before the day of civic garbage pickup.

And so, tossing on my heaviest clothes, grabbing from the bar rack some bags of nuts and jerky, I make ready to take the van.

When you're driving the sweet empty roads between home and Fargo, endless and empty possibilities surround you. That's the view I like, all nothing particular. Sky, field, and the signs of human attempts to alter same so small and unimportant and forgettable as you whiz by. I like blending into the distance. Passing shelter belts and fields that divide the world into squares, I always think of the chaos underneath. The signs and boundaries and markers on the surface are laid out strict, so recent that they make me remember how little time has passed since everything was high grass, taller than we stand, thicker, with no end. Beasts covered it. Birds by the million. Buffalo. If you sat still in one place they would parade past you for three days, head to head. Goose flocks blotted the sun, their cries like great storms. Bears. No ditches. Sloughs, rivers, and over all the winds, the vast winds blowing and careening with nothing in the way to stop them— no buildings, fence lines to strum, no drive-in movie screens to bang against, not even trees.

I park outside Art's Arcade, a twenty-four-hour video gaming enterprise. No sign of Gerry, not

260

yet. I walk inside and after I carefully scout the men's room, outskirts, the other players, I myself start playing, so as not to arouse suspicion. For about an hour, I play, then all of the drop-outs enter, the hooky-players. Beeps accelerate, mass destruction occurs, shifting futures. Blips of light dodge mad mummies and mine disasters, and street fighters groan and gripe at each other. From time to time, I am sure I feel Gerry's gaze rub through my jacket, hear his voice at my sleeve. But the minutes skim by into hours as the quarters flash off my fingers. I keep playing because I want him to see me winning when he enters. And so I spend quarter after quarter, save worlds without name, only to find when I turn around he has still not shown.

Morning floats by, dead on its feet, then afternoon.

I try to calculate what has happened. Outside, in the deepening cold, he might have stolen a car only to find that the battery dies. There is probably corrosion on his spark plugs, a frosted gas line, cracked tires. One picture in my mind features Dad with a pair of jumper cables coiled in his arms. I see him patiently attach them to his terminals, and then step back while I press down the gas. Life roars into the engine. Still, he doesn't show. The afternoon drags out and in time another episode forms. This one has my dad bound and handcuffed, sitting tight in the backseat between two smokies, who are writing in their pocket notebooks.

Gerry Nanapush is wanted by the entire combined police force of North America, but no

261

sooner do they catch him, he dissolves their shackles. He's not made of human stuff. Rain melts him. Snow turns him to clay. The sun revives him. He's a Chippewa. Yet in spite of his talents, he always does end up getting caught, and that is my fear, that is why I play hour after hour, until I have just one quarter remaining.

I turn around, sly, but Art himself catches me and points to the sign One Play Every Half Hour or Get Lost. He stands behind his register, cracking Russian peanuts and blowing the shells between his teeth. I pull my quarter out and hold it up for his approval. It is damp and sleek from touching, not just a piece of money, but a cool little circle of hope. I flip it once, and play an old-time classic.

A special current floats through me when the asteroids come whirling from all sides. Desperate concerns have tuned my reflexes razor fine. The controls warm to my hand, fuse flush to my nerves so I cannot miss. My mind pulls apart from my body, tugs off the screen, and hovers over me, impervious, in calm control. The watchers bunch around me, exploding their lips, punching air, urging me along. I don't need them. The score ticks high, higher. I go to the limit where there is no contest and the machine plays with me. I hit the edge. And then, I go further. I punch through all resistance into the white center of my mind.

Where I know he won't be waiting.

That's when the nerve cuts. My hands fly off the buttons. I turn, push my way out through the crowd, and another kid jumps into my place and starts firing. But he can't pull it out. The boulders

262

keep falling and dividing until they crush his rocket in a flash of pulsing noise.

Outside, it's so far below zero that the wind stiffens my face to a paper mask. It's early dark, and I get right into the bingo van to start it warming. I put the key into the ignition. I turn the key. Something clicks. There is an instant in which I'm completely hollowed, then I revive. I push the gas down, let up. I turn the key again with confidence. A twanging click, this time. The worst sound in dead of winter. I wait, freezing, turn the key again. I'm frantic, but no matter how I sweat and beg nothing happens any different. I've left the headlights on all day and run the battery down to nothing. There's no one up the street, no one down. I don't even have a dime to call a tow truck.

I zip up my army jacket, pull down my Vikings face mask, stick my hands in my pockets, and start walking toward the library, the second possibility I heard or misheard on our telephone conversation. All I can bank on is that when I find Dad he'll know how to hot-wire the vehicle, how to get it going. At the very least, he's bound to have ideas on how to scare up some cash.

The wind barges against me and I draw my hands up into my sleeves. The air is dangerous, thin to breathe as a scaling knife. My footsteps crackle. No one is outdoors. I keep walking, watching from the eye holes of my mask for some bar, hotel lobby, garage, anyplace to stand for a moment out of the wind. But the spaces grow between the buildings. The streets turn longer, wider, and I cross the downtown mall. It is too cold for life-forms in downtown Fargo, too cold for even me. I am thinking that I might end up as a municipal lawn ornament, a parking meter, mouth froze open to receive the night's spare change, when among the leftover Christmas mangers and hydrants the lighted castle of a building draws me across the snowy street. And there it is.

There are great squares of glass, rectangles of golden warmth that stream onto the snow in a rich, full invitation. I walk up the stone steps, push through the doors with my elbows, stand there, a stunned animal. Forced hot air blows over me, gentle and from far away. The mask has shifted on my face so I can hardly see out, and my arms are still locked around my chest.

As long as I walk around pretending to browse for something to read, chances are no one will tell me to leave. Behind my face mask I'm not anyone special, not an Indian even, just another half-froze Vikings fan. I put my hands through the sleeves, through cylinders of trapped and frozen air, and hold my breath. Then I walk upstairs and down the carpet, down the narrow rows.

In my line of work as night watchman, I depend on books. I read terror for the purpose of staying alert, I seek out mysterious crime, scare myself so bad that each creak means doom at the hands of the Undead, or a psychopath, and only the rising sun brings guaranteed safety. In the library, here, I look for the terror, the crime adventure, the space wars or weird occurrence titles to keep my motivation. As I wander the rows searching for Gerry, I warm too quickly, and now suddenly I'm

264

tired. My arms and legs are huge and heavy. My brain fills with star noise. I want to stretch out on the floor between the rows, drift into a blessed sleep. But I have to keep moving, up and down, grab books and pretend to scan the first page. I can't help stumbling from time to time and I'm afraid the authorities will think I'm drunk, kick me out. Snow is falling through my mind.

"Can I help you?"

It's a man's voice. I make like I don't hear him and walk quickly through the shelter of stacks of volumes.

Fateful coincidence. Things happen you can't deny. Good advice speaks from graves and love hints from the hearts of trees. Bags of light float through open windows on a summer night. Horses count with the knock of their hooves. Children are born who can add up unbelievable numbers. These things are possible.

I see the book through the gunner's vision of the eye holes in my face mask and my hands reach for it without any command of my conscious brain. Luckily, I know enough to brace myself before I read the title.

Fear and Trembling, it says, *and the Sickness unto Death*.

I shut my eyes and for a minute I sway in the mystery. I am staring down, off the railings of a bridge, into a river that is treacherous, full of suck holes and underground streams. I have looked into that river once, and thought I'd crossed it for good on my way back to reservation home ground. The title of that book drives back upon me like the current of that river, flowing north, certain in its course with no meandering, no pardon. I feel how fragile I've strung my own heart above that river, like a bridge of spiderwebs.

I open my eyes. It is a small dark volume with a covering like burnt skin. The title confronts me again, no letup. I stare straight back. I hold the book, careful, in my hands, and then I open it, random, to see my fate or pick a name out of it. I drop my finger on the words. *If, at the foundation of things, there lay only a wildly seething power . . .* I read. I consider. I think of the river in its misdirection, the fickle current, and the flood that washes out bridges and the porches of homes. I want to believe in the spirit, the order, the will, the blame. I want to believe in the blessed book where no stone can crumble, no arrow fall. But God won't be watching when they take my father up the hill.

The Sons of Norway lodge is large, as are the Sons of Norway who belong to it, strapping and bold. At the back of the building, I find the trash cans, covered by one large drift that has heavily swirled down and through which I try to dig with my hands. It is like trying to force a rock apart, and I fail as the snow is packed too tight. Dad has to be in there, I think in panic, Dad sealed alive.

I turn away from the snow-packed dumpster behind the lodge, and go looking for a shovel, but in all of the surrounding blocks there is nothing even useful or resembling one—just shut buildings. The great lights burn high on their poles and by counting their vague halos I keep track of where I am, know how to get back, and yet, though I continue to walk neat square upon neat expanding square I do not find what I am looking for. I only pass empty doorways, barred windows, lightless, empty, as if Fargo was all taped-up boxes and the people inside stunned and still as shoes.

And then, as I walk through a bleak alleyway, back toward the Sons of Norway, a gust of brash wind slings the giant Frisbee of an aluminum garbage-can lid right into my chest, knocking out my wind but giving me the proper tool. I barrel back, holding the lid hard to me against the wind. When I get to the place I dig into that drift with the top of the can and I pull snow, drag it, clear it. I manage to get down to the lid. I pry it open, lift it up, and then wait for my father to jump out like a spring-loaded child's toy.

Around me the wind swirls and blows and whistles through the lamps and roofs of the city like a flock of crazed swans. Nothing. I climb up, peer in. Not only is there nobody home in the dumpster but there is no scrap of garbage, not a cardboard box, a wisp of paper. Immediately, in my mind, expectations and pictures bloom. I see my father tumbled out of sleep into a big white Scandinavian garbage truck and hear those gears grind, those strong jaws champ. My thoughts reel shut on the possibilities, my mind is overstrained. I stumble along the lodge wall until I meet his open arms.

There, in the driving wind, Gerry Nanapush. Regular size and big as life.

Or not so big, maybe, for it looks to me that even covered in shelves of wool and parka hood and blanket though he is, my father is smaller, even diminished beneath. His face has contracted

267

around the bones, and there are tired lines around his eyes, so deep that I can see them in the faint aura of the parking lot spotlights. We stand against the wall breathing hard. Neither of us speaks and for a while there is just the sound of the wind sighing and battering. He finally leans over and asks where our transportation is, and then I have to tell him that June's car is stolen and my van's frozen dead. When he understands this, he seems to lose his control. Whirling, he turns and slams his arms once against the building. Then he flips around and hops up and down to bring the blood back to his feet. He drags me down to a little side-cellar just next to the door, where a vent blows heat straight upon us, melting, at least, my strained lips so I can talk. We cut right through the greeting, through the where-the-hell-were-you's, and come immediately to the desperate business of what-the-hell-we-do-next.

CHAPTER TWENTY-THREE

ZELDA'S LUCK

One afternoon during the first months after Shawnee and Redford left her house, Zelda Kashpaw walked in the front door and found, lying on her spangled kitchen counter, the softly tanned and quilled bag containing her father's ceremonial pipe—an object she hadn't seen since well before his death. She knew it came from Marie through Lipsha, from him through the hands of Lyman Lamartine. She knew it was his

268

way of reaching her and of conceding the unspoken failure of their truce. She walked around the pipe all that day, without touching or moving it, cooked her dinner, boiled her coffee the old way, in a blue enamel pot on top of the stove.

From a dark sleep that same night, her heart woke her, loudly drumming. The pounding in her chest was so sudden that she didn't recognize the sound as coming from her own body. A painful lightness bloomed beneath her ribs and her heart surged powerfully, gathering speed, galloping until she gasped and sat bolt upright in fear. She saw her heart explode from her chest and continue to dance, hot and fierce, alone along the snowy fields, the frozen sloughs, the staggered lines of fences. It twirled out of her and broke in the raving dusk. A pigeon in halves, a dove in threes, ripped velvet pillows.

Zelda shook her head, reached over and pressed the switch on her little bulldog lamp. In its soft glare she inhaled cautiously, trying to quiet the valves and pumps, but her breath squeezed in and out. Her chest muscles hurt, she gasped profusely, and it became clear at last that she was having a heart attack. When that fact sank in, she immediately became more calm. Death, she understood. She grew officious about herself, slammed pillows around to prop her back and then leaned into them, arranged herself to be found. She smoothed her hair along her shoulders, placed the lines in her quilt just so. She did not call for help because she did not want saving. No CPR. Preparing a serene pose, she brushed her face into a smile,

269

threaded her rosary between her fingers, and said an act of perfect contrition.

She couldn't think of anything that she was sorry for, at first, and then the sight of Redford's stunned, chocolate-stained face, the sounds of his sudden night terrors, caused her to grip the beads tighter in her fist. Small things came back, losses of her temper, pieces of rage she could not control around her father and her mother. She made a devout penance, and then, right in the middle of her Hail Mary, the picture thudded. Zelda saw herself twisted in bedsheets, naked, lying with her arms around a man with long, dark hair, and she took her breath so harshly that the immediate pain made her cry out. The pictures kept on coming. The scenes she'd missed would not stop, not blur, and that is when she came to realize that, in her life, she was sorrier for the things she had not done than for the things that she had.

The wrong things! She was sorry for the wrong things!

Light shortened and built in the gray windows of her bedroom, and the breeze stirred. Far off in a neighbor's field she heard the groan of a cow, and although she knew what the sound was, she pictured something else. Her hands trembled, her breath again weakened. The sounds came closer and her whole body shook.

She was a house coming apart, the nails, each in turn, wrenched from the wood with a sob, the boards bounding off like blows, wheeling end over end in a dark wind, punishing the fields, the house in pieces gliding over dark snow, the inner beams

270

shouting *huhnh, huhnh, huhnh*, panting with the sound of a woman giving birth.

She closed her eyes. A startling and painful radiance flooded her. Ice shattered. Her heart thawed unbearably, an unfrozen fist.

Another thing! She glared, thrashed her arms. In her mind someone stood before her. Another thing! She'd heard this old medicine could still be worked. Someone was trying to kill her. Someone had scratched a bark drawing of her, detailed, meticulous, all her insides etched out in empty strings. Into those lines that person had rubbed red clay, ochre, rouge, an owl's thick blood, until the color reached her heart's knob. So let it burst! Her heart was an old hand-iron that clanged against her ribs, hot and hissing. She wouldn't mind setting down such a heavy weight.

Quit, she ordered. *Quit!*

But the grip of her own life continued so strong it amazed and disgusted her. She braced herself, rose for a glass of water, and her hair fanned, deep as rain, across her rigid shoulders. She was afraid to look in the mirror, afraid to see an old woman with her father's stern face, so instead she peered into the dawn window. But her father was there, watching her with her own eyes, the fire of the sunrise surrounding his features.

It was the same fire that bent behind him thirty years ago, peculiar and sudden, the wall of bursting darts. Flames rose in her eyes again, the brand and shame of Lulu Lamartine's house, raging out of control. And she there to see it and see her father, she the one who had to drag him

271

back home to her mother, while she let the witch burn. But she wouldn't burn.

That was the effect of passion on a life. Zelda nodded, caught up in seeing it all happen again. She passed her hands before Nector Kashpaw's features, pushed them back into the frieze of leaping flames. He started the fire that bounded cat-like through wastepaper and rags, up a gas line, and destroyed his lover's house. To get even with him, Zelda would unmake him inside of herself. She never would be subject to love, never would be overtaken. Able to choose, to use her head and starve her heart, that was Zelda. She was capable of hovering in a blanket, in a room where her own breath rose and fell, a plume of longing, all night. She could exist in the dark cell of her body. She was capable of denying herself everything tender, unspoken, sweet, generous, and desperate. She could do it because she willed it. She could live in the shell of her quilt as the cold night lengthened, and she could let a man's fires flash and burn, flash and burn, until they disappeared. Again, she watched Xavier waste his fingers to the stubs like candles, one by one.

Her heart strummed sickeningly, now, and she stumbled back to her bed. She was sure that she could hold in these emotions—she had done so all of her life! Instead, she cried out, as she never had allowed herself in birth, and her cry was the old desire, a groan deep as a tree pulled over in a storm. Roots surged from the dirt. Curved arms dragged boulders to light. When the taproot came, violent, she leaned over on her bed certain that she'd die, but something else happened.

She took one calm breath, another, and then her heart grew quiet. It tipped back and forth, a muted bell. In that stilled ring disturbing thoughts were forced upon her—faint pictures, portraits. She saw Xavier Toose, how his arms were wrapped like clubs for a solid year while they healed into a shape that would never hold her. She saw his face, the haunted starkness of that arrested smile. Hollowed, drained, she overheard him when they sang at the drum those years after. He left his hair loose, as if in mourning, and it flowed down his back, heavy, with an animal scent. She stood behind him, breathing in the darkness of his neck, his throat, the woodsmoke and the clean male sweat, the tannins of his hide shoes. She heard his voice—loose, low, raw—the spirit voice that came on him deep in song, like the voice in the shaking tent, unseen, a rejoicing howl. Her chest was hot, split open. Shame covered her as she recalled a time she had been sitting to one side and not quite listening as he talked to some younger men. They asked how he acquired so many women, what his secret could be, and he raised his one blunt hand.

"True," he said, "I don't have everything you guys have. And yet . . ." He gazed thoughtfully and fixedly down past his belt buckle, so that all of their eyes followed and witnessed the obedient and sudden alertness there.

She had turned furiously away from their laughter. Now, she fought the understanding that all of her grown life she had cared for him with a secret unkilled feeling stronger than acids, unquenched, a coal fire set inside of her and

273

running through each vein with a steady heat. She loved Xavier Toose.

"And I always will, and I always will," she said out loud, beating a fist on her chest.

She struck herself like a person begging to be admitted to her own unworthy house. *Mea culpa, mea maxima culpa.* She hit her chest with unceasing regularity and monotony until her arm fell, the muscles spent, until the day came full on and she slept.

She woke slowly the next time and the thought of her father's pipe struck suddenly into her mind. She didn't need to see it, to hold it, but she pictured it there on her counter. Earth and heaven, connecting, the fire between that burned in everything alive. She lay straining for the familiar sounds of the day beginning, the small pleasurable noises of a woman caring for a child, and then she remembered that she was alone. A holy fire exists in all we touch, she thought, even in the flames that fed my father's heart. Framed and finished in the anguish, she felt her own face take on his depth.

It was too late for them to do anything but smoke the pipe together, she and Xavier. But that small thing was possible. She rose and showered in the little stall next to her room, calmer as the water coursed down, smoother as she soaped and rubbed. She wrapped a worn towel around her waist, her breasts. She dried her thick hair in which there was still so little gray, and she brushed her teeth twice. She wasn't hungry or anxious. Her heart was again docile in her chest, except when she thought directly of Xavier. Then, it yawned open like a greedy young bird, ready to be fed.

When she drove into his yard near Matchimanito and stopped, she was suddenly aware that her visit was strange and unnatural. Thirty years had passed. Between them there had been no word exchanged, and at the thought of what she possibly could say, she put her hand to her cheek, uneasy and afraid. Her actions would be unfathomable, the behavior of a crazy woman. Still, she did not turn the car around but sat for a long while, staring at the house, watching for a sign. The place was small, hand built, not a prefabricated government box but an old cabin like hers, shored up through the years. It was painted neatly and well shoveled, the snow heaped to each side of the walk. Zelda knew that Xavier had special tools built for his arms, that he could do anything, that he never believed or allowed himself to be treated like a man with something missing, but rather, it always seemed he had more than other people. The young came to him, sought him out, just the way she was seeking him now. He had simplified his heart.

She saw the window curtain drop, then Xavier appeared. Although they hadn't looked into each other's eyes since she refused him in the breath of horses, although they were more strange to one another than strangers, upon approaching her there was no hint of awkwardness in Xavier. He was wearing a heavy red and black hunting jacket, leather boots, an old billed hat. He leaned down to her window and Zelda's face bloomed toward

275

his as though his features gave out warmth. Deep vertical gashes of age ran from the corners of his eyes to his chin and folded like a carved fan in symmetrical weavings. They held one another in long regard, and as their stillness remained unbroken a mysterious peace descended. Light dashed itself upon Zelda, but she wasn't shaken. Her hands floated off the steering wheel and gestured, but she wasn't helpless. She left the car, stood before Xavier, new as if naked, but she had no shame. They walked toward the house and left the pipe in its leather wrappings in the front seat, buckled carefully as a child.

CHAPTER TWENTY-FOUR

LIPSHA

I'M A MAD DOG BITING MYSELF FOR SYMPATHY

We are at Metro Drug in downtown Fargo, passing time waiting for the right moment. When the next train pulls into the Amtrak station two blocks north, we think a car might be left outside, idling, keys in the ignition. That's our hope, but we don't dare hang too near the tracks. I never stole a thing as big as a car before and I keep having to turn my mind off. I wander the aisles of the big drugstore just to hear the canned leftover carols over the loudspeaker, and Gerry frowns at the pages of a magazine.

"Maybe there's a Santa Claus," Gerry says.

276

"Maybe we'll get lucky." I walk away from him and then, instead of lucky, I see the bird.

You think you know everything about yourself, how much money it would take, for instance, to make you take it. How you would react when caught. But then you find yourself in the middle of planning to steal a car walking out the door with a stuffed toucan. I can't explain this right, just why, though I put it all upon myself. Perhaps it is to warm up to grand larceny, to see if I'll get spotted, which I do. Or maybe it is just to distract the two of us, which also happens.

And too, there is Shawnee Ray. I think of Christmas, how this bird should have sat underneath her tree. The minute I see that toucan, I wish I'd won it for her at a county fair, though we never went to a fair. I see myself throwing a half dozen softballs and hitting every wooden milk jug, or maybe tossing rings. But then, you never win because those things are weighted or loaded wrong, and that's another excuse. I never would have snagged this toucan for Shawnee Ray because life's a cheat in general.

I lift the bird.

Outside in the street it is the tag end of this bleak day, unpleasant and gray. A light snow is letting up now, having dusted a few hard clumps, but covered nothing. Yellow grass from last year even shows on the boulevards. The temperature is up in the last few hours. I like the smell in the air, the dry dirt, even the threat of new snow, too, in the gloom of the gathering night sky.

The usual stiff-neck turns to look at me, at Gerry, who walks in front toward the train station and has not seen my petty theft. This bird is really huge and furry, with green underneath its floppy wings and fat stuffed orange feet. I don't know why they'd sell a strange thing like this in Metro. Maybe a big promotion, maybe some kind of come-on left over from the holiday season. And then the manager yells at me from the door. I am halfway down the street when I hear him. "Come back here!" Probably he points at me, too, though there is no reason since I stick out plenty, and still more as I begin to run.

I pass Gerry, looking over my shoulder, and he rises up like he was shot and springs high on the balls of his feet right next to me.

First I put the bird underneath my arm, but it throws me off my balance, so I clutch it to my ribs. That is no better. Thinking back now I should have ditched it, slipped off through the alleyways and disappeared. Of course, I don't—otherwise none of all that happens would have gone down. I sit the bird on my shoulders and hold the lumpy feet under my chin, then I bear down, like going for the gold. My legs churn beneath me. I leap curbs, dodge among old men in long gray coats and babies in strollers, shoot up and over car hoods until I come to the railroad depot, the new Quonset hut aluminum one just beside the old brick building. It is our destination, after all, so I slip in the door and look out the window just as the train sighs and breathes its way toward us along the tracks.

A gathering crowd follows with the manager. There's a policewoman, a few mall-sitters, passersby. They are bustling and talking together and making big circles of their arms, to illustrate the size of the toucan, and closing in.

That's when our stroke of luck, good or bad is no telling, occurs. Gerry stands beside me, breathing hard, looking wild. Then a white car drives into the parking lot, a solid plastic luggage rack strapped on its roof. A man jumps out, eager for a relative maybe, and he leaves the car running in neutral. We ease out of the depot and stand beside the car. At that moment, it seems as though events are carrying us. I open up the hinges on the plastic rack, stuff the bird under its restraints. No one notices. Encouraged, Gerry and I casually get in, him behind the wheel. He takes the car out of neutral and we start to roll, backing out of the lot. Gerry changes gears, then stops at the cross street and looks both ways.

There we are, in a car. It isn't ours but for the time being that doesn't matter. We get to the corner and we look up the street one way. It is clear. We look down the other, to where a bunch of people are still arguing and trying to describe us with their hands. Either way, the road will take us straight out of the town.

Gerry lets the car idle, looks at me, his expression asking which way to turn.

I know we shouldn't show up on the reservation, not with Gerry, with the toucan, much less the car, but then the truth is we don't have nowhere else to go. I think of the bird. In a way, Shawnee Ray got us into this, I tell myself, even though I know it is more my wish than a thought that makes any sense. Maybe her bad sisters will take my dad in, hide him, get us over the border.

So I nod north and Gerry makes the turn, and then another complexity, although at the time I don't realize, occurs when the man at the depot, the one who has left the car, appears very suddenly in the rearview mirror.

We have just started moving when I hear a thump from behind. It is so surprising. Just imagine. He is there on the trunk, hanging on as though by magnetics. The man reaches up and grabs the hitches on the rooftop luggage rack, gets a better grip, and sprawls across the back window. He is a small man, young. Through the side view, I see his boots, blue Dr. Martens, kicking in the air, and the edge of his black coat. I hear him shrieking in an inhuman desperate way that horrifies Gerry so much he floors the gas.

We must go by everyone fast, but the effect is dreamlike, so slow. I see the faces of the people, their mouths falling open, their arms stretching and grasping. As we turn the corner the man rolls off, over and over like a seal in water. He flies from the trunk and bowls the followers before in his rush so they heap on the ground beneath him. The man is in their laps, they are holding him. They lay him down as though he is a live torpedo and start running after us.

"Scandinavians," I say to Gerry, because Aunt Zelda was married to one. "They don't give up the ghost."

I want to yell out, to tell them, "Okay, so it's stolen. It's gone! It's a cheap stuffed bird anyhow and I will *park* the car. I promise."

"We'll check the oil in Devils Lake. No sweat, Dad." I talk as though we've got everything under control. I point out the scenic route, and we take it at a fast clip, but I know the view anyway. We are down near the river when the worst thing comes about, when all of a sudden I understand the man with his eyes rearing back in his skull, his thick heels kicking. I understand the changed faces of the people in the group, their blurting voices, ". . . baby."

As from the backseat, it wails.

I have my first reaction: I don't know what I'm hearing. I think it is an animal, car trouble, anything else but the obvious. Gerry pulls to the curb and I turn around in a frantic whirl. I still can't see that it's a baby because I am behind on the new equipment. He sits in something round and firm, shaped like a big football, strapped down at the chest and over the waist, held tight by a padded cushion. I guess he is a boy because he is dressed in blue. His blanket features flying baseball bats and hockey sticks. Above his face there is a little diamond attachment made of plastic, a bunch of keys and brilliant balls that dangle out of reach.

His face is small and dark, almost copper, and his fingers, splayed out against his cheeks, are tiny as the feet of a sparrow. There is a bottle of juice in a bag beside him. I reach back, put the nipple in the baby's mouth and the little guy sucks, but he can't hold the bottle by himself.

"Don't drop it!" I warn as the car sways and lurches.

Gerry pulls onto the road, gasping.

"Let's get the fuck out of here."

"We should leave off the baby," I say.

281

"No, keep him."

Gerry guns right out of there. The baby's cry begins again and I wish I knew how to stop him from suffering. I know he feels the confusion in the air, the strangeness, the whiff of threat. I feel like I should convince the baby that things will be all right, but I don't know how and also I don't know for sure. I would be lying if I said I did. Gerry has to slow down to get through traffic. Sirens rush ahead on their way to the interstate, passing in a squeal which surprises me. This car, this pack on top, it is so obvious. I say to Gerry that maybe we should ditch it at the old King Leo's, get out and run. But then we pass the place. Over us, the sky is bearing down and bearing down, so I think now maybe snow will really fall. A white Christmas like the music in my brain. I know Gerry must remember how to drive in snow and this car has decent tires, I can feel them. They never lose grip or plane above the road. They just keep rolling, humming, all four in this unified direction, so dull that after some time it all seems normal again.

The baby stops crying and drops off to sleep. He shouldn't be there. I have to realize the situation. There is no use in thinking back, in saying to myself, *You shouldn't have stole the damn bird in the first place*, because I did do that and then, well as you see, it is like I went along with the arrangement of things as they took shape.

Of course, a few miles farther on there is a smoky waiting, which we knew would happen, but not whether it would be before or behind us. So now our answer comes. The officer's car turns

282

out of a dirt road and starts flashing, starts coming at us from the rear. We take it up to eighty and then a hundred and we move, *move*, so the frozen snow standing in the fields flashes by like scarves and the silver snow whirls out of nowhere to either side of us, and what rushes up before us is a heat of road and earth.

I am not all that afraid, but now I realize why I feel sure that they will not use their weapons. The baby. I can't believe that Gerry thought to keep him with us for that purpose, though, and I try to put that thought out of mind—but it keeps popping in. We keep driving and then, as we take a turn, as we bound across a railroad intersection, I hear the roof rack snap open with a cracking thump. I twist around and see the bird as it dives out of the sky, big and plush, a purple blur that plunges its yellow beak into the windshield of the police car and throws the state police off course so their cruiser skids, rolls over once, comes back with such force the car rights itself and sits quiet in shock.

We slow back to eighty. The pack blows off too, and I reason that now the car is not so easy to identify. I should have thought about that in the first place, but then the bird would not have hatched out and attacked. About this time, being as the toucan is gone, I begin to feel perhaps there is no point in traveling farther. I begin to think that we should just stop at the nearest farm, dump the car and the baby with someone else, and disappear into the fields. I start to feel positive that if I show up at Shawnee Ray's, even with nothing, even with a convict criminal, she will not throw

283

me out. She'll have to take me in, let me sleep on the couch. I fast-forward. She will live with another man, someday, a guy of world experience. Soon she will visit restaurants and zoos, go camping in the wilderness, ski. She will know things and I will still be the same person that I was the day before I got this phone call from my dad. And I am glad about the toucan, then, which would have made me look ridiculous—me, showing up there like a kid in junior high school with a stuffed animal, when her tastes are becoming so enlarged. I should send her chocolates in a little red and green box. I wish I had. And then I look past the road in front of me and realize it is seriously snowing.

It isn't just like ordinary snow even from the first. It's like that rhyme or story in the second grade, the sky falling and let's go and tell the king. It comes down. I think to myself, Well, let it come down. Gerry keeps on driving. I know you'll say it, you'll wonder, you'll think what about the child in the backseat, that baby, not even one year old? Because he does have an age and all, but what could I know of that?

Gerry talks to the baby. He says, in a funny voice, "You little bastard you, what are you doing here?"

"Don't call him bastard."

My state of mind is lowering. I roll the passenger window open. Snow whites out the windshield and I can't see the road in front of us. I watch the margin, try to follow the white border before it is obscured by a twisting cyclone of snow. My attention vanishes when the baby bawls. My ears fill. He roars and I hear the wind screaming like his father on the trunk yelled, but there is something about that baby that is like a weight in me, heavier than a shrunk-down star, older than gravity. I don't mind the cries because they make a certain sense in this situation, and I understand him in a way, his misery, his wish for the tried and true. I can tell that he knows something is wrong, his world is fucked, some essential thing.

The sky grows darker, the snow is near solid in the air, and we are hitting zero-definition. The sky is in our face. The car's a hollow toy, and we're struggling for purchase when we chance in behind a snowplow. We almost run into it at first, but I see the faint glow of its lamps and flashers. Gerry whoops and he's pounding the wheel and the baby shrieks out still louder. Carefully, with sure belligerence, deliberate patience, the plow grumbles on in front of us, heading due north. Like a big, clumsy angel, like an ocean liner, clanking and mournful, the snowplow parts the waves and makes us our way.

We fall into the cleave of its wake and hang there, held fast, as it cruises into the boundless wastes beyond. We slow when it slows, stop when it pauses for breath, then go on into the deeper spaces of the night. It rumbles past the lights and past the farms and lighted elevators. We keep its tail in our sight, breathe easy. Gerry has me light a cigarette for him, in reprieve he takes a deep, slow, drag. It all seems simple now, for this one moment, it seems to me that we're saved. Never mind the fact we have stolen this car, not to mention the baby who needs rocking, feeding, never mind what comes next.

I reach back to joggle the plastic egg and reassure the baby that we're doing better, but I have to keep my hand there because I feel the car give on the road, shake and rattle, as another vehicle plunges alongside us. Out of nowhere, like a star, it rushes in a hollow of wind. This car gives off its own light, a flash of fire and deep blue, and it stays steady with us, almost glowing in the wall of snow. Running neck and neck to us, it breasts the impossible drifts, floats over them like a soundless ice blue skiff.

I suppose I should be more amazed than I am to see that it is June's car, and that she is driving. We see her silhouette, the barest outline of her, head high, hands resting on the wheel, one elbow on the open window ledge. Her hair is a black net, her back is held straight. We see her shrug her shoulders once, and smile through the clouds and frost.

My dad leans forward, grips the wheel, his voice ragged and amazed.

"June!"

He calls to her, begging her to stop although of course she can't hear. And then he starts to follow her car, turns out of the safety of the snowplow's salvation. He deviates. I lean over, wrench the wheel, try to take it from him in a struggle, and I manage to get him back into the tracks for a moment. I am all of a sudden shaking and cold with the dread. He strains to the windshield glass, looking after her, weaving for a glance of her through the sheets of irregular snow. He wants

286

her so hard that the desire takes me over too and I can't catch him back because I'm caught up in the anxious necessity. He swerves into line behind the blue car's trail. He follows even when she pulls calmly from the plow's path and leaves the blacktop highway.

The snow is packed so hard underneath that we continue across the fields at a steady pace, following her red taillights, which shine and wink as we travel unbounded through the perfectly flat land that runs along the interstate. Of course, here and there, the ground falls away, hollow and uncertain. Each time we falter, I turn to Gerry and open my mouth, but each time, before I can prepare myself to argue, he hits my shoulder and cries out not to stop him. He's fascinated, gripped, won't talk to me now, and doesn't notice how the tracks narrow into one, and then widen, go from wheel tracks to no tracks to unbroken snow.

In a sudden clearing in the blizzard, her car stops before us. We see it calmly waiting there, no lights on, lounging still and dark. Just like in a cartoon, like Dumbo flying and he realizes that he isn't supposed to be up in the air, Gerry panics and we get stuck.

"Dad?"

There is silence. No answer. He just turns his head slow and looks at me with an air of sad puzzlement and hard choice. I want to ask him not to go, but my lips are frozen still and frosted shut. His eyes are deep and the shadows on his face roar in my ears, blue receding, flooding out of my life as if sucked back from creation. The blackened moon shocks out somewhere in back of

287

the blizzard's violence. I take a deep breath of the stale smoke and desperation of my father, but already he's halfway out the door. Into the diamond swirl of radiance and chance, he vaults. He's drawn to June, lost in the surge of his own feelings.

The door slams. I sit waiting for a moment, hoping, watching. I see him slide into the passenger's side of the blue car and then, a small pause, and her headlamps go on. It isn't that he doesn't care for me, I know that, it's just that his own want is too deep to resist. June's beams trace the air, open spaces in the dark wind, and the car begins to move. I watch it until snow slams down over us, covering the windshield.

I am out in the middle of nothing, in a storm that can go on for three more minutes or three more days. And remember this: it is a white car we stole. Most difficult kind to spot. I can't recall what they say in the papers every fall, the advice about how to survive when a blizzard hits. Whether to stay on the road with the car, or to set out on foot for help. Plus, there's the baby. I know I shouldn't let the car run, use up the gas and the heater, but for a moment I do. I crawl into the back and unstrap the boy from the egg seat and I hold him in my arms. The heater roars, though I've got it on low, and in the breath of warmth I'm suddenly so very tired.

I think about my father and my mother, about how they have already taught me about the cold so I don't have to be afraid of it. And yet, this baby doesn't know. Cold sinks in, there to stay.

And people, they'll leave you, sure. There's no return to what was and no way back. There's just emptiness all around, and you in it, like singing up from the bottom of a well, like nothing else, until you harm yourself, until you are a mad dog biting yourself for sympathy. Because there is no relenting. There is no hand that falls. There is no woman reaching down to take you in her arms.

My father taught me his last lesson in those hours, in that night. He and my mother, June, have always been inside of me, dark and shining, their absence about the size of a coin, something I have touched against and slipped. And when that happens, I call out in my bewilderment—*"What is this?"*—and the thing is I never knew until now it was a piece of thin ice they had put there.

Come what might when we are found, I stay curled around this baby. The heater snaps off, the motor dies down. I rummage in the seat for whatever I can find to keep us warm and find small blankets, baby size. I know it will be a long night that maybe will not end. But at least I can say, as I drift, as the cold begins to take me, as I pull the baby closer to me, zipping him inside of my jacket, here is one child who was never left behind. I bite my own hands like the dog, but already they are numb. The shooting star is in my mouth, cold fire blazing into nothing, but at least this baby never was alone. At least he always had someone, even if it was just a no-account like me, a waste, a reservation load.

As I fall away into my sleep, I'm almost happy things have turned out this way. I am not afraid. An unknown path opens up before us, an empty trail shuts behind. Snow closes over our tracks, and then keeps moving like the tide. There is no trace where we were. Nor any arrows pointing to the place we're headed. We are the trackless beat, the invisible light, the thought without a word to speak. Poured water, struck match. Before the nothing, we are the moment.

Chapter Twenty-Five

LULU'S CAPTURE

They say that she was ready for the federal marshals when they drove up to the doors, though they were quiet, their tires hardly crunching snow. The rest of us had no wind and no warning, no inkling, but we were mostly awake anyway in the dark chill of a day that began with a plunging degree of cold. That below-zero chill burned our feet through the covers. We shivered, twisting deeper. Old bones need warm caves. From outside, in the insulated halls and behind the doors, we heard the shuffling, we heard the boot steps, the noise of their invasion, but most of us turned over into a sleep that would soon go on forever. We dreamed the young dreams, missed the beginning of what happened, missed Lulu's capture.

Of course, there was always Josette Bizhieu to tell us what occurred. There was Marie Kashpaw, who maintained calm and smiled past her questioners. There was Maurice Morris—man about town, he called himself—just returning to his

290

apartment around the time the federals entered Lulu's door.

They did not knock, they did not give her a chance to form an answer, just busted their way into her apartment and discovered her sitting there, ready. And she was prepared. All was in perfect order for their arrival. No possible doubt about it, none at all. For who else was attired in her full regalia at that hour, dressed traditional, decked out in black velvet with flowers from the woodlands beaded into the shining nap—red rose, yellow heart, white leaves, and winking petals—who else was dressed like Lulu? She carried her fan of pure white eagle tailfeathers. Four of them, upright, in her hand of a sexy grandmother. On the wrist of the other arm, there dangled her beaded carrying pouch, full of cosmetics and papers and identity proof. Of that, they disarmed her as with drawn guns they searched rudely through her precious things.

Let's say they found a knife, they found a weapon, they found something besides that machinery and bundled newspaper and Congressional material that she quoted as she took our money while playing cards. Let's say they found an Illinois matchbook, a pair of sawed-apart handcuffs, some direct proof her son had been to see her. Or let's say they didn't find a thing, but that motherhood itself was more than enough.

Whatever the reasoning, they questioned her. At this, we have to laugh.

We hide our smiles back behind our hands, to be polite to our government, for which so many of our men have died and suffered, and our women

291

too, but we can't help but say it was a useless cause for them to offer Lulu Lamartine her own coffee from her own pot on the stove, to ask her if she would like to sit down in her own chair and encourage her to make herself at home in her own home. It was useless to set up the tape recorders and take out the pens and papers. For what question were they going to ask her, after all, what question that would receive a reliable answer? A truth? When her son and her grandson were the ones at issue? What truth but Lulu's own truth? What other possible response?

Maybe they thought Indians dressed that way all the time. Maybe they thought Indians dressed that way to go to bed at night. No one commented on or noticed Lulu's outfit, ceremonial and bold, as if she was ready to be honored. Her moccasins, she always called them works of art: smoked deer-hide, expertly tanned. Little roses were beaded on the toes, white rabbit fur sewed inside, and meanwhile the rest of us wore house slippers, thin quilted robes. Listening at doorways, we called softly between ourselves, and shuddered with cold. Underneath her powwow dress, Lulu wore a pair of red long johns, we were sure. Winter is not gentle with us old ones and she anticipated drafts, who wouldn't, during the entry and seizure.

They were very smart, these federals. No doubt they were wise. They had seen a lot of hard cases, chased a lot of criminals, solved a great many crimes that would stump us ordinary Chippewas. And yet, the fact is, they had never encountered Lulu. For that reason, they spent a long time

292

questioning a fish in the river, they spent a longer time talking to a turtle in its shell, they tried to intimidate a female badger guarding the mouth of its den and then, to fool an old lady coyote who trotted wide of the marks her pups had left. They spent hours, in which they should have been tracking down their wary escapee, asking Lulu one question, in many different ways, until she seemed to break down, shaking her hands and fanning herself with feigned distress.

"Yes, yes," she whispered. "Something happened."

They got a story all right. One hour passed, then two, but then it's frustrating to question an old woman who is losing her memory. In shock, she gets the past mixed up into the present and cannot recall what age her son is now, or when, just precisely, these things occurred that all the clever and keen-eyed men describe to her, and then of course, when they bring in a woman, more sympathetic, there is a great deal of additional confusing material to relate, all of the normals and particulars of her son's habits and childhood behaviors that were so impressive at the time.

Heads are spinning and just then, when their tongues are sticking in their cheeks and their brows are going up, she remembers perfectly.

"Of course, of course he was here. He came home."

And at those words, of course, the ears perk and the recorders whir, but then the sense retreats, the poor old woman faints, slumps dead away, and must be revived with a strong fresh cup of coffee.

"Where else would he go?" she says when she

wakes up, and hours later, it turns out that she has just returned from taking him up north across the border in her automobile. Where? That takes quite a while more to figure out. She tries to help but the world is going vague, losing its shape and everything is getting mashed around inside her stumbling brain, although she frowns helpfully and often hums to herself, annoyingly, in order to aid her memory.

"Where? Where?"

Dreamy, she smiles, in her own time and place perhaps, but maybe they are onto her at last. Maybe they have lost their patience, it is true, or have finally understood that they are playing with a cat whose claws are plump and sheathed. They have dusted everything for fingerprints. They have examined every surface for nail clips and hair. They have looked into each drawer and sounded walls. Gone over each of her possessions, in turn. Including the wanted poster, nicely framed.

We told her, we reminded her that she'd done wrong. We scolded Lulu Lamartine to read the warning, heed the label, pointed out that she harbored stolen government property upon her shelf. For that offense, they finally take her in, arrest her, cart her off but with a kind of ceremony that does not confuse a single one of us, for she has planned it. And all so perfectly! By this time, outside the door, in the hallway, so many popping lights of cameras, whining shutters. All of the North Dakota newspapers. By that time, the local tribal officials. The Chippewa police. Jurisdiction issues? Sure, plenty of them right there to worry over.

There goes Lulu Lamartine, powwow perfect, chained at the wrists but still clutching the eagle-feather fan. Lulu Lamartine surrounded, walked off by muscle-bound agents, as if she would escape, and so frail! Removed from an old people's home! Lulu Lamartine luring dogs away, diverting attention, making such a big statewide fracas, and with her story, sending agents on a new goose chase. It is perfect, it is sinful, and any one of us could have told them they were getting into something like a mazy woods when talking to that woman.

They should have backed out early. They should not have taken her into custody, brandishing her hooked wrists with simple dignity. They should not have let her do the thing that she does, the act that gets onto the six o'clock news, everywhere, all through the country.

Down the frosted squares of the sidewalk, Lulu Lamartine dances the old-lady traditional, a simple step, but complex in its quiet balance, striking. She dances with a tucked-in wildness, exactly like an old-time Pillager. And then, at the door to the official vehicle, just before they whisk her inside, she raises her fan. Noises stop, cameras roll. Out of her mouth comes the old-lady trill, the victory yell that runs up our necks. Microphones squeal. Children cry. Chills form at Lulu's call, fierce and tingling. What can we do? Drawing deep breaths, hearts shaking, we can't help join her.

CHAPTER TWENTY-SIX

SHAWNEE'S MORNING

Stones or earth had shifted directly underneath, or maybe the university housing was like most new construction—cheap, uneven. Whatever the reason, Shawnee Ray woke cold every morning. Shivering as she prowled the apartment, a cup of coffee in one hand, a piece of clothing or a towel in the other, she usually managed to find the source of the draft before waking Redford. Cracks beside the windows where the frame and Sheetrock had separated away were stuffed with washcloths. All of her summer T-shirts insulated cold black squares through which tangled plumbing ran into the cinderblock bathroom. Most of her underwear was rolled under one broad sill with a northwest exposure. She was shedding herself slowly into the walls, pressing scarves and socks against thready fingers of wind.

And then one morning she woke, warm, from a dream. She must have finally managed to fill every one of the builder's mistakes. Her windows were frosted over in pale etchings of glittering and mysteriously detailed ferns. The dream still hung close, and she saw Lipsha.

There is so little time, just the warmth of a breath.

She touched her face, took a swallow of air. Dizzily, she pressed her hot fingers to the icy window and kept them there even though the frost

296

burned. Peering through the melted spot on the glass, she saw that deep snow had fallen, an overnight blizzard. The world was thickly covered and arrested, a place of sudden peace.

On the radio, lists of cancellations. No classes, no day care. No milk. She turned the radio onto a station of generic musical sounds, heard that Gerry Nanapush had still not been apprehended. She and Redford ate handfuls of cereal, drank juice with slivers of slush frozen off the side of the bottle. Partway through the morning, there was more news. Gerry Nanapush still at large. A hostage found in good condition. She turned off the radio and when Lyman called she put Redford on the phone. He spoke seriously, thoughtfully, full of plans. The sun blazed through cottony clouds. After the call was over, they ate a lunch of more cereal and then Shawnee Ray fitted Redford into his quilted nylon snowsuit, pulled thickly knitted mittens onto his hands, stuffed his three-layer stockinged feet into boots. The two went outside and Shawnee began to shovel her car free of the enormous dolphin swoop of drift that covered the front end. This was work she liked, and as she bent and swung to it she grew excited, along with her son, and they moved snow until his feet pinched with cold.

Back inside, Redford fell asleep as Shawnee Ray carefully spread her patterns and materials and drawings across the kitchen table and began to work, first in the slowly failing light and then in the deep glow of the lamp. She was making a ribbon shirt for Lipsha, interest on his loan, the whole amount now stuffed into a sealed manila envelope. Brown calico, blue, cream, salmon trim—she was fitting collar to shoulders, figuring out the way she would join the ribbons at the yoke. At the end of one ribbon, she had thought of attaching a dime-store wedding ring. As a joke, except it wasn't. Lipsha's absence was a constant ache. Maybe she would buy two rings with that two hundred dollars.

Scraps of other projects—turquoise, black and yellow satin littered the floor and twirled as she kicked the table restlessly. She had begun to paint and draw, and her tackle boxes full of materials were neatly stored upon the counter. As she worked out the design for Lipsha's shirt in her head, she found her thoughts drifting. A deeper part of her was listening. From time to time, the wind picked up outside, whirling a scythe, sifting snow down the shingles, sending clouds skittering into the frozen night. When the air boomed against the glass or scraped the splintered siding of the apartment house, Shawnee Ray raised her face and stared into the darkened window glass, as if to question the invisible presences.

In her dream, Lipsha had kissed her with a matter-of-fact joy, deep and long. The kiss still seemed so real that she could smell the smoke on his jacket. She closed her eyes—again his lips brushed hers once, twice, then carved a dark blossom.

CHAPTER TWENTY-SEVEN

PILLAGER BONES

In the dead cold of winter, Fleur Pillager went out. It was said by those who came to call on her, who came to take her house away with signed papers, that to move at all the old woman had to oil her joints with a thin grease she kept by her door. They examined the details, deciphered what they could and imagined the rest. After rubbing her elbows and knees with the bear's fat, she burned a wand of sage, breathed the pure smoke, and let her eyes shut. She sat in the dim and fading warmth of her house until the sun struck the center of the roof, at its zenith. Then she smoothed her thin braids back underneath a white headscarf and stood, ravenous and stooped. She shifted her arms slowly into the husk of an elegantly cut black coat that smelled of burnt leaves and cedar. The smooth lining, blanket-heavy satin, draped her shoulders. The collar was a curled swale of fur. She paused a moment, frowning, her face pressed to the worn nap, then hooked a pair of Lulu's child moccasins off the wall and put them in her pocket. The small hide shoes were pierced with tiny holes so that if death approached Lulu her mother could always make an argument. *My daughter cannot come with you, see the holes in her shoes? The journey is too long for her. Now go.* Fleur's own moccasins, knee high and embroidered in a looping tangle of flowers, were lined

299

with the snowy pelts of rabbits she'd snared. Her hat was woven of owl feathers. Onto her hands, she pulled a pair of leather mittens.

She didn't take the written walls, she didn't take the storehouse facts. She didn't take the tangled scribe of her table or the headboard, the walls, the obscured and veiny writing on the tamped logs and her bed. She didn't take the yellow newspapers, brittle as the wings of butterflies, scrawled in the margins, or the bound railroad ledgers or the linen sheets or scribbled mats. No, all of the writing, the tracked-up old cabin, she left for the rest of us to find. Fleur Pillager only took those things she carried with her all of her life.

Outdoors, into a day of deep cold and brilliance that often succeeds a long disruptive blizzard, she went, thinking of the boy out there. Annoyed, she took his place. Snow stars caught light in the packed yard and the toboggan that she dragged from the shed, a simple wooden frame loaded with skin-wrapped packages, was dusted with glitter, too. Her earrings blazed, silver-green circles, at the jaw of her fiercely cut and unchangeable face. The wooden runners that slightly elevated the bed of the drag squeaked against the packed whiteness as her dark form moved, a hole in the dazzling air.

The shore of Matchimanito Lake was iced perfectly to its broad lip of stone, and the night's relentless wind had carved the snow on its surface into mock waves delicate as shells. The island in the center of the lake was another core of darkness toward which Fleur traveled, dragging her toboggan of bones.

All afternoon, on into the fast-falling dusk, she

walked. Her step was brisk and driving at first, but then slowed, and she often had to rest. Her breath sawed in and out, the cold searing her lungs. On the island there was a cave and in that place her cousin sat grinning from his skull chair, waiting for her to settle into the whiteness and the raving dust along with all of their relatives. Steadily, slowly, her clean steps pressed down between the runner's trails. She stopped in the still breeze, she listened.

Her sisters bickered and argued, threw the marked pits of wild plum, gambled their rings and beads and copper bracelets back and forth. Her grandmother, Four Soul, who had given Fleur the burdensome gift of outliving nearly all of those whom she loved, sang quietly with her thin arms open, waiting. Nanapush was there to smooth her face and again he was a young man, straight as birch, rubbing his clever hands with pollen, and talking without cease. With the twig of a pine, her mother was combing her father's hair calm about his shoulders. The child she lost whimpered, rocked safe by the wind that swirled through and scoured clean the cave where Moses Pillager had slept with his child and his one love between him and the *windigo*. As she walked over the frozen waves she felt the lake bottom buckle far below her feet. The water trembled in its sleep. She waited to catch her halting breath and felt the years slide through her arms so that she braced herself, dizzy, almost weeping to see how far it was that she still had to travel.

It was then that the old strength that had served her in her hardest times seized her, lifted and set

301

her again on the unmarked path. In later days, there would be some who claimed they found her tracks and followed to see where they changed, the pad broadened, the claw pressed into the snow. Others heard songs rise, eager, old songs that haven't been sung since that winter. There is enough we can't account for, however, we need no more. Her tracks should have been obscured. Her tracks should have filled with snow. They should have blown away with those rough songs from the wild dead we cannot hush. Somehow, we should have learned not to tamper with what's beyond us. And yet on clear and brilliant days and nights of black stars they are sometimes again left among us, Fleur's tracks, once more, so it is said that she still walks.

We understand that from her island, when the lake is hard and deep, she covers ground easily, skims back to watch us in our brilliant houses. We believe she follows our hands with her underwater eyes as we deal the cards on green baize, as we drown our past in love of chance, as our money collects, as we set fires and make personal wars over what to do with its weight, as we go forward into our own unsteady hopes.

She doesn't tap our panes of glass or leave her claw marks on eaves and doors. She only coughs, low, to make her presence known. You have heard the bear laugh—that is the chuffing noise we hear and it is unmistakable. Yet no matter how we strain to decipher the sound it never quite makes sense, never relieves our certainty or our suspicion that there is more to be told, more than we know, more than can be caught in the sieve of our thinking. For that day we heard the voices, the trills and resounding cries that greeted the old woman when she arrived on that pine-dark island, and all night our lesser hearts beat to the sound of the spirit's drum, through those anxious hours when we call our lives to question.

IF YOU HAVE ENJOYED READING THIS LARGE PRINT BOOK AND YOU WOULD LIKE MORE INFORMATION ON HOW TO ORDER A WHEELER LARGE PRINT BOOK, PLEASE WRITE TO:

WHEELER PUBLISHING, INC.
P.O. BOX 531-ACCORD STATION
HINGHAM, MA 02018-0531